# CHASING A RUGBY DREAM

## BOOK ONE

# KICK-OFF

CHASING A RUGBY DREAM

BOOK ONE

# KICK-OFF

# JAMES HOOK

with **DAVID BRAYLEY**

**POLARIS**
PUBLISHING

This edition first published in 2020 by

POLARIS PUBLISHING LTD
c/o Aberdein Considine
2nd Floor, Elder House
Multrees Walk
Edinburgh
EH1 3DX

Distributed by
Birlinn Limited

www.polarispublishing.com

British Library Cataloguing-in-Publication Data
A catalogue record for this book is available on request from the British Library.

Designed and typeset by Polaris Publishing, Edinburgh
Printed in Great Britain by Clays, St Ives

This book is dedicated to my wife, Kim, and my three
boys, Harrison, Ollie and George, along with my parents,
grandparents, brother, sister and my in-laws.
Thanks for always backing me.

*J.H.*

For Debbie, Georgia and Olivia, thanks, always, for your
support. Also, my mum, Marilyn, my biggest supporter.

*D.B.*

# RUGBY DREAMS

JIMMY WATCHED the ball as it looped down towards him, swirling in the still sky. Without thinking, he shifted his weight to his left side, caught the ball in the crook of his arms and clutched it firmly to his chest as the onrushing defenders closed in to tackle him. As the opposition flanker readied himself for a bone-crushing hit, Jimmy stopped dead on the spot then jinked to the right, sending the flanker flying past him. Not even waiting to see who was next to try to smash him, Jimmy dropped the ball to the floor right in front of him, planted his left foot firmly into the turf, and just as the point of the oval ball kissed the lush green grass and bounced briefly upwards, Jimmy swung his right foot effortlessly through it, sending the ball sailing skywards. Time seemed to stand still. The capacity crowd in the stadium fell silent as they watched the ball on its way, arrowing towards the perfect white posts, spinning end-over-end into the floodlit sky. Everyone was focused on the ball – 80,000 spectators in the stands, millions more watching on TV. Everyone except Jimmy. He was looking at the clock. He knew when he struck the ball that it would go over – it was the time that was more important. Just one second after the clock turned to 80:00 and changed to red, Jimmy's incredible fifty-eight-metre drop-kick dived over the bar and into the arms of the distraught All Black full back, standing behind the posts. Jimmy swung around and jumped as high as he could, punching the air and screaming with delight.

'Get in!' he cried and ran to the touchline to celebrate with his adoring fans, who were uncontrollable with delight. Scoring the winning drop-goal in a Rugby World Cup final against New Zealand in the last minute should be enjoyed, and Jimmy was determined to make the most of it.

Among the cheers ringing in Jimmy's ears was a voice. A voice he recognised.

'Jimmy,' it called. 'Jimmy!' It got louder. 'JIMMY!' He recognised it . . . it was his mum.

Jimmy swung around, embarrassed. The screaming crowds at the stadium vanished. His cheering teammates disappeared instantly like ghosts. The Kiwi flanker lying on the turf in disbelief and despair, gone.

'What have I told you about kicking that blinking rugby ball so near the windows? You've broken two already, if you do it again, I'm throwing that stupid ball out . . . now be more careful!'

And with that, Jimmy's mother turned around, walked over the pavement, up to the open front door of their small terraced house they shared with Jimmy's younger sister Julie and older brother Jonny, and slammed the door behind her.

Jimmy looked down at the rough tarmac surface he was

kneeling on. It was not the beautiful green grass that he had so vividly imagined he'd been playing on. He looked towards the fence that led to the empty waste ground behind his house and searched for his ball. The fence was about as far removed from the tall white posts he had imagined as it was possible to get. He saw his scruffy, dirty and worn old rugby ball lying beside a tyre that was half hidden among tufts of long grass in the dusty earth of the waste ground. It wasn't the World Cup match ball he always pretended he was playing with.

Dreams over, back to reality.

But as he climbed over the fence to retrieve his ball, the sense of joy from his perfectly struck kick still coursed through him. He loved that he could lose himself so easily in his dreams. The street and the waste ground were his own personal rugby fields. He was never happier than kicking his ball about on them, believing that he was running out at some of the world's greatest rugby stadiums, playing through hundreds of different scenarios in his head – snatching victory at the death, side-stepping and pirouetting his way to glory, performing feats that would leave commentators breathless and his name on the lips of every rugby fan on the planet.

Jimmy walked to his ball and toe poked it so that it bounced off the tyre, then flicked it up behind him with his right foot before turning and catching it. He threw a smooth dummy to an imaginary teammate, then dropped the ball onto his left foot, deftly chipping it over a would-be defender before regathering the ball as it bounced up from the uneven ground, pleased that he'd put just the right amount of backspin on it. Then, in one flowing movement, he dummied again, tying the covering wing in knots, before sidestepping the full back and running in another match-winning try under the posts.

'And it's Jimmy Joseph with another spectacular finish! Is there anything this boy can't do?'

Jimmy looked around, a little embarrassed, but beamed when he caught sight of his grandfather, Will, leaning over the garden fence at the back of his house, which was just a couple of doors along from his own.

'You'll be playing for the Wolves in no time,' called Will.

Jimmy jogged back towards him, chipping the ball to himself as he ran. 'Thanks, Gramp,' he said, his face still lightly flushed.

'Honestly, I've not seen many with talent like yours,' said Will, 'and I've been watching rugby for sixty years!'

He took a sip from his white tin mug and Jimmy watched as the steam from the hot, strong tea drifted away on the gentle late-summer breeze. Clearly surprised by how hot the tea was, Will let out a little yelp as it burnt his tongue, and accidently sent his false teeth clattering into the mug.

'Urgh, Gramp, that's gross!' cried Jimmy, but he was barely able to get the words out through his laughter as Will scooped up his teeth and jammed them back in his mouth.

'Perils of war, my lad,' coughed Will, also laughing.

'What, you lost your teeth in the war, did you? Mum said it was because you ate loads of sweets as a kid.'

'Libel! Nonsense! Fake news! I hate sweet things.'

'So there aren't five sugars in your tea, then?'

'No, not a drop,' said Will, covering the tea with his hand as if the sugar granules might float to the surface.

'Uh-huh,' said Jimmy dryly. 'All right then, tell me what

happened to your teeth in the war . . .' He always loved listening to his grandfather's stories, even though he never really knew if they were made up or not.

'Well, it was back in 1967. Long time before you were born. I was stationed out in Aden—'

'Where's that?'

'Ah, well, it's not called that anymore, of course. It's South Yemen now, in the Middle East, south of Saudi Arabia. But back then it was Aden. And it was hot . . . hotter than hell – hotter than this tea, which I appear to have made with lava.'

Jimmy barked a laugh.

'Anyway, Aden. Hot, dusty, and there we are: a bunch of pasty boys out fighting a war. We used to ride camels in the desert and one day one of my mates bet me a week's rations that I wouldn't kiss one of the camels. So I went in for this big smooch but the camel was having none of it. He turned his face and slapped me with his hoof – and all my teeth fell out. Can you imagine, rejected by a camel! And it costs me all my lovely, perfect teeth!'

Jimmy was bent over with laughter. 'That never happened! No way!'

'I'm telling you. All true.' But there was a glint in Will's eye.

'Actually, talking about Aden,' he continued, 'there was a boy out there with me who you remind me of. He was from Gloucester, was rugby daft. Good player, too. Small like you, but quick like you, too. Skills not quite as good as you, though.' He paused, frowning a little. 'I think his name was Harry . . . Harry Dyer? Harry Dalton? Oh, it was such a long time ago, I can't quite remember. Anyway, there was this one time we were out on patrol and the rebel forces had just taken Crater, which was an important town. We were on patrol, trying to get a foothold back in Crater when we were shot at by a sniper. We had to take cover and were pinned down behind a low wall. We couldn't move because of the sniper, so we all just had to keep our heads down and wait for reinforcements. It was a serious situation. But then Harry saw it, and he just had to have it . . . silly fool.' Will stopped, as if suddenly lost in the details of the story.

'Saw what, Gramp? The sniper?'

'No, no, not the sniper,' said Will, snapping back to the moment. 'None of us could see *him*, he was totally hidden, we didn't have a clue where he was. No, what Harry saw was a rugby ball – a tattered old rugby ball, just lying out in the rubble.'

'A rugby ball? In a battle? Come on, that can't be right, Gramp.' Jimmy was beginning to think that this was going to be yet another tall tale.

'Yes, a rugby ball!' Will cried. His eyes were wide and Jimmy could see he was telling the truth. 'You see, just a few weeks before, Crater had been just a normal town with streets and houses and shops and people living and going about their business. When the rebels moved in, the civilians were all forced out and just scarpered, leaving all their belongings behind. And one of those things was a rugby ball!

'I can remember it so clearly. It was about ten yards from where we were and it was clear it had once been a cracker – brown leather and with laces – and there it was, just sitting in the gutter. Well, as soon as he saw it, Harry shouted to me, "I'm having that, Will!" and he crawled out to go and get it.'

'Was he insane? What happened?' asked Jimmy.

Will threw his head back and started to roar with laughter.

'No, he wasn't insane – just a kid who was obsessed with rugby! So he crawled out to go get this ball but just as he moved out from behind the wall, a shot rang out, like a firecracker in an empty church. The shot was followed straight away by a big "clang". We all looked at young Harry, thinking he must be dead. But all we could see was him sitting there, startled, bolt upright like a telegraph pole, with the tin hat on his head spinning round like a tornado where the sniper's bullet had glanced off it! It was the funniest thing we'd ever seen.'

Jimmy's eyes were wide, now as lost in the story as Will was in the telling.

'But before we could even start to laugh, our huge Sergeant Major – I remember *him*, Fred Ridge – shouted out "GET DOWN, PRIVATE!" which, luckily, Harry did. Just as Harry hit the floor, another shot from the sniper thumped into the wall behind him. That one woke Harry up a bit, so he spun round on a sixpence, dragged himself across the floor to the wall like the fastest snake you've ever seen, and somehow managed to clamber back behind cover before a third shot rang out. This one was close, and hit the frame of the rifle that Harry had slung over his shoulder. It broke his rifle, but saved his life. I'll never forget the sound of the bullet ricocheting over our heads and into the wall behind us. It was just like you hear in the films. Incredible.'

Jimmy paused for a moment, absorbed in the detail of his grandfather's story.

'Wow, that must have been really scary, Gramp.'

'Scary? No, not really,' said Will, chuckling again as he spoke, running his fingers through the thinning grey hair on his head.

'As I say, it was one of the funniest things any of us had ever seen! And what was even funnier, was that just as Harry peeked out to see if the ball was still there, another shot rang out, but this time it completely destroyed the thing the sniper was aiming at. He'd got his prize.'

Jimmy's face changed from one of interest to one of horror.

'What? He hit Harry, Gramp? In the head? Was he killed?'

'No!' cried Will. 'The *ball*. The sniper shot the ball! It just exploded in front of us! He obviously wasn't a rugby fan like we all were. And poor Harry was more disappointed that the ball was destroyed than horrified that he'd nearly been shot dead on a dusty street thousands of miles from home!'

Will paused for a moment, shaking his head at the memories, before he took some more tea from his mug – this time, just a sip.

'They were great days, Jimmy, great days. And you know what, it reminds me of rugby.'

'What, war does?'

'No, no, no. Being part of a team. Working together. Sharing goals and achieving them as a group. Having a laugh with your friends. Those are the things you remember most as you get older. That's the point – rugby's a *game*. Take it seriously, go out and try to win, work hard to make yourself better – but when you're out there, enjoy being with your pals on the field. You can be the most talented player in the world, but if you don't work with the team, if you don't support them and look after them, then they won't support and look after you. And without them, you'll achieve nothing. You understand?'

'Yeah, s'pose so.'

'Good lad.'

Jimmy's mum came out in her garden then and stared across the wasteland for a moment before spotting Will and Jimmy chatting. 'All right you two, enough gabbing. Jimmy, it's time for tea and then homework.'

'Ugh, do I have to?' moaned Jimmy.

'In here, *now*. Otherwise that ball's getting thrown in the bin.'

'I'd get going if I were you,' whispered Will with a knowing wink. 'We both know she's a terror if she gets cross.'

Jimmy smiled and rolled his eyes. He flicked the ball onto the tips of his fingers and spun it around like a top before walking the few strides to his garden fence. He leapt over it in one fluid motion and disappeared inside, still spinning the ball as he went, as if what he'd just done was the easiest thing in the world.

Catherine stared after him, with a small shake of her head. 'Kids. What can you do with them, eh, Dad?'

Will smiled. 'Listen to you! You were a right handful when you were growing up . . .'

'I was not—'

'I tell you what, mind, he's got talent,' interrupted Will, his smile broadening into a grin. 'I keep forgetting he's only ten.' He let out a long whistle in admiration. 'Even Jonny wasn't as good at that age.'

Catherine nodded slowly. She knew both her sons were talented rugby players, and she wanted to support them with all their sporting dreams – but she also knew it was tough for anyone to make it to the top in sport. Of all the millions of kids who dreamed of being a professional footballer or rugby player or golfer – or a professional in whatever sport they loved – only a few ever achieved it. And fewer still went on to cement their name in legend as Jonny and Jimmy dreamed of doing.

Will seemed to read her mind. 'Believe me, he's got it all,' he said quietly. 'I've never seen a kid like him. *If* he works hard, he could be special.' He paused, before continuing. 'If he works hard.'

# OFF TO SCHOOL

'Jimmy! Come on, you're going to be late!' shouted Catherine up the stairs. 'What's the Monday motto?'

'Start Monday with purpose, and the rest of the week will take care of itself,' mouthed Jimmy in perfect timing as his mother called out the words. Jimmy leant forward and reached for his tube of gel on the sink. Squirting a little bit on to his fingertips, he swept it quickly through his dark brown hair until the floppy fringe was transformed into a proud peak. Happy with his work, he washed his hands, swept up his black framed glasses and ran straight back into his bedroom to grab his back pack.

By the time he made it downstairs, his little sister Julie and big brother Jonny were both already out of the door and on their way to school.

'Why are you always the last in the mornings?' sighed Catherine, throwing his backpack over his shoulders and bustling him towards the door. 'You know I haven't got time to mess about with you before work – why can't you be more like your brother and sister?'

Jimmy knew his mum was right, but he always loved to watch rugby films on YouTube on her iPad first thing in the morning. He'd find one from the *Rugby Greats* channel and lose himself watching the legendary players of the past. It was the perfect way to start his day. But he always tried to squeeze an extra play out and, inevitably, he would end up being last out the door.

Despite his protestations that he wasn't hungry, she crammed two slices of toast in his hand as he swept out the door. 'It's the most important meal of the day!' she cried as he skipped down the short path to the pavement, before turning right and jogging down the road, dodging the dog poo on the pavement that had been left by Mrs Lewis's Great Dane. *Why doesn't she just pick it up?* Jimmy thought to himself as he narrowly missed a mound that was like a mini Mount Everest of disgustingness! But he knew that Mrs Lewis had been having a difficult time of late, so it wasn't her fault really, he just wished her huge dog would do his mountain-sized poos somewhere else. 'Doesn't she realise that's the halfway line?' he asked under his breath.

Managing to make it through the minefield of dog dirt unscathed, Jimmy reached the end of his road and turned right towards his school. It was less than half a mile to Central Primary and his mum usually liked to walk him there if she could.

'I just don't know why more parents don't let their kids walk to school,' had been her favourite topic of conversation in recent days with her friend, Jeanette. 'It's ridiculous, all these mothers in their Land Rovers in our little village, clogging up the pavements just so they can all get in the yard for a gossip before they go to the hairdressers . . . they want to get jobs like us, Jeanette, and see how the other half live!'

Jimmy loved his mum. He knew she'd had it hard since his dad had left home and she often had to work double-shifts to help pay the bills – that, as much as anything, fuelled his dream to be a professional athlete one day. He'd buy her a new house, one of those cars she was always complaining about, and she could do any job she wanted, not just the one she *had* to do to make ends meet.

Jimmy felt a bump on his shoulder, which woke him out of his daydream and nearly knocked his glasses off.

'All right, Jim?' It was his best mate, Matt.

'Hey, watch the glasses!' said Jimmy, swiping a playful punch at Matt, who dodged out of the way.

'Ooooooh, stroppy boy on a Monday morning,' laughed Matt as he bumped into Jimmy's shoulder again. 'No need to get all Anthony Joshua on me!'

'You break them more often than I do!' muttered Jimmy, sliding his glasses back in place, but keeping hold of one arm just in case Matt jumped on him again.

Before Matt could have another go, they were joined by Manu, another of their rugby-playing gang.

'All right, boooooooys?' shouted Manu, 'you heard the news about old Mr Lloyd?'

'What? He's not giving us another one of those surprise tests, is he?' asked Jimmy, his face sagging at the prospect of a Monday morning maths test.

'Oh man, hope not,' said Matt. 'He absolutely *slaughtered* me last time when I only got five right.'

'Old Mr Lloyd won't be slaughtering anyone anymore,' interrupted Manu.

'Why?' asked both Jimmy and Matt in unison.

'Haven't you heard?'

'Heard *what*?'

'You know he wasn't in last week?'

'Yeah,' said Jimmy.

'He was on a course, wasn't he?' asked Matt.

'Nah, that's just what they told us. My mum's best friend is Debbie, the school secretary. She was over at ours last night, and I heard her telling Mum that Mr Lloyd wasn't away on a course – he's *ill*, and he might not be coming back. *Ever*. No Monday morning maths test today, boys . . . no need to worry about that.'

Manu skipped happily ahead, before shouting back over his shoulder.

'We've got a new teacher.'

# THE STRAY KICK

OLD MR Lloyd was the only topic of conversation in the schoolyard that morning.

By the time Jimmy, Matt and Manu made it to the old Victorian shelter at the end of the top yard, to dump their bags by the column that made one of the two rugby posts of their imaginary break-time stadium, they'd been told by various friends exactly what had happened to the unfortunate Mr Lloyd.

Depending on who they spoke to, he'd either had a stroke, a heart attack, got cancer, had a car crash, had brain surgery, had died, had not died, was in a home, had Alzheimer's or had broken his neck falling off a balcony at the golf club. Oh, or he might have been kidnapped. He sounded as if he was the unluckiest man alive. Or dead. Nobody really knew.

The three boys got together and Manu reached into his backpack and pulled out a rugby ball.

'We'll find out about Old Lloydy soon enough,' he shouted. 'Quick game of touch before registration?' and he drop-kicked the ball to Jimmy, who caught it effortlessly, leant back and punted the ball as high as he could into the sky above the yard – the little party piece he always did before they began their first game of the day.

As the boys watched the ball climb higher and higher into the sky – everyone always marvelled at this, nobody could kick the ball as powerfully as Jimmy, not even the Year 6 boys – the head teacher, Mr Davies, walked into the top yard, accompanied by a tall, stern-looking man in a tracksuit.

Mr Davies was deep in conversation with the man, pointing out various parts of the school buildings. None of the boys paid much notice to Mr Davies and his visitor, who was probably just a parent of a new kid in school; they were too focussed on the ball high above them.

They watched as the ball soared into the morning sky, until it stopped, seemed to hover for a moment, and then began to hurtle back down towards them.

But then from nowhere, a gust of wind swept across the yard. It caught the ball, and swerved it away from the area by the shelter, where the boys were standing, towards the centre of the yard. Right to where Mr Davies and the man were walking away, back towards the school reception.

The entire yard full of children seemed to freeze as they watched the spinning ball arrow downwards towards the head teacher.

Jimmy, Matt and Manu all wanted to shout out a warning, but as they opened their mouths, no sound came out. It was too late anyway.

Just as it looked as if the ball was going to hit Mr Davies smack on top of the head, the flight of the ball curved on the wind and it bounced directly behind him, an enormous thump echoing around the yard as it hit the ground. The visitor's head snapped around at the sound – just as the ball bounced up off its tip . . . and hit him square in the face. His head jolted back and his glasses were sent flying. They skittered across the hard tarmac yard, a lens popping out of the frame.

A chorus of 'Ooooooh!' reverberated around the schoolyard as the visitor gave a blood-curdling growl and clutched his nose. Mr Davies swung round in a rage and screamed, 'WHO KICKED THAT BALL?'

Silence.

'*WHO* KICKED THAT BALL?' he bellowed again.

More silence, broken only by the scrape of the visitor picking up his broken glasses.

'For the last time,' said Mr Davies, his voice now quiet and infinitely more menacing, 'who kicked that ball?'

Mr Davies was a man not to be messed with. All the children in school were extremely wary of him, petrified of how angry he could sometimes get, yet they all respected him too – he was always fair . . . but only if you were honest with him.

Jimmy gulped. It was time to be honest.

'It was me, sir,' he said in barely more than a whisper. But it was loud enough to cut through the silence of the yard.

'I might have guessed,' said Mr Davies coldly. 'Our resident rugby dreamer. Jimmy Joseph. Come here, boy. NOW!'

On legs that felt like they had turned to jelly, Jimmy sloped forwards, his head bowed, his cheeks flushed. He could feel every eye in the yard on him.

'I-I'm sorry, sir, I'm sorry,' he stammered. 'The wind took it, there was nothing I could do—'

'The wind couldn't have taken it, lad, if you hadn't kicked the thing, could it?'

Jimmy stood in silence.

'COULD IT?' roared Mr Davies.

'No, sir,' whispered Jimmy, his head bowed so low the back of his neck hurt.

'No, sir,' repeated Mr Davies flatly. 'What have I told you about kicking that ball, boy?'

'Not to do it, sir.'

'That's right, not to do it, sir. And why have I told you not to do it?'

'In case it hits someone, sir.'

'Yes, in case it hits someone, sir. Well it *has* hit someone, hasn't it, boy?'

'I know, I'm sorry. I didn't mean it to hit a parent, sir. I'm really sorry.'

'I'm no parent,' growled the other man, speaking for the first time. Jimmy glanced up at him. He hadn't appreciated until now just how huge the man was. He was like a bear towering over Jimmy. At least six foot four, with a big scar over his right eyebrow, slightly bald, with wispy blond hair around his ears. His ears! Jimmy couldn't believe them. They were gross! They were fat and warped and knobbled with scars, as if they'd been repeatedly hit by a plank of wood. They looked like two great big cauliflowers stuck on the side of his head. And in the centre of his face, between two beady eyes that were glaring viciously down at him, was a battered and crooked nose – from which a trickle of blood was now creeping.

Jimmy opened his mouth to speak, to apologise again, but he was too confused to say anything. Mr Davies always showed new parents around the school when their children arrived for the first time. But if this man wasn't a parent—

'What's your name?' asked the man, peering down at him through those narrowed, dark eyes, as if trying to memorise every feature of Jimmy's face.

'J-Jimmy,' managed Jimmy. 'Jimmy Joseph.'

'Jimmy Joseph,' repeated the man thoughtfully, nodding to himself. 'Year?'

'F-five.'

Another nod. Then a small snort that caused a bubble of blood to pop from his nostril.

Jimmy looked to Mr Davies for help. He was just too bamboozled by what was happening – and he couldn't help but feel a little scared around this giant man.

'Well, this is an unfortunate way to meet,' sighed Mr Davies. 'Of course, you're in Mr Lloyd's class, aren't you, Jimmy?'

This time it was Jimmy's turn to nod silently. His stomach felt like it was turning to lead. *Oh, no, please not that . . .*

'This is Mr Kane,' continued Mr Davies. 'I was showing him around because he is joining us at Central Primary . . . He's your new teacher.'

Jimmy didn't say a word in reply but watched as Mr Kane raised one huge forearm and dabbed some blood from his nose with his sleeve, his eyes never leaving Jimmy's.

*Oh, no . . .*

# FROM BAD TO WORSE

'FLIPPIN' HECK, Jimmy,' said Manu angrily as he snatched up his backpack from the foot of the rusty, green column of the shelter. 'Davies will keep my ball for the week now because he thinks it's yours. My dad will *kill* me, he brought it back from visiting family in Samoa! Why didn't you tell him it was mine?'

Jimmy said nothing. He was still in shock.

Manu stormed off to registration.

Jimmy looked at Matt for support. Matt looked as shaken as Jimmy, and stood there, returning the gaze in silence. Then his right shoulder started to twitch. Followed by his left. His head started to move slightly, before he couldn't hold it any longer and just burst out laughing into the loudest guffaw that Jimmy had ever heard. 'Your face, your face! You should've seen your face!' laughed Matt, before copying Jimmy's look when he found out Mr Kane was their new teacher

'Shut up,' Jimmy said, snatching up Matt's Eagles backpack and throwing it at him, which made Matt laugh even more. 'You're not the one that just assaulted a teacher.'

Matt swung his backpack over his shoulder and tried to compose himself. 'Oh, man, did you see the size of him! And those ears! Wow. He's a monster!' Matt shook his head in wonder and then started laughing again. 'Our new teacher's a monster, and you just cracked him in the face with a ball!'

Jimmy spun around, and pretended to lunge towards Matt, as if to attack him.

'All right, all right!' protested Matt smiling, throwing his hands up in mock surrender, 'I'll stop. I'll stop. I'm off now anyway . . . to meet our new teacher . . . the monster!'

And with that, Matt turned and jogged towards the doors of the school, shaking his head and still laughing as he went.

Soon, Jimmy was all alone in the yard, putting off the moment that he would have to confront Mr Kane for as long as he could.

Then he heard a soft voice. 'You okay, Jim?' He recognised it instantly. It was his friend, Kitty.

'Yeah, I'm all right,' he said, but he could feel his cheeks burning. He'd known Kitty since they were babies, growing up together on the same street and he'd never been able to hide anything from her. With Kitty, it was impossible for him to pretend that he wasn't embarrassed about what had just happened.

'Don't let it get it get you down,' she said, simply.

'But what am I supposed to do now? That guy – Mr Kane – he's going to *hate* me.'

'No, he's not,' she said, soothingly, picking up his backpack and handing it to him. 'It was obvious it was an accident – and by the look of Mr Kane's face, I think he's had worse.'

They laughed at that and Jimmy started to feel a little better.

'You know,' she continued, 'I couldn't believe Mr Davies got so angry. What was that about?'

'Dunno,' muttered, Jimmy. 'In fairness, he has told me about a million times not to kick the ball in the yard.'

'Still, it was unlucky. Bet you couldn't have hit Mr Kane in the face even if you'd been trying.'

'Yeah, I could,' he said and they both laughed again. They reached the door to the classroom and Jimmy took a nervous breath.

'It'll be all right,' she assured him, reading his body language. 'He's clearly a tough guy that Mr Kane – but you can see he used to play rugby. He'll like you as soon as he sees how good you are. And you never know, maybe you've just helped to straighten his nose out.'

Jimmy smiled but the laughter didn't come so easily this time. They were at the door and no matter what Kitty said, he didn't want to go in and face Mr Kane.

But Kitty didn't give him a chance to wait any longer. She swept her long, straight brown hair away from her eyes, then grabbed Jimmy by the back of his backpack and pushed him into the classroom.

Mr Kane had his back to them, talking to the teaching assistant, Miss Ayres, and didn't see them come in. They slinked quietly to their desks at the back of the room that Jimmy shared with Matt and Kitty shared with Rachel.

Jimmy put his backpack on the desk and looked at Matt, who whispered hoarsely, 'Fancy a game of rugby, mate?'

'You're hilarious, you know that?' replied Jimmy, 'You should have your own YouTube channel.'

'Good idea, I'd smash it. Billion hits in no time—'

A booming voice suddenly thundered across the classroom. 'What are you doing back there?'

Jimmy was relieved it wasn't him getting into trouble this time – he wasn't doing anything, so he just took his usual seat next to Matt, and kept his head down.

'I said, what are you doing back *there?*' boomed the voice again.

Jimmy looked up to see Mr Kane, looking straight at him. His eyes were like daggers.

'Me, sir?' questioned Jimmy respectfully. He glanced at Matt in the faint hope that Mr Kane was talking to him. But he knew he wasn't.

'Yes, *you*,' exploded Mr Kane. 'Don't answer me back, boy.'

Jimmy remained silent, just looking at his angry – make that *extremely* angry – new teacher. He didn't know what to do.

'Why are you sitting all the way back there?' asked Mr Kane.

'This is my seat sir, it's where I always sit.'

'Not anymore you don't. Get down here at the front with me, where I can see you, where I can make sure you're not spending your whole day daydreaming. I've been told about you.'

Jimmy was confused and hesitated, before looking at Matt for some support. Matt was staring intently at his desk as if all the secrets of the world had been scratched on its surface.

'You,' said Mr Kane, snapping his fingers at Ryan Lewis in the front row. 'Swap.'

Ryan looked a little startled at the command and stared straight down at his desk. He'd already started to unload his school bag of his supplies for the morning: two energy bars, a banana, packet of crisps – cheese and onion, of course – three buffet pork pies and bottle of Lucozade sport.

'And pack all that rubbish away, it's not lunchtime yet.'

'It's not my lunch,' replied Ryan with a quizzical look, 'this is for break. I'm just getting it organised. My mother drops my lunch down later. I can't fit it all in my bag.'

Mr Kane glared at the stocky, sandy-haired boy in front of him. Ryan could see his new teacher wasn't in the mood for a conversation about his dietary habits, so with a sigh of indignance, he picked up his mid-morning buffet, stuffed it all back into his bag, and made his way to the back of the class, rolling his eyes at Jimmy as they passed in opposite directions.

Jimmy took his seat, flopped down and had an awful feeling in his stomach as he looked at Mr Kane who was logging into the old laptop on his desk and waiting for the projector to warm up. He was sitting so close to him, he could actually smell the garlic on Mr Kane's breath as he breathed in and out impatiently, waiting for the computer to load.

After a couple of minutes, which felt like two hours to Jimmy, the laptop and projector sprung to life at the same time, and Mr Kane finally stood up.

He really was huge. He looked even bigger in the classroom than he had outside. As he introduced himself to the rest of the class, explaining that Mr Lloyd had suffered a heart attack, which would mean he would be unlikely to return to teaching, Jimmy took advantage of his new seat to check the giant out.

He was quickly drawn to those ears again. They were incredible. They were swollen, scarred, puffy, red and almost closed up; Jimmy had never seen anything like them before. He noticed that Mr Kane had several scars on his face, around his eyes, not as big as the one above his brow, but he counted at least six or seven of them. Then there was another running along his top lip for about an inch, and another across the bridge of his large, swollen, nose. Close up, Jimmy thought, he looked like an old patchwork quilt.

As Mr Kane spoke to the class, Jimmy noticed that he used his hands a lot. He wasn't surprised, they were enormous. It was as if he didn't have fingers, just two bunches of bananas attached to shovel-like palms. At one point, Mr Kane pulled up the cuffs of his tracksuit top – one of which was smeared with blood from his nose – to reveal the most powerful set of forearms that Jimmy had ever seen.

Then, as Mr Kane pointed to something on one of the displays at the back of the class, Jimmy saw it. The scar.

It was incredible. It ran from the point of Mr Kane's elbow, all along the edge of his arm, right the way down to the side of his wrist. Either side of the scar, about every half inch, were small dots that were clearly where the stitches had once held the wound together. The scar itself was as thick as a piece of string and seemed to have formed a raised ridge of flesh, all along the length of his arm. It was also a different colour to the rest of the skin – much pinker, maybe even purple in parts. Jimmy couldn't take his eyes off it.

Mr Kane glanced down at Jimmy, who quickly turned his gaze to the information projected onto the whiteboard. Mr Kane paused for a moment before continuing, pulling the tracksuit sleeve back down to hide the scar as he did so.

'Right then, that's enough of the introductions. I'm sure we'll get to know one another better as the days and weeks pass.' He sat down and started tapping on the keyboard, opening up some of Mr Lloyd's old work folders.

'Now, one thing you'll get to learn about me is that I don't like wasting time. I've been placed in this classroom to make you learn, and nothing will distract me from that . . . not even fools kicking rugby balls.' He didn't look at Jimmy, but everyone knew who he meant.

'So, while I'm looking for this file on here, get your maths books out, along with your pens. Apparently, Mr Lloyd has left some work here that he had planned . . . ah, here it is.'

Mr Kane double clicked on the file in the folder and it sprung into life on the enormous whiteboard.

*Monday Morning Maths Test* flashed up in bold letters followed by a groan from the class.

Jimmy closed his eyes for a moment.

He'd had better days.

# RUGBY HOMEWORK

'EAT YOUR tea, Jim,' said his mother, 'stop pushing your food around your plate like you're shovelling snow!'

*Snow,* thought Jimmy, *that would be good. They'd close the school then and I wouldn't have to face Mr Kane.*

'What's up with you today?' she asked, spooning a second helping of mashed potatoes onto Jonny's plate. 'You've had a face like thunder since you came home. Has something happened at school?'

'No, nothing,' lied Jimmy.

'Yeah, Jimmy's had a *ball* at school today,' murmured Julie under her breath. She shot him a little grin as he kicked out at her under the table and her legs danced out of the way.

'I'm just not really hungry, that's all,' he said, pulling a face at his little sister. He got up to take his plate to the sink, but Jonny grabbed it out of his hands and scraped the leftover food onto his own plate.

'Ta,' muttered Jonny, his mouth full of potato. Jonny was *always* hungry. And despite how much food he shovelled away, he was still thin as a rake – it was all the rugby he played. And the football; and the swimming; and all the extra running he did. He'd started doing hill sprints in the summer and going for long rambling runs through the hills that rose up steeply to the south of the village. It seemed like every step he took on one of those runs meant that he needed an extra mouthful of food to compensate.

'Hey, have you broken your glasses again?' called out Catherine as Jimmy passed her, heading for the stairs.

Jimmy reached up and felt the new piece of sellotape that he'd had to put on the arm of his thick black-rimmed glasses earlier, after having them knocked off in the yard playing rugby after school. He used to hate that he had to wear glasses, but he'd got used to them now. When he'd started to wear them, in Year 2, he was teased a little bit, but not anymore, people just accepted that Jimmy wore thick glasses, it was no big deal. The only real problem was that he kept breaking them. He'd become an expert in fixing them with sellotape, but his mother still got annoyed when he did it, especially as the lenses often popped out and got scratched.

'No,' he replied, 'the tape just came loose today, so I changed it.' Jimmy didn't like not telling the truth, but a little white lie now and again was okay, he reckoned.

'Mmm,' replied Jimmy's mum, disbelievingly. 'Well, try to look after them, love, they're expensive.'

'Yes, I know, okay,' replied Jimmy, and he carried on upstairs.

He slumped down on his bed and stared up at the ceiling. He thought long and hard about his day with Mr Kane, and how bad it had been. What was he going to do? He had always got on really well with Mr Lloyd – bad maths test results aside. Mr Lloyd understood Jimmy and his love for all things rugby, but there was something just so . . . *horrible* about Mr Kane.

Jimmy remembered the chilling words Mr Kane had uttered as they all left the class at 3.20 that afternoon: 'Right, everyone, just so you know, I'm going to be the new rugby coach for this school, and I'm looking for big, tough boys who listen to orders. The headmaster has already told me that we don't have enough Year 6 players to fill the team, so I'll be looking for some of you here to come to a trial match after school tomorrow. Bring your kit if you want to take part.' Then, looking straight at Jimmy he said, 'But if you're one of those players who thinks the game is all about them and how far they can kick a ball or sidestep everyone without passing . . . my advice would be: don't bother.'

It was the fact that Mr Kane hadn't taken his eyes off him at all when he'd said that last bit that really hit Jimmy hard. All he wanted to do was play for the school rugby team, it had been his aim ever since he'd begun taking an interest in rugby when he went into Year 2, after his granddad had given him his first ever rugby ball. Under Mr Lloyd, Jimmy had been getting close, and before he had been taken ill, Mr Lloyd had told Jimmy that he thought the next trial might be the time he would break into the Year 6 team. But he had warned him not to be disappointed if he didn't, because there were some big lads in Year 6 ahead of Jimmy who had more experience and might be picked instead.

'But don't worry if that happens,' Mr Lloyd had told him, kindly. 'It'll just mean you have to wait another season. Another year and you'll be bigger and stronger and will walk into the team anyway.'

On the one hand, Jimmy thought, it was a good thing that he now had a new teacher to impress to see if he could make it into the team. But on the other hand, this teacher clearly already disliked him, so maybe his chance was over for another year. All because of a stupid kick that went wrong!

Jimmy slunk through to his mum's room to see if her iPad was charged. It was. He tapped on the YouTube app. He followed lots of channels on YouTube. There were some that just focused on past tours of the British & Irish Lions, there was another called *Six Nations Action* that featured compilation films of each Six Nations season going back until before Jimmy had been born, and there were lots of individual channels focussing on the leading players from around the world.

Jimmy went back to his room and threw himself on his bed, quickly finding the channel he was looking for. It was called *Life at Number 10* and it was a channel devoted to players that had played the pivotal, play-making position. There was one film on it that started by showing flashes of all the great fly-halves that had played rugby from years and years ago, moving through the decades until they hit the present day. The action included players that had been around even when Jimmy's dad had been young, moving through the years and the countries showing off incredible play from the likes of Tony Ward, Ollie Campbell, Ronan O'Gara and Johnny Sexton of Ireland; Barry John, Phil Bennett, Jonathan Davies and Dan Biggar of Wales; from Scotland there was John Rutherford, Craig Chalmers, Gregor Townsend and Finn Russell; England were represented by Rob

Andrew, Paul Grayson, Jonny Wilkinson, Owen Farrell and George Ford. Then there were the southern hemisphere greats: Grant Fox, Andrew Mehrtens, Carlos Spencer, Dan Carter and Beauden Barrett from New Zealand; Mark Ella, Michael Lynagh, Stephen Larkham and Quade Cooper from Australia; Naas Botha, Joel Stransky, Henry Honiball and Handrè Pollard from South Africa; and Hugo Porta, Felipe Contepomi and Juan Martín Hernández from Argentina.

Jimmy tapped on the link and while it buffered, he noticed another video on the sidebar with the face of the great Welsh and Lions winger Shane Williams in its preview frame. It made Jimmy think of all the players who had done what he wanted to: play for the British and Irish Lions. His grandfather had once told him something Jimmy had never forgotten. 'It's all very well playing for your country, son,' he'd said, 'that's a great achievement and huge honour, make no mistake about it. But playing for the *Lions*? Well, that's another thing altogether. To be picked as the best in your position of all the players from England, Scotland, Ireland and Wales . . . well, that's just the peak. It only happens once every four years too. Remember son, you've got to be the best of the best to play for the Lions.'

*The best of the best*, thought Jimmy. And then, with a groan, he muttered out loud, to nobody in particular: 'And I can't even get in the school team.'

Next to the preview frame of Williams's video was its title: 'Shane Williams offers advice to rugby players deemed "too small"'. Intrigued, Jimmy clicked the link.

'I've been asked a question on Facebook by Lewis Juliff,' said Williams, staring straight down the camera, 'about whether I

have any advice for players that have been told they're too small
. . . In school I was in the B team because I was too small. When
I finished school I was asked, when I played my first senior match
against big guys, whether I wanted to continue playing or not.
And I did.

'I became a professional in 1999 and from the first moment
I was told by the press and the media that I was always going to
be too small and not good enough to be an international player.
When I became an international player, I was still told I was too
small and I was dropped from the squad.

'All I can say, really, is that what you've got to do is just keep
going. If you get smashed, you get up, you dust yourself off and
you go to the next play. Rather than running over the top of
people, I had to learn to sidestep, to become quicker and more
agile in the way I played and beat defenders in a different way.
And it helped and it made me the player I was. So when you're
told that you're too small – whether it be by your teachers or
your coaches or anyone, really, use that to motivate you . . . And
trust me, if I can do it, you can certainly do it.'

Jimmy knew Shane Williams's stats well enough. He had won
five major trophies with the Ospreys, played eighty-seven times
for Wales and scored fifty-eight tries for them. He had won three
Six Nations' Grand Slams and had also toured with the British &
Irish Lions three times. In 2008 he had been named the World
Player of the Year. He was one of the sport's all-time greats. And
he had been written off by so many people, time and time again,
for being too small.

When the short film finished, Jimmy tapped the 'replay'
button. He watched it again and again, five times in total. Was

32

it fate that had made Jimmy notice Shane Williams's film on the sidebar? Jimmy made up his mind: he was going to do exactly what the great Shane Williams had once done – he was going to go to the trial and he was going to find different ways to beat defenders. If a Grand Slam-winner and British & Irish Lion was once in the same position as him, then there was no reason why Jimmy shouldn't try and change his teacher's mind either.

Just as Jimmy was about to watch Williams's interview for a sixth time, Catherine called up the stairs. 'Jimmy, Kitty's at the door, she's wondering if you want to go to The Rec to play rugby?'

With a grin, Jimmy threw the iPad down on his duvet. He loved playing rugby with Kitty – she was the best player in their year (well, after him, *obviously*). And now he was in the mood to go out there and play like Shane Williams used to – but with an added sprinkle of Beauden Barrett's flair, Finn Russell's tricks, Handrè Pollard's kicking and . . . and . . . well, a little bit from *all* of his heroes. And a whole lot of Jimmy Joseph.

The cloud that had hung over him all day finally had lifted. Jimmy sprinted out of his room in search of his boots.

# KITTY

'So WHAT did your mum say when you told her about Mr Kane?' asked Kitty, chipping the ball up off her heel so that it sailed over her shoulder and into her hands as they walked down their street towards The Rec.

'I didn't tell her,' replied Jimmy, quietly.

'Why not?' she exclaimed, bouncing the ball off the side of his head as if it would knock some sense into him. 'I told mine and she said she wasn't surprised. Apparently, Dad played rugby with him when they were teenagers and nobody liked Mr Kane back then. She said he was a good player, but that he was a real bully in those days.'

'*How* good was he?'

Kitty rolled her eyes. 'I don't think that's the point of the story.'

'Yeah, all right, I get that. But seriously, how good was he meant to be?'

'I dunno. Pretty good. Very good. Who cares?'

'I just wanna know, Kitty,' said Jimmy, and dug her in the ribs with his elbow. She swatted him away and then dropped the ball onto her right foot and threaded it between his legs. It bounced up off the hard asphalt and she regathered it, shooting him a wink as she did so.

'Skiiiiiiiiills,' she sang and he shot her an exasperated look.

She sighed and chucked him the ball. 'She told me that he'd been spotted by a pro team near Manchester and went to play there,' she relented. 'Dad played international age-grade rugby with him and they all reckoned that if any of them was going to go to play full Test rugby, it was going to be Kane.'

'So what happened? I've never heard of him.'

'Apparently he had a really bad arm injury in his twenties and he had to retire. Had to give up playing altogether. Dad said nobody in the village seemed sorry to hear about it.'

'Sounds like he was a popular guy,' said Jimmy dryly.

'Yeah, exactly. Mum says he was horrible – she can't believe that he's ended up as a teacher. I tell you this, she's not exactly thrilled that he's now teaching *me*. She's hoping he'll remember my dad more fondly than Dad remembers him.'

'That explains the scar,' muttered Jimmy, his mind wandering back to the career-ending injury.

'The what?'

'The scar. Didn't you see it today?'

'No, I was sitting at the back, remember? It was only the naughty boy that got moved to the front.'

He pulled a rude face at her and she laughed.

'Well, he's got this *incredible* scar,' said Jimmy, tracing a copy of the scar on his own arm to show her. 'All the way from his elbow to his wrist. It's really horrible.'

'Urgh . . . I'll see if I can get a peek tomorrow,' said Kitty in gruesome wonderment. 'Horrible man: horrible scar. Makes sense.'

'Um, I don't think it works quite like that. We're not living in a fairy tale.'

'Fair enough – imagine if it did work like that, though. You'd have a shocker of a scar after that kick today!'

'Hey, it was the wind!'

'Whatever, whatever! I don't think Dan Biggar or Emily Scarratt or George Ford – or anyone else decent for that matter – would ever blame the wind like that, though. And I doubt whether any of them will have broken their terrifying teacher's nose either!'

'Aghh,' cried Jimmy, clutching his hair, 'I still can't believe that happened!'

They fell about laughing. Matt had been trying to get Jimmy to laugh about the whole episode all day, but it hadn't really worked. Not like this. Kitty had that kind of effect on Jimmy. She could make anything seem all right.

'Why did we have to have him at our school, though?' sighed Jimmy, as they turned the corner and saw the green expanse of The Rec opening up beyond a low wall ahead of them. 'Especially as he's going to pick the rugby team. I'm *never* going to get in.'

'Nah, don't worry about it, of course you will. Once he sees how far you can kick the ball, and how good you are at sidesteps and dummies, you'll be in!'

'I hope so . . . but did you hear what he said about players like me? *Don't bother!'* he suddenly rasped, mocking Mr Kane's deep, gravelly voice.

'Brilliant!' she roared. 'You sounded just like him . . . do it again!'

*'Don't bother!'* he rumbled again and then began coughing violently, making Kitty laugh even more.

Their next steps took them around another corner towards the gates of The Rec, and they nearly collided with a man putting some shopping into his car. For what felt like the millionth time that day, Jimmy froze.

It was Mr Kane.

Mr Kane looked at them, said nothing, and then looked away and walked to the driver's side of the car. He climbed in, fired up the engine and drove off, as if Jimmy and Kitty weren't even there.

'Do you think he heard me?' whispered Jimmy as they watched the car disappear down the street.

'Nah,' replied Kitty, although she didn't sound entirely convinced. 'We were too far around the corner. Anyway, he'd have said something otherwise, wouldn't he? But come on, forget about him . . . let's go and play!'

And with that, Kitty sprinted across the road and through the wrought iron gates decorated with the words *The Recreation Ground*, to the field where they practised their rugby nearly every day of the week , her long hair, flowing behind her in a dark brown slipstream.

Jimmy jogged behind, aware that there was no point trying to catch her – she was just too quick. Kitty had won the sprints at the school sports day ever since Jimmy could remember and she was now the fastest in the whole school, at just Year 5. And by the whole school, Jimmy meant *the whole school*. She was faster than any of the boys too. Jimmy always enjoyed it when she was challenged to a race in the yard by some of the Year 6 boys. He used to stand and watch and just think, *Why are you lads bothering?* Each time, Kitty just smashed them, leading from start to finish. Often the Year 6 boys just laughed off the defeat, giving her a high-five in congratulations, but some of them really didn't like it – particularly Keegan Miller and Jack Bain, who were both wingers in the rugby team and hated that they weren't the fastest in the school. And more than that, it really bothered them that it was a *girl* who was faster than them. Jimmy and his friends all thought it was hilarious how angry they got. Why did it matter that she was a girl? A race was just a race. Speed was speed. And that was that.

It was no surprise either, really. Kitty's dad was just about the fittest man in the village, which was saying something bearing in mind the number of rugby players that lived there. He was a personal trainer and did something called Cross Fit, which Jimmy didn't really understand. All he knew was that her dad did a ridiculous number of exercises, all in a short space of time, until he could hardly stand up due to exhaustion. Jimmy had been with Kitty to watch him train at the gym one evening and Jimmy just couldn't believe the intensity with which her dad approached his training. He found it quite inspirational and was interested to see how much Kitty clearly absorbed the information her dad was giving her when he explained the techniques behind all the different exercises he was doing. As Kitty sprinted off across The Rec, Jimmy realised it was no fluke that she was as fast as she was. It was natural talent combined with carefully practised technique and lots and lots of hard work.

As she darted around an imaginary defender, Jimmy looked beyond her to the large stand that backed on to The Rec. The stand overlooked a pitch on the far side which belonged to the Wolves, the former first-class rugby team of the village. Back in the day, the Wolves had been one of the biggest clubs in the country and thousands would regularly come to watch them play their games there. Even the mighty All Blacks had played there in the 1950s. But now, since rugby had become professional, everyone went to watch the local pro team, the Eagles, who were based down in Northsea, the nearest city, about six miles away. At best, you'd only get a couple of hundred spectators along to watch a Wolves game now.

But despite its diminished status, it was still Jimmy's dream to one day play for the Wolves. He wanted to run out on that pitch just like his dad and his grandfather had once done and make his family proud. Of course, the ultimate goal was to one day play for the Lions – but Jimmy appreciated that was the pinnacle of the sport. One dream at a time. And first it was the Wolves.

'Jimmy! Kick it here!'

He was snapped out of his daydream by Kitty's loud call. He looked up and saw that she was darting around on the other half of the pitch, just by the ten-metre line.

Jimmy smiled. 'You'll never catch it!'

'Oh, shut up and just kick it,' she shouted back. She was jogging on the spot and then stepping from side to side, as if warming up for a big match.

Jimmy jogged to the twenty-two-metre line, and looked across to the huge Wolves flag that flew on the top of the stand. It was blowing to Jimmy's left and was flapping strongly in the wind. He knew that this meant that the wind was behind him, and blowing quite strongly to the left-hand corner of the field. Because Kitty was standing near the centre of the pitch, he knew that he'd have to direct his kick out to the right, before allowing the wind to take it in-field. *If only I'd calculated all these kinds of things this morning . . .*

He shoved the what-if thought aside and stepped up to the twenty-two, and made a mark with his foot. He imagined that Nigel Owens, one of the world's best rugby referees, had just made the mark and told him it was a penalty kick. In his mind, he was playing for the Lions. Kitty was now a Springbok.

He looked down at the ball in his hands. Once perfectly white, it was now almost a muddy brown colour with much of the stitching worn to bursting point. Jimmy had been given the ball about three years before by his grandfather for his birthday, and Jimmy's almost permanent use of it on both The Rec and the waste land by his house, had made it look very ragged. But, despite it being worn, one thing Jimmy always made sure of was that it was pumped up fully. There was nothing worse than kicking a flat rugby ball.

Jimmy stood still. Focusing on the ball in his hands, he quickly looked down the pitch at Kitty, then quickly to the right touchline, where he would initially aim. In one swift movement, he flicked the ball about a stride ahead of him, and then springing off his left leg, which he had planted on the mark he'd made, Jimmy threw his right leg through the air, his foot connecting perfectly with the ball as it fell. His foot stopped at the point of impact, as if punching it, and as the ball flew on its way, Jimmy lifted his head to follow the direction it was flying. First it shot straight up into the air, in a perfect arc, heading for the touchline. Then, just as it seemed it would fly to the back of the stand, the wind caught it and sent it back in-field towards Kitty. But he hadn't struck it quite right. Despite the wind, it wasn't coming back in-field enough to reach Kitty. Jimmy was disappointed, he hated getting his kicks wrong.

In a flash, Kitty was off. Not taking her eye off the ball, she sprinted after it like the wind itself. At one point she slowed slightly, thinking that the spin on Jimmy's kick would bring it closer towards her, but it didn't. She accelerated again and, just as the flight of the ball was dying and it began to drop to earth like a stone, she put on one final burst of speed and, like a panther, dived to gather the ball just as it was an inch from the turf. In one seamless movement she had rolled over one shoulder and was back up onto her feet, sidestepping an imaginary tackler, before delivering an inch-perfect grubber kick back to Jimmy, who had jogged up to his own ten-metre line.

'Nice catch!' he shouted. 'Sorry about the kick, it wasn't my best,' and he held a hand up in apology.

'It was fine!' Kitty replied, breathlessly, 'it gave me the chance to look like a total legend.'

Jimmy barked a laugh as he scooped the ball up, and passed it back swiftly to Kitty, who caught it and delivered a perfect spin pass straight back to him.

Jimmy was about to launch an up-and-under when they heard some clapping from the shadows of the stand. There, on the edge of the pitch, stood a tall man who had paused his dog-walk to watch them.

Jimmy recognised him instantly and his breath caught in his chest. It was the tall, slender figure of Peter Clement, the legendary former Wolves fly-half who had played fifteen times for his country, before going to play rugby league for the Warriors and eventually win ten caps for Great Britain – the rugby league equivalent of the Lions. Everybody loved Peter, he was a hero in the village and because he still commentated on rugby for the BBC, he was still very well known all over the country. Jimmy's dad idolised him and he and Jimmy used to sit and watch old VHS recordings of Peter's Great Britain Test matches. Sitting cuddled up to his dad watching the fuzzy recording was one of Jimmy's first rugby memories and he too had soon grown to hero-worship the local legend that was Peter Clement.

Peter beckoned to Kitty and Jimmy to come over to the touchline.

Jimmy, for once, ran faster than Kitty to get there.

'Hello, Mr Clement,' he said before Peter could say anything. 'Don't suppose you fancy having a kick-about with us?'

'Ha!' Peter laughed. 'Not tonight, I'm afraid – I'm walking the dog and my wife would kill me if I came back all muddy!'

Kitty had now joined them. Peter gave her an appraising look. 'That was some catch,' he said, the admiration clear in his voice. 'You judged it perfectly. I could see that you initially thought it was going further towards you, until it died a bit,' he glanced at Jimmy when he said that, 'but you did the number one thing: you kept your eye on the ball and never gave up. It was a brilliant catch!'

Kitty blushed with pride.

Peter turned to Jimmy. 'How old are you, son?'

'Ten, sir.'

'Ten! Wow, that's pretty young to be able to kick as well – and as far – as that. Who taught you?'

'Nobody,' replied Jimmy. 'I watch streams on YouTube. I try and learn as much as I can by watching all the top players. They've got clips of everyone . . . even you're on there, when you were playing rugby league.'

'Haha, they go back that far do they? Well I'll be . . . The good old days when I could still run!' Peter thought for a moment. 'If you've only been watching, and not had people pointing things out to you, that'll explain your lack of follow-through on your kick. It's so important.'

Jimmy looked a bit lost at the comment.

'Right, I meant what I said about my wife,' continued Peter. 'Tea'll be ready soon and she'll kill me if I'm late or muddy. But I'd like to help. I can see that you've both got some talent. Listen, I'm in work late tomorrow night, but finish early on Wednesday. Can you be here at five o'clock on Wednesday? I'd like to show you how to really spiral punt a ball. The earlier you learn the correct way, the better. And I can sort out that follow-through straight away. How does that sound?'

Jimmy said nothing. He just stared, opened-mouthed at the elegant, middle aged man in front of him, until Kitty kicked him in the shin.

'Erm . . . yeah, that, that sounds great!' said Jimmy, his eyes so wide and earnest that Peter couldn't help but laugh.

'I can't, I'm afraid,' said Kitty, politely. 'I've got football on Wednesdays.'

'That's a shame. Another time then. But Wednesday at five o'clock's okay for you?' he said to Jimmy, who nodded. 'Good. That's a date then.' Peter held out his hand to Jimmy to shake on the deal.

Jimmy eagerly shook his hero's hand. 'Five o'clock, Wednesday . . . I'll be here!'

'Don't be late. I won't be hanging around here if you're not on time.'

'Oh, I'll be here at half past four,' replied Jimmy. 'Practising!'

'Good lad,' said Peter, and with a wink and another smile, he was off.

As Peter walked away, back into the shadows of the stand, Jimmy turned to Kitty and said, 'Wow! Peter Clement is going to teach me how to kick! I must've walked past his house a hundred times, kicking my ball, hoping that he'd come out and play, and now he's going to teach me! I've seen him in the shops loads as well but never had the courage to speak to him.'

'Really?' laughed Kitty. 'What a creepy stalker! Poor old Peter Clement. He probably only came to talk to us so you'd stop hanging around outside his house!'

Jimmy ignored her and instead drilled a drop-goal attempt into the wind, that just fell short of the posts.

'Race you to it, fanboy!' shouted Kitty. 'If you can get your jaw off the floor!' And with screams of delight they were off.

As they ran after the ball, from out of the shadows of the stand, another person was walking his dog. He had seen and heard everything.

'Five o'clock, Wednesday. We'll see about that,' he whispered.

Mike Green, the full back for the school team, and a member of the Year 6 class, yanked roughly at his dog's lead and turned to walk home. He was not happy.

# NO BREATH

It HAD been one of the worst days Jimmy had ever had at school. It had started in assembly – and got worse and worse.

They had been sitting in assembly when Keegan and Jack – the wingers from Year 6 – had started messing around, and a stray elbow from one of them hit had Jimmy on the back of the head. 'Ow!' Jimmy had exclaimed loudly, the instant pain from the elbow behind his ear, delivering instant shock – and anger. Instinct took over and Jimmy turned around quickly with a swinging arm, lashing out at both boys. He didn't connect with either, and the red mist that had settled over him disappeared as quickly as it had arrived but, unfortunately, Mr Kane had seen it.

'You, boy!' he bellowed at Jimmy. 'Get up and get out! There'll be no scuffling and swinging of arms in a school assembly!'

Jimmy could feel his face burning with embarrassment as he stood and shuffled out of the hall, the whole school watching him. He wanted to explain that it hadn't been his fault, and that he'd only reacted to being hit on the head, but he knew that Mr Kane wouldn't listen to him, so he quietly walked to the door.

Fortunately, Miss Ayres had seen Keegan and Jack larking about behind Jimmy, and she had told Mr Kane that Jimmy had received a nasty bump to the head and had only reacted out of instinct. There was no acceptance or understanding from Mr Kane, simply a terse, 'Just get to your seat, boy,' when assembly ended and they were back in class.

But it was only a temporary reprieve. A few moments later, to Jimmy's horror, Mr Kane began to read through the results of the maths test from the previous day. Not good. Jimmy had only got three out of ten. Mr Kane then spent ten minutes, using Jimmy's test paper as an example, of why maths was so important, and why a score of three was so bad. Jimmy had been close to tears at one point, until he felt a nudge in his back and someone passed him a note. It read, *Don't worry, I'll help you with maths.* It was from Kitty.

He slipped the note in his pocket, feeling a little better.

Then, after lunch, came the worst moment of the day. Trying his best to draw straight lines for a graph he was doing in geography, Jimmy stretched forward too far on his desk, and his ruler caught a stack of books on Mr Kane's desk and they toppled over, knocking his cup of tea all over his desk and onto his lap. He was so furious, Jimmy thought he was going to burst. A vein on Mr Kane's temple throbbed so violently that it made the scar above his brow wriggle like it had a life of its own. It might have been funny – if Mr Kane hadn't looked so terrifying.

For the second time that day, Jimmy was ordered out of a room. On the day of the rugby trial, too.

Once again, Miss Ayres had come to Jimmy's rescue and convinced Mr Kane it had been an accident, but apart from glowering at him when he was allowed back in, Mr Kane didn't speak to or look at Jimmy for the rest of the day.

But all that was behind him now. It was time for the rugby trial, and despite his bad day, Jimmy was going to follow Shane Williams's advice and prove his doubter wrong.

Jimmy was sitting on the old wooden benches in the run-down Victorian pavilion at The Rec that had acted as dressing rooms for Central Primary's sporting events for over a hundred years. It might've been dark and a bit dingy and smelly, but Jimmy loved it. Whenever he was in there, getting changed to play, he always imagined the former pupils and players that had changed there, exactly as he was doing, all those years before.

There was a glass case in the Central Primary hall that contained some international jerseys that had been donated by former pupils of the school. Jimmy looked at them every day and knew them all by heart. The first and oldest was W.O. 'Billy' Edwards, who had played for his country three times in 1937. Next to him, were two jerseys from the 1950s, worn by flying winger Les Shuttleworth and the tighthead prop, Benny Pickering. Next to those two was the best player of the 1970s, full back Andy Collins, who had played thirty-seven times for his country between 1972 and 1978. Jimmy's grandpa had also told him that Collins had been picked for the 1977 British & Irish Lions tour to New Zealand, but had been injured in the last match of the season for the Wolves and had missed out on the tour. 'A true sporting tragedy, that was,' his grandfather had told him.

Then there were two more jerseys, both belonging to Peter Clement. There was his national rugby union jersey and also one of his Great Britain rugby league jerseys. The Great Britain shirt, in particular, was magnificent.

As Jimmy reached down and put his left foot into his boot, he stopped for a second, looked around the grotty changing room, breathed in the smell of dust, sweat, bleach and liniment before thinking to himself, *They all sat here, like me now. They all did it. They all made the team. I'm going to do the same.*

Manu called across to Jimmy. 'Hey, Jim, have you got any of that black tape for this?'

For some reason, Manu was wrapping a white crepe bandage around his head, and he needed some tape to secure it. He looked ridiculous. Jimmy burst out laughing.

'What you doing that for?' he asked.

'What do you mean?' replied Manu. 'Elliot Daly wore one on Saturday, I saw him!'

'Yeah,' replied Jimmy quickly. 'But that's because he'd been kicked in the head, he had stitches!'

Manu burst out laughing, his freakishly wide shoulders heaving with every bark. 'Oh, was it? I didn't see that bit, I missed the first half. I don't care anyway, it looked cool so I'm going to wear it. Just chuck me the tape will you!'

Jimmy rolled his eyes, reached into his bag for the tape and threw it at Manu, hitting him square on his short cropped, dark haired head.

'Watch it!' shouted Manu. 'I don't really want stitches!'

The whole changing room roared. 'You may look like Elliot Daly, but you need to work on your catching if you're going to be anything like him out there,' called Matt.

Jimmy carried on sorting himself out, still chortling at Manu as he put his boots on and pulled up his socks. He didn't usually suffer from nerves like some did, but larking around with Manu always helped him take his mind off the game if the odd nerve began to creep in – which, today, was a real help.

Jimmy finished getting changed, sprayed a quick bit of Deep Heat on his thighs, then took a deep breath. It was cold in the changing room, and his chest felt tight. He wasn't surprised, he almost expected it on the nippy days. He just needed his inhaler.

Jimmy had suffered from asthma for as long as he could remember. It had been a problem when he was young, especially when he had a cold or if he did too much exercise on a chilly day. But once the doctors had sorted it out, and given him the brown steroid inhaler to take twice a day – morning and night – and his blue salbutamol inhaler when his chest got tight, he was usually fine. It was the blue inhaler that was key though, because when his chest tightened, just as it was doing now, he would grab it quickly, take a couple of puffs, and within seconds he would feel as good as new.

Jimmy reached into his kit bag for his inhaler. He always kept it in the small zip pocket inside his bag, next to his gum shield.

*That's strange*, he thought. The zip of the inside pocket was open. Jimmy always made sure it was shut. He found his gum shield straight away . . . but no inhaler. Jimmy looked again, scrabbling around inside his bag. It wasn't there.

Jimmy's chest tightened some more. He let out a slight wheeze as he started to panic. He *needed* his inhaler.

He took his bag to the table by the door, nearer the light. He looked again. Nothing. He started to rummage through every corner and every zip. There were spare studs, old sweets, snapped laces, rolls of tape, mud . . . plenty of mud . . . but no inhaler.

Totally frustrated, Jimmy strangled an angry scream, and tipped the bag up onto the table . . . just as Mr Kane walked in.

'You again, boy! What on earth are you doing making a mess in here? Clean that up straight away!'

'But sir,' Jimmy replied forlornly, 'I've lost my inhal—'

Mr Kane cut across him before he could finish. 'And I'm about to lose my temper with you. What did I tell you earlier?'

Jimmy didn't reply as he started to sweep up the contents of his bag and tidy them away.

'*Well?*' shouted Mr Kane.

Jimmy jumped. He thought the question had been rhetorical. 'You said if I cause trouble again,' he stammered, fighting hard to get the words out. 'I'm going to have detention after school tomorrow.'

'That's right,' growled Mr Kane, 'so if I was you, boy, I'd sit back down and keep out of my way.'

Jimmy knew he couldn't win, but he was more worried about his chest and the missing inhaler than he was about Mr Kane's threats. He picked up his bag, attempted to take a deep breath, but only managed a three-quarter one accompanied by a rattling wheeze. *He had to find his inhaler.*

Jimmy sat down and tried to relax his chest, while Mr Kane outlined the details of the trial. Unseen, in the row behind Jimmy, sat Mike Green. He was looking at the floor, grinning.

After Mr Kane had finished calling out the names of the pupils who would start the trial, he said finally, 'Right, everyone, let's get out there, do your best, tackle hard and don't forget your gum shields.'

Mike reached into his bag for his gum shield. He found it straight away. It was in a side pocket next to an asthma inhaler. Except, the inhaler wasn't his. Mike didn't have asthma.

## GIRLS CAN PLAY TOO

OUT ON The Rec, Jimmy was starting to panic. His chest was
getting worse by the minute, but there was nothing he could do.
Mr Kane had picked two sides, one called the Probables and one
called the Possibles – reflecting the chances that the players on
each side had of making it into the final team selection. Jimmy
was on the bench for the Possibles – which showed just how far
down the pecking order he was. But for the first time in his life,
he was actually glad that he hadn't been picked to play. When
Mr Kane had read out the teams, it was clear what approach he
had in mind. It was as if he hadn't picked the Probables team due
to any rugby ability, he'd picked it just by sheer size.

Usually, the team would be mainly made up of boys from Year
6 because they just had more consistent rugby skills than the Year
5s at that age. But this time, some of the Year 6s who were the
most skilful and trickiest players, were overlooked and placed in
the Possibles team. Instead, Mr Kane had picked much bigger
boys in their place, including Andrew Beasley, the biggest boy in

the school. Andrew was a Year 5 boy who wasn't actually a great lover of sport, but he was big and that was all that seemed to matter to Mr Kane. So Andrew was in. Then, alongside Andrew was another Year 5 boy, John Cleverly, who everyone called 'John Cena' as he was nearly as big as the wrestler – but John was about as interested in playing rugby as Andrew. And on it went. He even picked Andrew Beasley's younger brother, Justin, from Year 4 – mainly because he was only just a bit smaller than his brother. *It's madness*, thought Jimmy, as again, he was robbed of another full breath as he stood shivering on the touchline.

Matt and Manu ran across, smiling. They'd been picked in the Probables, Matt as scrum-half, Manu at centre. Jimmy was genuinely pleased for them.

But as soon as they got close to Jimmy, their smiles disappeared.

'What's the matter, Jim?' asked Matt. 'You look awful.'

'Asthma,' wheezed a downbeat Jimmy, tapping his chest.

'Where's your inhaler, mate?' asked a concerned Manu.

'No idea,' shrugged Jimmy. 'I definitely had it earlier, I needed it in the yard lunchtime when we were playing British Bulldogs – after you clattered me, Manu.'

'Oh, yeah, sorry about that,' said Manu with a grimace, fearing that he was somehow responsible for the lost inhaler.

'Nah, it's not your fault,' said Jimmy, his voice now little more than a hoarse croak. 'I was fine. When I got back to class, I put my inhaler straight back in my bag, next to my gum shield where I always put it, and zipped it up. Then, when I needed it in the changing room just now, it wasn't there. I just don't understand it. Nobody would take it, surely?'

Just as Jimmy finished his words, a huge shout of 'Heads!' rang out from those near to the three friends. They just had time to duck before a ball landed right between them, narrowly missing Jimmy as it bounced up and spun over the heads of the small group of parents who had come down to watch the trial. The three boys swung round to see who'd kicked it. It was Mike Green. Mike laughed at their startled faces and made a mocking, coughing sound, as if to mimic Jimmy.

'I hate that guy,' muttered Matt, glaring at Mike. 'That's the one downside to being in the team – having him as a teammate.'

'He's a good full back though,' said Manu.

His two friends scowled at him.

'Sorry, sorry,' cried Manu, raising his hands in defence. 'Just saying.'

Jimmy coughed again, and this time, he struggled to control it. The coughing fits were the worst. His chest tightened even more as the coughs grew, meaning he couldn't get any air into his lungs between them. His eyes bulged with the strain, and soon they ran pink like the early evening sky above them and were streaming with tears. Manu rushed forward and started smacking his back; it wasn't helping.

Manu's mother ran over and could see Jimmy was struggling. She was a nurse. 'Come here, Jimmy, love,' she said, and tried to straighten Jimmy up from his hunched position. His coughing started to ease a little. 'Small breaths, small breaths,' she said gently, and reached into her bag. She pulled out a blue inhaler. 'Here, have some of this. I always carry one for emergencies.'

Jimmy snatched at it like a drowning swimmer finding a piece of driftwood to cling to. He quickly flipped off the cap and gulped down two, three, then four puffs. 'That's enough, Jimmy, not too many,' said Manu's mum and she eased the inhaler from his hand.

Jimmy felt the relief immediately. Even though he felt a little light headed, at least he could breathe properly again. It was like magic.

The whistle blew.

'All of those picked to start, in here, now!' bellowed Mr Kane from the centre of the pitch.

Matt and Manu glanced at their friend, clearly disappointed that he wasn't joining them, but also relieved to see that he'd recovered quickly from the asthma attack.

'Go on, don't worry about me,' called Jimmy, waving them away. 'I'll get on soon, and when I do, you better be ready: I'm gonna take you to pieces.'

'Yeah, yeah, nice one,' scoffed Manu, while Matt chuckled.

Smiling, they ran off towards the looming figure of their teacher, who was standing with his tree trunk-like legs either side of the halfway line like some kind of hideous statue.

Now that his chest was under control, Jimmy was at last able to focus on the trial. He knew that Mr Kane would never have picked him for the Probables, but couldn't believe it when he had left him out of the starting team of Possibles too.

He had felt himself welling up when he was named amongst the replacements, but he had managed to keep control . . . just. He closed his eyes for a moment and remembered Shane Williams's story. He was going to be like Shane. He was going to prove Mr Kane wrong.

As Jimmy watched the teams spread out on either side of

halfway, he saw Kitty take up her position on the wing for the Possibles – although her being there at all had caused a bit of a stir earlier in the day.

When Mr Kane had asked for the pupils wanting to take part in the trial to put up their hands, he'd ignored Kitty's until it was the very last held up.

'What do you want?' he'd snapped.

'Um, to play, of course,' said Kitty.

Mr Kane laughed out loud. 'Sorry, my dear,' he said with a patronising shake of his head, 'rugby is a man's game, you'll have to wait until I have time to start a girls' team.'

Before an embarrassed – and angry – Kitty could reply, Miss Ayres stood up at the back of the class.

'Excuse me, Mr Kane,' she said with an edge to her voice that none of the kids had ever heard before. 'There is no such thing as male and female sports in primary education. As long as sensible precautions are followed, girls can play anything . . . I thought you would be aware of that?' She stared at him unblinking, her gaze like an invisible lance in the air between them.

Everyone had looked straight at Mr Kane, who, for the first time since he had joined the school, looked a little flustered. He cleared his throat and looked away, shuffling his feet under the furious heat of her glare.

'Oh, erm, well, erm, yes of course . . . I was just teasing the girl, just having a little fun, you know . . .'

If the whole class could have spoken up at that point, they would have cried a collective, 'Yeah, right!'

With a face like thunder, Mr Kane added Kitty's name to his list of players.

'Right, there you are,' said Mr Kane without looking up. 'Although I've no idea what position you'll play. I'll have to think about that.'

'Wing, sir,' volunteered Jimmy. 'Kitty's the fastest in the school.'

Mr Kane shot Jimmy a filthy look, but then averted his gaze again before Miss Ayres could see it. Jimmy glanced across at a smiling Kitty and when Mr Kane turned to the whiteboard, they bumped fists.

# WAITING ON THE LINE

Mr Kane blew the whistle and Ollie Snell, the Probables fly-half, took the drop-kick to start the match. But he struck it horribly – he was leaning back and his boot scooped under the ball. It hardly made five metres. It was so bad, everybody stopped. Apart from Mr Kane, 'Play on, play on!' he bellowed. Everybody knew that he was wrong – according to the laws, it should be a scrum on halfway to the Possibles, but he seemed to ignore it. He even shouted, 'Good kick, Ollie'.

*Good kick?* thought Jimmy to himself. *I could kick it better than that with my left foot and my eyes closed.* And just to prove it, he turned around, and did just that, sending a spare ball fifteen metres down towards the nearby swings.

Jimmy had nothing against Ollie, he was a really nice lad and not a bad player, but even Ollie himself knew he wasn't in Jimmy's class as a kicker. He was just much taller, and that's what Mr Kane clearly liked. *But then maybe Mr Kane was just trying to be encouraging,* thought Jimmy about the kick. *Perhaps he's going to be like that with all the players. Maybe he isn't so bad after all . . .*

It was wishful thinking.

Jimmy jogged after the ball, sprinted as he got closer to it, swept it up one-handed and, imagining he had a flying flanker on him like Sam Underhill or Pieter-Steph du Toit, threw a dummy, spun and then launched a high chip over his left shoulder, which he chased and regathered.

'Nice skills, son.'

He recognised the voice immediately – it was Peter Clement. He could barely believe his hero had come to watch the trial.

'I managed to finish early after all,' said Peter, wandering over, 'so I thought I'd come and take a look. But I thought you'd be playing! They must have a pretty decent squad to leave you out.'

'Mr Kane thinks I'm too small,' muttered Jimmy, feeling a little embarrassed. He tried to puff himself up to his maximum height.

Just then a big 'Ooh' went up from the crowd as Andrew Beasley ran over the top of a tiny Year 5 centre to score the first try for the Probables.

Peter shook his head slightly as the Year 5 boy dragged himself off the turf and went to join his teammates behind the posts. 'Yes, I can see your teacher likes to have a bit of bulk in his team. Oh well. I happen to think there's always room for skill and it shouldn't matter how big you are. Think of Shane Williams. Think of Cheslin Kolbe. Think of George Ford and George Horne. Think of Aaron Smith!'

Before he could list anymore, one of the dads saw Peter and called, 'Pete, Pete, come over here, pal. I can show you how good my boy Mike is doing – he's an animal! Just like his old man!' It was Mike Green's dad, a thick-set, powerful-looking man. Peter looked at Jimmy and rolled his eyes. 'Oh well, here we go, this will be ten minutes of my life I'll never get back,' and he turned and walked away.

As Jimmy watched him, Peter stopped and glanced back. 'You'll get your chance, son, and when you do, look to play attacking rugby. And always try to do something special. Make a statement. Otherwise, what's the point in playing? It's a *game*, remember? Oh, and don't forget . . . five o'clock tomorrow. Don't be late!'

He turned and continued towards Mike's father, who was bellowing at his son to smash anyone who came near him. 'Hammer them, son, hammer them!' yelled Gary Green. 'Take no prisoners!'

'Always look to do something special . . . make a statement,' repeated Jimmy as he walked back to the touchline to watch the game. *Yes, I can do that.*

As he edged to the sideline, Manu's mother found him again. 'How are you doing now Jimmy?'

'I'm fine now, thanks,' he replied. 'The inhaler always works.'

'That's good, you had me worried for a second!'

Jimmy smiled, and then remembered something.

'Oh, could you do me another favour? Because I was worrying about my inhaler, I forgot to take my glasses off earlier, could you put them in your bag until after the game, please?'

'Yes, of course,' she replied, 'pass them here.'

Jimmy took off his glasses and blinked, letting his eyes adjust to the change.

'Gosh, Jimmy, what have you done to these? There's more sellotape on them than they sell in Wilko's!'

'I know,' grimaced Jimmy. 'My mum always shouts at me about that!'

'I don't blame her! Listen, if you can do without them for an hour or two, I'll get our technician down in the hospital to fix them for you. Manu can drop them over after tea?'

'Oh, yes please,' said Jimmy gratefully, 'I've got a spare pair in my bag – and I won't be in mum's bad books for a change!'

'I'm not sure about that,' laughed Manu's mum. 'You'll still have to tell her you lost your inhaler.'

Jimmy pulled a face at that, which made her laugh even more and she ruffled his hair. They turned their attention back to the match. He could still see more or less everything, it was just things in the far distance that were a little blurred without his glasses, and that was usually fine for rugby – although he did wish he could play in his glasses. Some kids had those sporting glasses, like goggles that some top basketball players wore – and he'd even seen a couple of rugby players wearing them on the TV – but neither of Jimmy's parents could afford them, so they were out of the question. Maybe one day he could get lenses or even laser eye surgery like Brian O'Driscoll—

There was another 'Ooh' from the crowd. This time, the blond-haired giant Andrew Beasley, offering his best Alun Wyn Jones impression, had run straight over the Possibles tighthead prop, Ryan Lewis. Ryan wasn't the most athletic player on the pitch, but he was one of the most determined and committed. Even as he'd been dumped into a crumpled heap by Beasley's rampaging charge, Ryan had somehow managed to tap-tackle the monster just as he was getting away. Keeping his balance elegantly for a big lad, Beasley flicked the ball on the inside to his equally monstrous Year 4 brother, who then ran straight over the nearest tackler. Just as he was stopped by the Possibles outside centre, the younger Beasley, copying his brother, managed to flick it out to John Cena who headed straight towards Kitty on the wing.

What happened next caused some controversy later as some parents were sure they heard Mr Kane shout, 'Smash her!' – but he denied it and said it only sounded like that because he had the whistle in his mouth, claiming he only said, 'Watch her!' This seemed to satisfy the parents but Jimmy didn't believe him for a second.

But nobody need have worried. The 'Ooh' wasn't for John Cena running in for a try, it was for Kitty's brilliant tackle, diving straight at his ankles, bringing him down in a heap, and managing to get him in to touch too. She'd saved a certain try.

All the parents applauded, including Peter Clement who was shouting, 'Way to go, girl! Great tackle, *great* tackle!'

Jimmy grinned broadly and cheered as loudly as anyone.

There was only time for a quick line out, followed by a knock on, before Mr Kane blew the whistle for half-time.

He called everyone in to the middle, including the replacements, who brought on a drink of water and a slice of orange for everyone.

Just as Jimmy started to talk to Kitty about her brilliant tackle, Mr Kane blew his whistle, 'All replacements, over here to me.'

Along with the others, Jimmy jogged over to Mr Kane.

'Right you lot, while they're having a breather, down to the posts and back three times to warm up. You'll all be going on for the start of the second half.'

Jimmy was delighted and reached into his sock for his gum shield. He loved to wear it when he warmed up, it helped him focus.

'Not you, Jimmy,' said Mr Kane. 'The two fly-halves are playing magnificently, there's no point you coming on. You're not going to get in the team in front of those two. You can warm up with the others if you want to, but you won't be coming on.'

With that, he turned away and called both the fly-halves together, patting them on their backs and then pulling them into a huddle to discuss their tactics.

Jimmy turned away, on the brink of tears. It felt like he'd been punched in the stomach. It was all so *unfair*. He looked up and saw Peter Clement, who quietly called him over.

'Hey,' he said, fixing him with a clear, firm gaze. 'Get that chin up. Stay positive. And don't worry, you'll get on. I'll make sure of that. Just make sure that when you do, you make that statement. You got me? Make that statement.'

Jimmy was at a loss as to how Peter would get him on, but he nodded and pulled himself together, running off to join the others. He'd make a statement all right, and it would start now. And for the next five minutes he warmed up as if he was going to play for the All Blacks. He held nothing back.

And if he got on, he was going to make a statement Mr Kane would remember for a long time.

# THE STATEMENT

Jimmy sat forlornly on one of the spare balls. He'd been sitting there for about ten minutes, watching the second half of the trial continue without him. The two fly-halves had both played well, but Jimmy knew he was better than both of them; he just couldn't believe he wasn't getting a chance to get on the pitch to show everyone else.

The ball came out of the scrum, and Matt quickly scooped it up and sent a perfect spin pass out to his waiting fly-half, Ollie Snell. Ollie looked up for a split second and saw a huge gap behind the Possibles left wing. He also noticed that their full back had been sucked over to their right, in case Matt had decided to make a break down the blindside. It was a perfect opportunity to kick. Just as he shaped to punt the ball into the space and gain some precious metres for his team, Mr Kane, reading Ollie's mind, screamed: 'No kicking, take the contact, take the contact!'

Not wishing to upset his coach, Ollie did just that and instead of kicking, ran straight at his opposing fly-half, George Stapleton.

George was a good player but wasn't much of a fan of tackling. Bravely, however, he tried his best to stop the onrushing player . . . but got the angle of his tackle all wrong. The tackle, whilst being poorly carried out in terms of technique, was actually a very powerful one. So powerful that it dislodged the ball from Ollie's grasp and both players went down in a painful heap. Mr Kane's whistle rang out for the knock on and play was stopped. Several parents, concerned that the boys – particularly George – had seriously injured themselves, sprinted on from the sidelines to give them some aid. One of the adults who ran on was Peter Clement.

They knelt over George, who was struggling to breathe. He'd taken the impact of the tackle right in his stomach – his solar plexus – and was winded. He looked in a bad way.

'Take it easy, son, take it easy,' said Peter Clement gently. 'Just try and catch your breath. You'll be okay.'

Mr Kane walked over and parted the crowd of anxious mums and dads to take a look.

'Winded, that's all,' he said dismissively. 'Get him up on his feet and we can carry on. We've got nobody to take his place anyway.'

Peter glared at him, then looked back down to the breathless boy, who was trying to get up after hearing his teacher's comments.

'Stay there, son,' said Peter firmly, 'take your time.' He looked straight up at Mr Kane. 'What about him?' he asked, pointing at Jimmy who was jogging on the spot, hoping this unfortunate incident would be the moment he'd finally take the field.

Mr Kane looked over at Jimmy, then back at Peter.

'No need, this boy will be fine in a minute.'

'No, he *won't*,' replied Peter, 'he's going to need a few minutes to get his breath, that was a hell of a bang he took.'

'I agree,' said George's father, who, helped by Peter, lifted up his shaken son and helped him towards the touchline.

Before Mr Kane could say anything, Peter called over to Jimmy, 'Hey, son, take that bib off, you're on.'

Jimmy's face lit up as he quickly pulled the yellow bib over his head, threw it to the ground, pulled his gum shield from his sock and ran onto the field. He took a deep breath and was relieved that his chest felt fine.

As he ran past him, Peter winked at Jimmy again. Jimmy knew what he had to do. Make a statement.

Mr Kane blew his whistle and called for a scrum. Before continuing, he looked coldly at Jimmy. 'No kicking,' he growled. 'This is a running and tackling trial. People work too hard for the ball just for somebody else to kick it away.' In reply, Jimmy just made a noncommittal shrug and ran to take up his position.

The Possibles scrum-half fed the ball into the scrum, but it was won by the Probables hooker, who heeled the ball straight back for his team.

Quick as a flash, Matt scooped the ball up from the back of the scrum and darted down the blind side, catching the defending wing, Kitty, completely unawares. She'd expected her side to win the scrum and had already moved into an attacking position in-field. Matt was sharp and spotted his chance in an instant, hurtling into the space she had left down the wing. The only other player who had anticipated Matt's move, was Jimmy.

Turning on a sixpence when he saw the ball hit Matt's hands, Jimmy worked out the best angle to catch his friend. He knew he was quicker than Matt, he just had to make sure he ran at the best angle to cut him off.

To all the parents, it looked like Matt was going to streak ahead and score a spectacular try. Despite being one of the smaller players on the field, Matt was a classic pocket battleship of a scrum-half, and his all-action running style, which actually made him look as if he was moving faster than he actually was, would surely see him over for his touchdown. But as everyone was screaming and cheering for Matt, Jimmy flew across – almost unseen by everyone – and with a perfect dive, he swept Matt's legs from under him and bundled him in to touch, deep inside the Possibles' half. It had been a brilliant passage of rugby – a great break followed by a great tackle.

Every adult watching cheered and clapped, except one. Mr Kane.

'Line out to the Possibles,' was all he said.

As the rest of the Possibles forwards took their places for the line out, Jimmy walked quickly up to the hooker. He took his gum shield out, put his hand over his mouth and whispered to the hooker, 'Throw it to the tail.'

He ran past the scrum-half, Billy O'Reilly, and whispered, 'Tail,' then looked straight at the player at the back of the line out, their tall second-row, Mark Smith, and winked. Mark understood.

Mr Kane walked through the middle of the line out, making sure there was a gap between the two packs of forwards. When he got to the tail, he looked straight at Jimmy. 'No kicking,' he reiterated. 'We run and try to bust the tackles.' This time, Jimmy didn't even look at him.

The whistle blew and the ball arced to the back of the line out, where Mark leapt like a salmon and superbly caught and passed the ball to Billy in one movement. Taking the ball in front of him, the scrum-half quickly passed the ball on to Jimmy.

In Jimmy's mind, everything was clear. It took him a split second to see how flat the Probables back line had got, and notice that the full back had moved way too far up the field.

In one, wonderfully silky movement, Jimmy dropped the ball onto his right foot and drilled the most perfect and precise kick, straight up field. It was hit with such timing and power that there was a collective 'Ooh' from the watching parents.

At the precise moment the ball left his boot, only one person on the field moved. Jimmy.

He chased his kick as if his life depended on it.

The first two players to react in the Probables defence were full back, Mike Green, and the right wing, Keegan Miller. Jimmy saw them and realised that Green was his major problem. Ignoring any negative thoughts, Jimmy chased the ball as it came rolling to a stop in the opposition half.

As he reached it, he knew that Mike was almost on him. He could hear his feet and virtually feel his breath on the back of his neck.

At that point he also heard, 'Jimmy, Jimmy, right pop!' It was Kitty, haring up from the right wing.

The safe thing to do was to fall on the ball, gather it and hope that some of his teammates would be there in support to help secure the ball. But Jimmy had other ideas.

Hardly breaking stride, Jimmy dipped his body forward and scooped the ball up with his left hand. As he did so, Mike clattered into him. Just before Jimmy hit the ground, he switched the ball to his right hand, and flicking the ball behind him, popped it into the air. Right into Kitty's path.

Kitty caught the ball in one fluid movement, sidestepped inside the despairing dive of the covering Keegan, and jogged in under the posts, touching the ball down as casually as if she had just walked it in.

The parents went mad. It was a superb piece of play. Jimmy looked up from the mud to see his teammates celebrating, then across to Peter Clement, who was smiling, nodding and clapping. He threw Jimmy a triumphant thumbs-up.

'Yeah, boooooy!' cried Matt as he jogged back to the line. 'That was brilliant.'

'Hey, you're not even on his team!' spat Mike, incredulously. 'Don't go congratulating him.'

'Shut it, Mike, it's a trial,' muttered Matt, without looking at him. 'We're supposed to want people to play well.'

As Mike spluttered something inaudible, Kitty ran across and gave Jimmy a high-five as he hauled himself to his feet. 'Nice one, Jim!' She tossed him the ball. 'Now slot the extra two points for us as well.'

Jimmy had forgotten all about the conversion. As he looked to see where he should take the kick from, Mr Kane loomed over him.

'Ball!' he snarled.

Jimmy looked confused, but passed him the ball.

Mr Kane looked across to George Stapleton, who was standing beside Peter Clement.

'Got your wind back?' called Mr Kane.

'Erm, yes sir, I think so,' replied George, slightly bewildered.

'Good,' said Mr Kane. 'You have a conversion to take.' And looking straight at Jimmy, quickly added, 'Which means you can get off, we don't need you anymore.' Then he turned and walked away.

On the sideline, Peter just stood there, shaking his head at Mr Kane.

Jimmy shrugged his shoulders, put his gum shield in his sock and brushed a clump of mud off his knee. Strangely, he didn't mind too much. He'd done the only thing that mattered. He had made his statement. And everybody had seen it.

# THE FIGHT

THE ATMOSPHERE in the old changing room at The Rec was bouncing. It had been a cracking game of rugby, with the Possibles, helped by Jimmy's amazing try-making break, managing to beat the Probables by a single point, 33–32.

It seemed that nearly all of Jimmy's friends had contributed to the quality of the game, especially Kitty, who had scored two tries, Manu who had scored one, and Matt whose three tries from scrum-half had won him the man of the match award.

Jimmy sat on his bench, peeling off his socks, and although he'd only been on the field for about two minutes, he was feeling pretty happy.

He knew he should really be annoyed by Mr Kane's refusal to let him stay on the field, but what he'd done in the short time he'd been given had been pretty special. He was delighted with his kick, maybe more so because he knew Mr Kane didn't want him to do it – but that wasn't why Jimmy had done it. Jimmy had kicked it for one simple reason: it was the best opportunity to score a try . . . it was the right rugby decision. It was as simple as that.

With all the noise and larking about going on around him, Jimmy allowed himself a quiet moment to reflect on his brief, but important part in the game. He enjoyed the kick, but it was his flick pass out of the back of his hand that he took the most pleasure in. He'd seen one of his heroes, Sonny Bill Williams – who had played for the All Blacks – do it many times and he was chuffed to bits that it had come off and set up Kitty to go in under the posts.

George had missed the conversion. Although Jimmy liked George, he had been quite relieved to see him miss it. They were friends, but they were also rivals for that number ten jersey.

As Jimmy dumped his grassy boots in his bag, Mr Kane strode into the changing room. He didn't look pleased.

Just behind Jimmy, Mike Green, intimidating as ever with his grade one shaved haircut and permanent sneer, sat quietly. Watching. Waiting. Clutched in his hand was a blue asthma inhaler. He sat still and waited for Mr Kane to start speaking.

'Right then, listen up everyone,' said Mr Kane. 'I've just had to listen to thirty-odd parents out there telling me what a fantastic game of rugby they've just seen. Nothing changes round here . . . they still don't know a thing about rugby.' He paused, looking at all the faces staring back at him. 'That game was *littered* with mistakes,' he continued, gruffly, the vein on his temple beginning to throb. 'Handling errors, knock-ons, poor positional play and missed tackles. If you'd have all listened to what I was telling you out there, well, it would have been more like 15–3 than that ridiculous score line. And as for *you*,' he said, pointing a huge crooked finger at Jimmy, 'the last thing I told you was *not* to kick it! If you disobey a direct order from me again, you won't ever get a chance to play for this school.'

Jimmy stared at the floor, a mixture of frustration, embarrassment and anger shuddering through him.

With that, another voice broke in from the back of the changing room. It was Mike.

'Sir, do you know whose this is?'

Everyone looked around to see what he had. Jimmy was one of the last to turn. And when he did, he saw Mike looking straight at him, smirking and holding the missing asthma inhaler out in front of him.

A feeling of rage, the likes of which he had never felt before, surged through Jimmy, and he ran across the room and pounced on Mike, quickly landing three rapid punches to the top of Mike's head. Before Mike could retaliate and before Jimmy could add to his surprisingly impressive and fast combination of punches, Jimmy was dragged away by Mr Kane.

'Sit back down there, boy. NOW!' Nobody ever lays a hand on one of their own teammates . . . EVER!

'But sir,' cried Jimmy, his outrage making his voice tremble, 'he stole my asthma inhaler! He did it on purpose so that I wouldn't be able to play!'

'Be quiet, boy!' raged Mr Kane. 'Detention for you after school tomorrow. I'll get a letter home to your mother later. Now get changed and get home, you've caused enough trouble for one day!'

A bad day had ended awfully for Jimmy. As he finished dressing, he put his spare glasses on and picked up his bag, then he glanced across at Mike, who was sitting there laughing with one of the other Year 6 boys. A surge of something that Jimmy had never truly experienced before flowed right through him.

It was hatred.

## BULLY, BULLY

Tired as he was after the trial, Mike Green didn't go home at once. He wandered around The Rec for a while, checking the abandoned farm compound where he often hung out with his gang to see if any of them were around – but they weren't. He pulled out his phone to send his group on WhatsApp a message, but saw that the battery was dead. He wanted to tell them all about the inhaler – he was so pleased with how his plan had worked out, first by getting Jimmy worked up before the game and then getting him in to detention by goading him into their fight. It had all panned out better than he could have hoped. He couldn't have been certain how Jimmy would react or even if Mr Kane would give him detention, but it had worked like a dream – and Jimmy would now miss the coaching session with Peter Clement. Mike smiled at the thought of a job well done.

Now he just wanted to tell his friends about it. They would find it hilarious. They would think he was so cunning. He'd lived up to the Green family name once again! His thoughts faltered for a moment. He didn't want to think too much about that. It was like picking at a scab that wasn't ready to come off. But still . . . he couldn't help it.

It all came down to the Green family name.

*Pick.*

The others followed him because he was a Green. Because of who his father was. Because of who his brothers were.

*Pick.*

Was it really anything to do with *him?*

*Pick.*

Did any of them really like him? Or were they just afraid of him?

*Pick.*

He tried to force the whispers in his head away and focussed again on his triumph over Jimmy Joseph. That little rat thought he had it all. Thought he was the man when it came to rugby. Wrong! Mike was the team captain. He was number one. He was the best player in the school. Not that speccy little twig.

Yeah, Jimmy could kick. Yeah, he was light on his feet . . . whatever. He had nothing on Mike Green. And he was going to prove it every time they went on the pitch, every time he saw Jimmy in school or around the village. Mike knew well enough what it was like to live in the shadow of a Joseph. His brother Paul had to deal with Jonny Joseph being the star player in their year. There was no way Mike was going to let that happen to him as well. He lived in no one's shadow.

*Except your father's,* whispered a little voice in his head. *Except your brothers'.*

'Shut up!' he shouted at the darkening sky.

The wind was blowing in cold off the mountains now and Mike shivered. He was tired and hungry and cold. He had no choice. He had to go home.

He walked back slowly, playing over the events of the day again in his mind, congratulating himself again and again on his cleverness. A job well done.

As he reached the gate at the end of the path that led to his front door, he heard a crash from inside the house and shuddered. There were loud voices. It was his dad, Gary. Mike winced and nearly turned around to walk back to The Rec, but before he could make that choice, the tatty, brown front door was yanked open, and there stood his father – tall, bald, tattooed and menacing. A living, breathing ball of fury.

'And where the 'ell have you been, eh?' The question was delivered coldly, eyes narrowed, lip curled into a barely concealed sneer. the sunlight glinting off the three earrings in each ear lobe and from the huge gold chain that adorned his enormous, bare chest. 'Getting your nails done?'

Mike cowered slightly as he replied, not taking his eyes off the ground in front of him, 'I – I, no. 'Course not. I was playing rugby, remember?'

Gary's eyes narrowed still further. 'Until *now?*' He stared at his watch disbelievingly.

'Eh, yeah. I did some extras afterwards. You know, game wasn't hard enough so I wanted to do some extra running and stuff.'

'You're right it wasn't hard enough – it was pathetic. I couldn't stand it, so I left at half-time, I had some . . . business to attend to. But you won, yeah?'

'Yeah . . . 'course,' lied Mike, praying that his father would never learn that the team he'd captained had lost to a bunch of losers and misfits. And a *girl*.

'Good. At least you can do *something* right.'

Mike nodded, still staring at his feet.

'Look at me when I talk to you,' growled his dad suddenly, jabbing an enormous finger into Mike's chest as he spoke. 'You show me some respect, you hear me?'

Mike looked up, trying to hide the terror in his eyes, knowing that if his father saw any fear there, he would be in for trouble.

He tried as hard as he could. But he failed.

'God, you're pathetic, aren't you?' spat Gary, witheringly. He shook his head. 'Get inside!'

As Mike slunk towards the door, Gary turned and shouted into the house, 'Come on, Joe, I haven't got all day. We need to get to that new car dealers' yard before the security guard gets there. I want to be long gone by the time he shows up . . .' Gary Green's face broke into a satisfied, lopsided grin as his criminal mind turned to the thought of his next, lucrative job – in just a few minutes' time he be driving away in a brand-new car.

Then without another glance at Mike, he walked to the battered truck that was parked on the roadside and jumped in. As he slammed the door, Mike's second eldest brother, Joe, jogged down the stairs. At seventeen, he was the carbon copy of his father. Head shaved down to a number one, so blond that he looked as if he was completely bald, with biceps bulging out of his knock-off Under Armour t-shirt. As he pushed past Mike, he jerked his head and shouted, 'Boo!' loudly in his face, making Mike jump back.

'Freak!' shouted Joe, cackling as he jumped in the truck beside his dad, who was now revving the engine impatiently.

Even before Joe had time to fully close the door, Gary had pulled away with a screech, getting the car up to thirty miles per hour before he was halfway down the street, doing so just as he passed a twenty-miles-per-hour sign. Mrs Roderick, the school cook who lived opposite the Greens, tutted to herself as she watched the vehicle shoot past her, way over the speed limit. She felt like saying something, but she'd learned many years ago to ignore Gary Green's antics if she wanted a quiet life.

The whole incident with his father had lasted no more than a couple of minutes, but the adrenaline coursing through Mike's veins was even more intense than it had been during the entire rugby match. He closed the door behind him and leant his head against it, his backpack containing his rugby kit and school books weighing on his back as heavily as the guilt of being aware of his father's latest criminal venture.

'Come on, toughen up,' he whispered quietly to himself. 'You're better than this. You're *tougher* than this . . .'

*Pick.*

# DETENTION

Jimmy sat in detention on his own. In silence.

He'd tried to tell his mother to come to the school to complain about his treatment, but she'd refused.

'Life isn't always fair, Jimmy,' she'd told him. 'Of course what Mike did was wrong, but you shouldn't have reacted in the way that you did – no matter how badly people goad you, Jimmy, never give them the satisfaction of seeing you react. And in this case that is even truer, because your teacher had warned you about your behaviour.'

Jimmy had tried to explain that Mr Kane had it in for him, but she was having none of it.

'He's a new teacher, Jimmy, and he's just trying to lay the law down. You might feel that he's against you at the moment, but I'm sure it's nothing personal. It'll change in a few days. It will make things worse if I go to him and complain. You shouldn't have attacked Mike – no matter what he did – so you'll just have to accept the punishment.'

Jimmy's silent response slightly upset his mother, but she had always promised herself never to spoil her children and to always make them understand right from wrong. She was determined to make them grow up and realise that they would always have to accept the consequences of their actions, no matter how unfair they felt that was.

Jimmy understood what his mother meant, and agreed with most of it. He knew he had been wrong to go for Mike Green in the way he had, it was just that with all the other disappointments he'd had on the day, it had been the straw that broke the camel's back. One thing his mother was wrong about, though, was her assessment of Mr Kane. He wasn't just trying to lay the law down, he just didn't like Jimmy at all. It was so unfair.

Jimmy looked at the clock. It was 4.35. It would take him ten minutes to get to The Rec to meet Peter Clement, and he was desperate to get there on time. Mr Kane said he was keeping him until 5.00, but surely he would let him go early – Jimmy had done everything he'd asked, he'd even redone his maths test and got seven out of ten this time.

Jimmy just sat there in silence, watching the second hand of the clock. It seemed that every second was taking a minute.

At 4.45, Jimmy decided to speak.

'Sir?' he enquired politely.

No response. Mr Kane just sat there, carrying on with his marking.

Jimmy waited fifteen seconds. 'Sir?'

Without looking up, Mr Kane replied coldly, 'You will not leave a second before five o'clock. If you speak again, it will be quarter past. I don't mind, I've got lots to do.'

Jimmy slumped back in his chair, dejected, and continued to stare at the clock.

At the stroke of five, he grabbed his bag silently and looked to his captor.

'Go on then, get out,' said Mr Kane, still not looking up.

Jimmy didn't need a second invitation. He was up and out of his desk like a shot, out of the room, down the corridor past Mr Davies' office, around the corner into the reception area, before pausing to tap the button to release the lock on the front door.

Like a flash, he was out, across the yard to the school gate, before turning left and sprinting down the road to The Rec. He ran like the wind.

When he got there, it was eight minutes past five. No matter how fast he'd run, he was still late. He looked all around The Rec, there was no sign of Peter anywhere. His heart sank.

Just as he turned around to head to Peter's house to explain the horrible situation, Jimmy heard a familiar voice.

'He's gone. He looked angry too.' The statement was followed by laughter. Jimmy spun around but he already knew who the voice belonged to. It was Mike Green.

Jimmy looked at him and he could feel his face flushing with anger. He wanted to rush at Mike, to hit him, to scream in his face that this was all his fault. But he remembered his mother's words: *Whatever people do, don't react.*

Jimmy took a long, slow breath and then gently exhaled as if his breath was fluttering a candle flame. *Choose your battles, Jimmy,* he said to himself. *Now's not the time.* He turned and continued his run to Peter's house.

'That's right, you chicken,' crowed Mike. 'Just run away . . . like you always do.'

Every part of Jimmy's body wanted to stop, turn around and confront Mike, but he had more important things to do. He ducked his head and continued on. He needed to explain himself to Peter.

Peter answered the door, munching a mouthful of food.

'I told you I wouldn't wait, son,' he said with a disappointed shake of his head. 'If you haven't got the discipline to be somewhere on time as arranged, then I'm not going to waste my time. If you want to be a professional, you have to have a professional attitude from the start.'

He began to shut the door so Jimmy spoke hastily, 'I know, I'm really sorry, Mr Clement, but I had detention until five o'clock. I ran as fast as I could. I'm really sorry I was late.'

Peter paused and appraised Jimmy's face, searching the boy's sorry features for a trace of a lie.

'Detention, eh?' he said at last, his hand paused on the door. 'What did you have that for?'

Jimmy cleared his throat. 'I, er, I tried to punch Mike Green in the changing room. He stole my asthma inhaler.'

'Did he?' replied Peter, thoughtfully. 'That's Gary Green's son, isn't? Well, that doesn't surprise me too much, to be honest. But fighting? There's only one way to get back at people like him, and that's by being better than them on the field.'

Peter continued to stand there looking at Jimmy. He didn't know what it was, but he liked this boy. Saw something of himself in him. He could see his apology was sincere and, judging by how red and breathless Jimmy was, he had clearly done his best to get there as soon as he could. *Okay. Maybe time to give him a break.*

'I don't normally give people second chances,' said Peter, his mouth breaking into a small, crooked smile. 'But I'm willing to make an exception this once. After my tea, I'm going across to the Wolves to take a session with their backs. I should be done by 6.30. If you can be there by then, we'll have a chat after that. That sound okay? Oh, and bring your boots!'

'Yes, Mr Clement, of course. Thank you, *thank you.*'

'That's okay, son,' replied Peter, giving him a wink. 'I'll see you then. Oh, and call me Peter.'

Jimmy nodded and picked up his bag. He was thrilled. And so relieved.

'Just don't be late!' called Peter as Jimmy headed for home. 'Remember, be professional – always.'

Jimmy clenched his jaw. He was determined to show Peter just how professional he could be.

# RUGBY ON THE BRAIN

WHEN JIMMY got home he found a note from his mother on the hall table saying that she was working an extra shift and that Jonny would sort out dinner. Jimmy knew that this would involve reheating some meatballs and boiling up a pot of pasta and he was hoping to find it ready for him – but he found his brother ensconced in the front room watching a highlights programme of that week's Top 14 rugby while his sister lay sprawled on the couch behind him, reading a book, an annoyed expression on her face. She looked up and gave Jimmy a pained look.

'Jim, can you get him to listen to me? I'm *starving* but he's not going to make tea until the stupid rugby's finished.'

Jimmy's stomach was almost aching with hunger too, but his eyes had already been drawn to the French rugby on the TV. He tossed down his schoolbag on the end of the couch – hitting Julie's feet, which led to a loud complaint – and slumped down beside Jonny, who was sitting on the floor just a foot or two away from the screen.

'Is that Damian Penaud?' asked Jimmy, leaning forwards slightly to take in the picture.

'Yeah,' replied Jonny. 'And look at this, they're just about to do a replay. Look! See that!'

'Man, that's *class*,' breathed Jimmy, goggling at the screen.

'Honestly, I sometimes wonder if there's anything in those brains of yours except rugby,' muttered Julie. '*Helloooo . . .*' she added when neither boy replied. She threw her book at Jonny.

'Hey, if you're hungry, you know where the kitchen is,' cried Jonny, rubbing the back of his head. 'Or you can wait – this'll be finished in . . . uh, seven minutes.'

'But I'm hungry *now!* I've been hungry for *ages!* Jimmy, you're always starving, you not hungry?'

'Yeah, but . . . it's only seven minutes . . .' said Jimmy without taking his eyes off the screen. He was now transfixed by Romain Ntamack ghosting through the defensive line as if he were on skates and the surrounding tacklers were running through treacle.

'Uggh, you guys are the worst!' she shrieked and stormed into the kitchen where she began to crash pots around loudly.

'I reckon she has a big career ahead of her,' muttered Jonny. 'That much rage needs an outlet. Can you imagine her tackling someone? She'd *destroy* them.'

Jimmy laughed. 'Yeah, and then when she retires she could be a coach. No one would ever mess with her. She'd make Shaun Edwards look like a kitten.'

Eventually Julie's relentless racket – and their own guilt – drove them to abandon the final minutes of the programme and go and help her.

'So how was your session with the great Peter Clement?' asked Jonny as he spooned a mountain of pasta and meatballs into Jimmy's bowl.

'Not too much!' exclaimed Jimmy, and scraped half the food back into the pot.

'Eh? What's wrong with you? You normally eat twice that much.'

'I haven't *had* the session yet. I'm meeting him after the Wolves have trained tonight. I don't want to eat too much and be sick.'

Jonny nodded in understanding. Two-and-a-bit years older than Jimmy, Jonny had captained Central Primary during his last two years there, before being appointed captain of the Year Seven team at Bishopswood – the senior school – and, more recently, the Year 8s. He'd also played for his district and was part of the Eagles Under-13s Academy Squad. Anyone in the area who knew anything about young Jonny Joseph, knew that he was going to become a star. He had the lot, it was just a matter of time.

'How did you manage to persuade him to give you some coaching, anyway?' asked Jonny, sitting down at the table. 'I thought Peter just coached the seniors, not the kids?'

'I dunno, just lucky, I guess,' said Jimmy, making sure he chewed his food thoroughly. He didn't want any of it sitting heavily in his stomach if he was going to be running around soon. 'He saw me and Kitty playing on The Rec and then came over and said he thought I had some talent, and would I like some coaching on my kicking. It was pretty cool.'

'Too right it's cool,' breathed Jonny, his eyes wide. 'I'd love him to coach me. Can I come along too?'

Jimmy went quiet. He'd love to take his brother along, but Peter's repeated warning about being 'professional' kept ringing in his ears. The fact that he'd already messed up once also lay very heavily on his mind.

'I don't think you can, Jonny. I've let him down already and don't want to give him a chance to be annoyed at me again.'

'Let him down? What happened?'

'Well, I was supposed to meet him on The Rec earlier, but I had detention at school, so was late. He really wasn't happy about that, but gave me this last chance. That's why I want to go now, and get there early.'

'What did you have detention for, then?' asked Julie, through a mouthful of pasta.

Jimmy had really wanted to tell them both all about the stuff with Mike yesterday after it had happened, but he knew that Jonny himself was involved in a running battle with Paul Green, and he didn't want to get Jonny involved in his own troubles. And what was Julie going to do? Probably march up to Mike and give him a right earful – but that wouldn't help either. Imagine what Mike would say about Jimmy getting his little sister to fight his battles for him? It would just add more fuel on the fire.

'Oh, it was nothing really,' he said, his eyes fixed on the last scrap of pasta in his bowl. 'I was just caught messing around in the dressing room after the trials yesterday. The new teacher wasn't happy, so gave me detention.'

'What? Detention just for messing around in the dressing room?' cried Jonny. 'Our whole team would never play again if we all had detention for that. Are you sure that's all it was?'

Jonny didn't take his eyes off his young brother, who had now carried his bowl to the sink and was beginning to root through his kitbag.

'Well, it wasn't just for that,' said Jimmy, trying to work out just how much to tell them. 'I was also messing about in class earlier and I ended up knocking his cup of tea all over his desk. He did warn me after that – so it was my fault.'

'Oh, flipping heck, Jim, you know what mum says about behaviour in school . . .'

'*Once you get a bad reputation, it's going to stick,*' parroted Julie in a perfect imitation of their mother, which set them all howling with laughter.

Jonny glanced up at the kitchen clock. 'Well you'd better get going then, Wonderboy. Enjoy training with The Legend and maybe put in a good word for me for next time.'

'Sure thing,' said Jimmy with a smile. He snatched up his boots and shoved them in his kitbag.

'Oh, and Jim,' called Julie as he headed for the door, 'don't mess up and puke pasta all over him.'

Jimmy rolled his eyes and threw a clod of grass from his boots at her.

# THEATRE OF DREAMS

THE AIR was still and filled with the last drifting clouds of that summer's midges as Jimmy headed down towards the Memorial Ground, which had been home to the Wolves for the past 110 years. The sky above was a pale blue tinged with flashes of pink as the late summer sun began to sink towards the horizon, casting long lazy shadows from the mountain peaks that jutted high into the sky beyond the Memorial Ground's ancient stand.

As Jimmy approached the ground, the hairs on the back of his neck stood up. He absolutely loved the place.

He couldn't remember exactly how old he'd been when he'd first gone there – he thought he must have been about four or five – but he remembered so much about it. He could recall with perfect clarity the feel of his grandfather's hand as they walked down the street to the ground, the sound of his voice as the old man showed the gateman his season ticket and said to him, 'You don't mind if I lift this little one over, do you? We might only stay twenty minutes if he doesn't like it.' Then the thrill of being lifted over the turnstile.

His grandfather had expected him to last twenty minutes max before he got bored. But Jimmy had loved it. Every part of it. He loved the clank of the rusty, old-fashioned turnstile as his grandfather followed him into the ground. He loved the buzz of the supporters hanging around in the area beneath the stand, laughing and buying piping-hot cups of tea. He loved the hot dog that his grandfather bought him. He loved the first glimpse of that beautiful green grass, like the lushest carpet he'd ever seen. He loved the sound of the crowd when the players ran out, the crack of their studs as they crossed the stretch of red gravel that ran between the tunnel and the field. He loved the noise of the game, the smell of the liniment, the thuds and crashes, the speed, the colours, the tribal roars. He loved it all. And he'd begged to be taken back. And almost every home game since, he had been back.

Jimmy was also very lucky because of his dad's involvement at the club.

Saturday was the day that Jimmy got to spend the whole day with his dad – or, more accurately, with his dad and the Wolves. Jimmy's dad was a health and safety officer for the local council, but on Saturdays he was the physio for the Wolves. His job was to make sure that all the players were fit and well enough to take part in that day's match and to look after them if they picked up any injuries during the game. He would sit with his medical kit in the players' dugout on the sideline and Jimmy, Jonny and Julie got to sit there, too, if they wanted to. For Jimmy, it was dreamland. He knew the names of all the players, knew all their individual stats and he'd also read lots about the club's history. Sitting in the dugout alongside the substitute players really made him feel part of things, listening to the banter – not to mention the swearing! – as they bided their time, hoping to get their chance to get on the field. When a player went down injured his dad would leap into action, sprinting across the field like an Olympic gold medallist to treat the stricken player while one of the guys next to him would stand and stretch, towering over Jimmy, getting themselves ready in case they were needed.

And then, every now and then, Jimmy got to show off his own skills by fielding a ball that had been kicked to touch and had rolled into the dugout – returning it to the hooker for the line out either with a spin pass or a little chip or grubber kick. Yes, Jimmy's Saturdays were spent in rugby heaven.

It was Jimmy's obvious talent in fielding the odd stray ball that, eventually, gave him his greatest ever birthday present. When he was nine, his dad handed him a Wolves training top, that had been taken in and altered to fit his skinny frame. He had even had the initials *J.J.* sewn onto it. His dad then took him to the dugout and sat him down. It was a Saturday morning before a Wolves home game, but kick-off was still more than two hours away. The ground was empty and a light drizzle was blowing in off the mountains. The wind whistled through the stand and the posts swayed slightly at either end of the field.

'Listen, Jimmy,' his father started. 'I know it's your birthday, but I've got some bad news for you . . . you won't be able to sit next to me in this dugout anymore.'

Jimmy was so crestfallen he felt on the edge of tears. He felt unable to speak. What had he done wrong? He blinked rapidly and tried to swallow down the thick lump that had formed in his throat while staring mournfully at the wonderful woven Wolves badge on his jersey. He traced his fingers around its edges, not wanting to believe his dad's words.

'The reason,' his father continued, 'is that you'll have a job to do, which means you'll not be able to sit down here,' – he tapped the dugout seat – 'because you'll be out there, on the touchline now.' Jimmy looked up at him, his face a picture of confusion. But then a spark of hope flared in his eyes. He wondered if he could guess what his dad was about to say, but he didn't want to ask in case he jinxed it.

'Today, for your birthday, I've arranged for you to become a ball boy. And if you do well, the club have said you can do it for the rest of the year.'

Jimmy jumped up and punched the air. He'd never been so happy.

From that day on, Jimmy had been one of the club's ball boys – and he loved every second of it. He couldn't wait until a ball was kicked his way and he had the chance to catch it. He hardly ever dropped the ball and always drew great cheers from the crowd. This link with the Wolves, thanks to his dad, had deepened Jimmy's love for rugby even more and fired his dreams to, one day, pull on that famous red and black jersey. It was all Jimmy could think about.

Normally, on a match day, Jimmy went into the ground via the large gate at the corner of the stand that backed on to The Rec. It was where the St John Ambulance was driven in and where Jimmy met Mr Phillips, the chief steward, and the other ball boys and ball girls. But not tonight. Tonight, Peter Clement had given Jimmy instructions to enter the ground via the players' entrance in the opposite stand. This was a first for Jimmy, a really special moment.

Jimmy approached the main stand from the top of the street that ran from the back of The Rec. He looked up at the big, red-brick stand in awe as he approached it. Above the walls stood the massive canopy of the roof, a huge grey structure that stretched out like a giant umbrella to protect the watching fans from the winter weather that usually swept down from the mountains behind the stand or from the direction of the coast away to the south. Beyond the edge of the stand Jimmy could just about see the tops of the white posts at one end of the field, climbing into the sky like two enormous, white knitting needles. On top of each post were Jimmy's favourite things: small metal wolves that stood guard above the ground, surveying all that went on around them. Protecting their territory. Overlooking their pack. He thought they were so cool.

After spending a few moments just staring at the wolves, Jimmy moved off and walked halfway along the stand, and stopped again. There it was, the players' entrance. High above the wrought iron gate, which was adorned with an intricately designed wolf's head above a rugby ball, was the plaque that said it all.

Jimmy read it to himself in a whisper. 'Players and officials of Wolves RFC only. No unauthorised admittance.'

Just below it was the phrase that Jimmy had learnt by heart when he had been just five years old. *The strength of the pack is the wolf, and the strength of the wolf is the pack.* It was from *The Jungle Book* by Rudyard Kipling. It meant that the pack – or in this case, the team – was only as strong as the abilities of its individual players – the wolves; but the individual players were only as strong as the combined abilities of the team around them. Jimmy loved the idea so much. It encouraged individual brilliance while emphasising the importance of teamwork.

Jimmy hoped with all of his heart that he would one day become a Wolf. It would be his first step on his journey to becoming a British & Irish Lion.

He stepped through the gate and headed for the dark tunnel which led to the dressing room area. The gate creaked noisily as he pushed it open and before he could take another step, he heard a voice.

'Oi, where d'you think you're going, young man?'

It was Mr Price, the club secretary. He was a friend of Jimmy's grandfather.

'Erm, sorry, I, I, um, um, I'm here to see, erm . . .' Jimmy was so flustered, he'd forgotten Peter Clement's name.

'Ah, hold on. You're Will's grandson, aren't you? How is the old devil?'

Jimmy blushed with the recognition. 'Oh, yes, I am. He's fine, thank you.'

'That's good to hear,' replied the secretary, who was dressed smartly in grey trousers and navy blazer which had an enormous embroidered patch over the breast pocket with the club emblem. Jimmy couldn't take his eyes off it.

'Right, so why are you here, son?' continued Mr Price. 'Not just anyone can walk through the Players' Entrance. That has to be earned.'

For some reason, Jimmy froze, unable to say anything more. It was as if he'd been caught doing something he shouldn't have. He just stood there in silence.

'Hold on a minute,' said the secretary, looking closely at Jimmy. 'You're one of our ball boys, aren't you?'

Again, Jimmy said nothing, but he managed a nod.

'You should know better, son. Your entrance is through the big gates on the far stand, not here. Anyway, there's no game tonight, so what are you doing here? It's not allowed.'

Jimmy's brain finally sparked into life.

'Peter Clement told me to come down,' he blurted. 'He said to be here by 6.30. I'm a little bit early.'

'Oh, is that right?' said the secretary, a little surprised. He glanced at his watch. 'Well it's only just gone six o'clock and the team are still out training.' He thought for a moment and then offered Jimmy a kind smile. 'Come with me.' He turned on his heels and walked quickly down the dark corridor that led to the changing rooms. He walked so quickly, Jimmy nearly had to break into a trot to keep up – all the while wishing that Mr Price would slow down so that he could take in every detail of this special place.

Indeed, almost before he had had time to blink, they had passed the door that Jimmy had wanted to stop and look at the most. It was a normal brown, wooden door, but in the middle of it was a bright white sign bearing a single word in red capital letters: 'HOME'.

Jimmy had never been allowed in there. Even when he used to sit next to his dad in the dugout, he'd always been told the tunnel and dressing rooms were off-limits. Jimmy would've given anything to have had a peek inside, but with Mr Price there, there was no chance.

'C'mon, lad, keep up,' shouted Mr Price over his shoulder.

With that, there was light. Lots of it. The tunnel opened out onto the pitch and the towering floodlights bathed the whole area in a dazzling glow. Mr Price turned left and began walking along to the coach's dugout and replacements' seats on halfway, but Jimmy just stopped for a moment and stared down at his feet. His tatty trainers were standing firmly on the red gravel that circled the pitch. He moved his feet over the top of the gravel, enjoying the crunching feeling under his toes, the grinding sound it made and the red dust that puffed up over his sky-blue trainers. He always loved the way the dust clouded around the players' boots as they ran out on a match day. Then he looked a few yards ahead of him. The grass. The pitch. It was raised above the gravel by about ten centimetres, almost like a grass step. Jimmy carried out his ball boy duties on the other side of the ground, and the natural slope of the pitch meant that there was no step there, just an end to the grass where the gravel began.

Jimmy looked at the step and wondered just how many players had run down this tunnel and onto this pitch over the last hundred years or so. Thousands probably. Jimmy was in awe. He was desperate to step onto the pitch as a player himself one day.

'Lad. Lad! Come on, no time to daydream.' It was Mr Price, waving to Jimmy to join him. Jimmy ran, kicking up more dust from the gravel as he went, to where Mr Price was climbing the steps to a row of seats behind the dugout.

'Come and sit here,' Mr Price instructed. 'This is where the chairman sits on match day, so it's a bit of an honour.'

Jimmy took his place, put his kit bag on the seat next to him, and made himself comfortable. Unlike the rest of the seats in the stand, these ones had cracked red-leather cushions attached to them.

'Bag on the floor please, lad,' bustled Mr Price. 'We don't want you scuffing the leather – that's the chairman's wife's seat!' And with that, this funny, chubby, red-faced old secretary spun around and was off, back towards the tunnel.

Jimmy threw his bag quickly to the floor and dusted the seat with his hand before casting his eyes to the field.

The gradually darkening sky, lit by the four massive floodlights, gave the ground a special, almost supernatural feeling. The sight and sounds coming from the players as they made calls to mark various passages of play as they ran around this magical arena made the whole scene the most perfect of pictures for Jimmy. The odd swear word that boomed across an otherwise silent stadium made him giggle too. Strangely, it made him feel as if he was part of some secret society that nobody else in the village ever got to witness. This was inside the wolf pack. This is where he longed to be.

As he craned his neck to see Liam Wyatt, the Wolves' fly-half, practising a place kick, he heard a familiar voice. It was Peter Clement.

'Good lad, you're early. Very professional. Get your boots on. Once Liam has done a few more kicks, we're both going to show you how best to use that big boot of yours. We'll be about fifteen minutes. I'll call you on.'

Jimmy couldn't even manage a reply. He just nodded and gave a little thumbs up, then scrabbled in his bag for his boots.

He was so excited, his hands were shaking as he drew them out of the bag.

# KICKING KING

Jimmy was literally sitting on the edge of his seat.

He had removed his Wolves training top to reveal the scarlet British & Irish Lions replica jersey his grandparents had bought him for his last birthday. He had tucked his tracksuit bottoms into his red and black socks, which themselves were secured tightly inside his boots. His eyes were as wide as two satellite dishes as they focused on Peter Clement and Liam Wyatt, who had been talking for about five minutes, in the far corner of the pitch.

The training session had ended a few minutes earlier. Most of the players had wandered off to the changing room for the well-deserved hot shower, but one or two remained, doing some light stretches with each other as part of their warm down routine, laughing and swearing loudly as they did so. Jimmy was captivated.

Jimmy saw Liam laughing at something Peter had said, then watched him spinning a ball around in his hands, before effortlessly drilling a drop-goal through the posts from the widest of angles. Peter gave Liam a mocking round of applause before Liam jogged towards the posts, then bending down to scoop up another ball, Peter turned around and motioned towards Jimmy. Jimmy was so on edge, he didn't think Peter meant him, so looked around to see if anyone was sitting behind him. There wasn't anyone else there. Jimmy realised that this was his moment.

He stood up, walked to the end of the row, skipped down the five or six steps onto the red gravel, then ran onto the pitch. And fell flat on his face.

He had forgotten about the grass step on this side of the pitch and the bottom of his studs had just caught on it and sent him sprawling. He couldn't believe it. He sprung up onto his feet as soon as he could, hoping that nobody had noticed, then looked down and saw that he now had two mud stains down both legs of his trackie bottoms and over the chest of his jersey. He quickly looked over to Peter to see if he'd seen his personal disaster, praying he hadn't.

He had.

Peter was laughing out loud. 'Wow! You certainly know how to make an entrance, son. Come on, don't worry about that, we've all done it!'

Jimmy wished the ground would open up and swallow him, but instead just laughed. 'Idiot,' he said to himself quietly, as he ran towards Peter.

'You won't believe this,' said Peter, who was surrounded by a dozen or so balls, 'but I had my first training session on this pitch with the first team when I was fifteen-and-a-half. Big Allan

Wheel was the captain . . . and I did exactly the same thing. The only difference was that I broke my finger, look.'

Peter held his left hand up for Jimmy to see, and he noticed the lump on Peter's little finger and the odd angle that the finger ran compared to his others.

'Oh, no!' exclaimed Jimmy. 'That's terrible. How long were you out for?'

'Out?' laughed Peter. 'For about ninety seconds! I ran straight over to big Al to show him, in some pain, expecting him to send me off to hospital, but he just looked at it and said, "Well, you're right-handed aren't you?" I nodded and said I was, so he said, "Well just use that one then," and he ran off! I did a full hour session before he'd let me have it strapped up.'

Jimmy was almost shell-shocked. 'Wow. That's brutal.'

Peter laughed. 'Yes, son, you're right, it was. But so is professional sport. Taught me a lesson that day, did Big Al. Play through the pain if you want to make it. He taught me another lesson too.'

'What was that?' asked Jimmy, slightly agog.

Peter leant down and whispered conspiratorially, 'Watch that grass step when you run out!' They both laughed out loud.

'What's the joke?' asked Liam as he joined them.

'Grass step story,' laughed Peter.

'It got me too when I played a schools' final here,' said Liam as he put his hand out to shake Jimmy's. 'You won't be the last, I tell you that. The best bit's when the opposition do it. A little home-advantage trick, that step!'

'Okay,' said Peter, clapping his hands together, 'let's get started . . . Liam, show him how it's done.'

Liam bent down and scooped up one of the balls that lay around them, and took a few steps in-field, away from the touchline.

'Right, Jimmy,' he said, looking across at him. 'We're going to do some punting. I'm going to pretend I've got a penalty right here. We're tight to the touchline, deep in our own twenty-two, right on the five-metre line. What I'm going to try to do is put the ball into touch, beyond halfway.'

Liam put his head down and focused on the ball in his hands. He looked up, as if aiming at an imaginary target, then looked back down at the ball. He took one giant stride, allowed the ball to roll out of his hand smoothly, then he brought his right leg through from behind him and struck the ball as it dropped with huge force, and, importantly, with great timing too.

Jimmy noticed two things. First, Liam had kept his head down after he'd struck the ball and second, the follow-through of his right leg was amazing . . . it nearly took his own head off!

The ball flew up the touchline like a rocket. But it didn't go straight.

First, it coiled to its left, like some sort of flying snake, sailing high, but over the touchline. But then, as the ball was still climbing, it came back in-field about five metres, away from the touchline, before passing the halfway line and spinning left again, into touch.

Jimmy was amazed. The ball must have travelled at least sixty metres, spiralling furiously as it went, before diving left, into touch. *Perfection*, thought Jimmy. He also had another thought.

'I'll never be able to do that.'

He was slightly startled to realise he had said this out loud.

'No such thing as "never" in professional sport,' corrected Peter. 'Just practice.'

Jimmy nodded in agreement.

'Okay, this is how we do it,' continued Peter and he flicked up a ball with his heel and caught it before striding in-field next to Liam. 'The key thing is how you hold the ball. You must be comfortable with it in your hand, and you must hold that arm out in front of your body, stretching it as long as you comfortably can.'

Peter demonstrated to Jimmy, stretching his right arm way out in front of his hips.

'Now, one thing you must stop doing, which I've noticed you do every time you kick the ball from hand, is tossing it up in front of you. The higher you throw the ball up in front of your body, the more things that can go wrong, a gust of wind may move it slightly, meaning you may slice or hook it. Does that make sense?'

'Yes,' replied Jimmy, his concentration as sharp as a laser.

'Good. So we want to reduce the amount of distance between letting the ball drop from your hand and your foot striking the ball. That way, not much can go wrong. What we're actually doing is holding onto the ball for as long as possible, even once we've begun to move our leg through to actually kick the ball. We are looking to let it drop at the last possible moment.'

Again, Jimmy nodded furiously. He was processing every word Peter was giving him, imagining himself carrying out every step of the instructions, his brain was whirring.

'Okay, good. The next bit is about timing. You've got great natural power when you kick the ball, son, it's effortless. The biggest mistake kickers make is to try to kick the ball too hard.

It's as if for important distance kicks, players think they have to try and kick the ball into space! You don't. You just swing through the ball with your foot in a controlled, natural manner with a lovely high follow-through. That will ensure perfect contact with the large area of your boot on the ball, and the natural "sweet spot" of the ball will do the rest. If you try to put too much power through it, then all you will be doing is kicking too fast, which means the accuracy of your foot making contact with the ball will be lost. That will probably just result in you hooking the ball and losing distance.'

'That sounds a bit like golf,' said Jimmy. 'I was watching Sky Sports at my grandparents' house the other day, and they were talking about Rory McIlroy, and saying how he had such a smooth swing, yet hits it so far.'

'Exactly!' exclaimed Peter with delight, 'that's *exactly* right! The smoother the kick and follow-through, the more in control of the ball you'll be and the more distance you'll get. Same as golf. Good lad.'

Jimmy blushed with delight. Finally there was a use for his obsession with watching any sport he could. *Wait until I tell Julie . . .*

'Right, last bit now,' said Peter, 'and this is a bit like golf too. Most people, think that to get the ball high and far, you have to lean back – it's a natural movement that the body will make. But instead of helping you kick it further, leaning back will just send the ball higher into the sky, meaning you will lose distance.'

Jimmy tried to take that bit of information in, because he always leant back when he kicked. Peter could see that he was thinking about it.

'Let me show you,' said Peter, 'but keep your eyes on me, not the ball.'

Peter stepped away from Jimmy and Liam. He moved forwards to strike the ball and Jimmy noticed that it was only at the last moment he held the ball out in front of him in his right hand, with his arm stretched out as far as possible. In Jimmy's mind, he would have had it stuck out in front of himself for ages like some sort of rugby robot! He was glad that he was able to watch Peter take the kick in the flesh like this, it all made so much more sense.

Jimmy continued to watch as Peter moved forward, then brought his right leg back, before bringing it forward into the kick, dropping the ball from his hand and then striking smoothly through it, with a nice, high follow-through. All the time, his upper body was straight and, if anything, leaning slightly forwards as he kicked through the ball. There was no sign whatsoever of leaning backwards. The ball flew down the touchline like a rocket. Jimmy understood instantly.

'See?' said Peter. 'No leaning back, just driving through the ball with my body moving forwards, even after I've kicked it. That and good timing gives you the power. The shape of the ball will do the rest and deliver that lovely spinning spiral we like to see in the air. Understand?'

'Yes,' said Jimmy enthusiastically.

'Good. Also, remember to plant that left foot nice and strongly in the ground for stability, alongside where the ball would make contact with the ground if we weren't going to kick it. That's very important.'

Jimmy looked down at his feet, and planted his left foot down in an exaggerated manner to feel how firm his stance was. 'Like this?' he asked.

'Exactly like that,' replied Peter, 'and remember to get that kicking leg straight through the line you are kicking. Resist the temptation to cut across the ball with your boot. That will only end in one thing.'

'The big old slice!' said Liam, laughing, making the shape of a banana in the air with his hand.

'Yes, you'd know all about that, Liam,' chuckled Peter. Then he looked back at Jimmy. 'Right then, time to have a go,' and Peter tossed Jimmy a ball, 'just remember the key points – arm long and low, out in front of you; keep hold of it as long as possible; drop it, don't toss it up; keep controlled and don't kick it too hard; don't lean back but drive forward through the ball. Easy.'

Jimmy took in everything that Peter had told him. There was a lot to remember, but it all made sense in Jimmy's mind. He was used to kicking the ball as far as he could, but what Peter was telling him was that he needed to be more controlled about his kicking, not to give it everything like he usually did. That seemed key. The timing.

He stepped up to the mark, and looked down at the ball, spinning it nervously in his hands. He stopped, took a deep breath, lifted his head and looked down the touchline to his imaginary target.

Poised, Jimmy stretched his arm out in front of him, took his big step forward, dropped the ball down onto his foot as it was coming up, trying to make contact with as much of his boot as he could. *Remember the follow-through, remember the follow-*

*through,* Jimmy thought to himself as he struck the ball. Then, as soon as he'd struck it, *Don't lean back, don't lean back, drive through the ball.*

The ball left Jimmy's boot, but before he even had time to look up, expecting to see the ball snaking its way along the touchline, he heard a strange *crash.*

The sound was the ball clattering into the seating of the stand that ran along the touchline. Instead of sending the ball fifty metres down the pitch, as he usually did, Jimmy had only succeeded in hooking the ball about twenty metres, straight left into the stand.

Jimmy's hand shot straight to his mouth. He was horrified. He looked at Peter and Liam, as if he had just shot someone. 'Oh God,' he said through the hand that covered his mouth, 'I'm really sorry, I've never done that before.'

'Don't apologise,' said Peter, with a twinkle in his eye. 'Try again.' He threw him another ball.

Jimmy caught it, and walked back to his mark. He looked down, and completed his routine again, reminding himself to follow through and keep his head down.

And then he did exactly the same thing, hooking the ball, horribly, straight into the stand.

His hand shot to his mouth again, and he looked at Peter and Liam for a second time.

'Again,' said Peter, throwing him another ball.

And again, Jimmy just dumped it straight into the stand. This time, he didn't look at Peter and Liam, he just stared straight at the floor close to tears. What was happening?

He felt a hand on his shoulder. It was Liam.

'It's okay, Jimmy. You're over thinking it. Just try and get the feel for your kicking, the way you always have. Try and relax. Don't think of all the things we've told you individually, just think of them as one complete thing – swing, contact, follow through, head down. Make it one whole thing, not lots of separate things. Relax and it will come. You're too good not to be able to do this.'

Jimmy felt much better hearing these words and Liam's patient, encouraging tone. He could do this. *Just stop worrying and put it all together.* He took a deep breath and cleared his mind, concentrating on the ball. He didn't even look up to his target.

He briefly closed his eyes, opened them, stepped forward to let the ball drop and struck it . . . almost with an empty mind. The ball flew off his boot like a bullet, arcing straight into the air, just as Liam's had done earlier. As it crossed the halfway line, it spiralled left and flew into the empty stand. It was a thing of beauty.

'Good. You had me worried for a minute,' said Peter quietly. Jimmy looked up and was pleased to see a satisfied smile on Peter's face.

'Never in doubt!' shouted Liam, who gave Jimmy a high-five. Then he looked at Jimmy and gave a small, wondering shake of the head. 'That was some strike. An absolute beast.'

'Again!' cried Peter, tossing another ball to Jimmy.

Jimmy kicked again, just as well as the last one. He followed it with three more, all expertly done.

'Right then, well done,' said Peter. 'You can do it, you know that – all you need now is practice." He paused for a second and looked at Jimmy intently. 'And that bit's up to you.'

Jimmy nodded.

'I'm taking Liam inside now to talk to the team about Saturday's game – you can kick a few more if you want.'

'I will,' said Jimmy. 'Thank you.'

He kicked twenty-five. And he only messed up one. He could do it.

# THE CHALLENGE

The following week came and went. Jimmy never found out if Mr Kane had picked him in the first squad of the season because the match that was due to be played on the Saturday was cancelled due to heavy rain. But that hadn't stopped Jimmy from practising his kicking.

Every night after school, he would rush home, head to The Rec and practise. Kick after kick, night after night. Most nights, Kitty, Jonny and Julie would come with him. Jonny and Kitty wanted to pick up tips, both constantly asking exactly what Peter and Liam had instructed Jimmy to do, while Julie sprinted around retrieving stray balls and, despite her protestations to the contrary, clearly listening carefully as she began to spiral punt the balls back to them. It was becoming a family event and Jimmy loved the fact that they were all helping each other to improve.

Some nights though, Jimmy would stay out on his own, long after Kitty, Jonny and Julie had popped home for tea – 'Tell

Mum I'll have mine warmed up later on,' Jimmy would shout as he eyed up another kick.

One evening, Peter drove past in his car, and could see Jimmy at the bottom of The Rec, making a perfect spiral kick fly along the line. The rain was pouring down in long lances through the dimming light, plastering Jimmy's hair to his head and his shirt to his skin. Peter was impressed. Out on a night like that, practising in the almost-dark. That was dedication, it showed Peter that Jimmy really wanted it.

On the Wednesday after lunch, Manu caught up with Jimmy who had been sitting chatting with Kitty and Matt, trying to explain to them all about the perfect spiral punt.

'Have you seen the notice board?' asked Manu. 'We've been entered in the Schools Cluster Cup. There are only seven teams, and we've been given a bye, so are straight into the semi-finals. If we win that, the final will be played on the Memorial Ground.'

'Wow! That's brilliant!' said Matt.

'It gets better,' continued Manu. 'The game will be played before a Wolves match, in front of a proper crowd!'

Jimmy said nothing. He just sat, silently, in abject disappointment.

'What do you think, Jim, that's fantastic, isn't it?' said Manu, not noticing Jimmy's desolation.

'Yeah,' replied Jimmy after a moment of silence, 'it's great for you guys. But there's more chance of a spaceship landing on the middle of the pitch than me getting picked to play. Kane hates me.'

'Ahhh, maybe normally,' said Manu, his eyes bright. 'But have you heard the news about George Stapleton?'

'No,' the friends replied together.

'He's leaving. His father's got a job in Swindon, so he's off. That means the only fly-halves in the school are you and Ollie Snell in Year 6. And you're way better than him.'

Jimmy looked pointedly at Manu. 'Not sure if that's going to make much of a difference, mate. Kane'll still pick Ollie ahead of me. Every time.'

'Yeah, well maybe he will,' said Kitty, 'but you know what, he'll have to pick you in the squad now.'

Jimmy realised that Kitty was right. There was nobody else in the school who could play fly-half, so with George leaving, maybe there was a chance that if Kane put him in the squad, there would be an opportunity to get on the field at some point. Jimmy felt a brief sense of hope rising inside him.

'When's the semi-final?' he asked Manu.

'The week after next, on the Thursday.'

Before the friends could consider the possibilities of maybe playing on their beloved Memorial Ground, they were interrupted by a group of Year 6 boys walking past, with one of them barging into Jimmy's back, and another clipping him around the ear and knocking his glasses to the floor. It was Mike and his mates.

'Look out, it's the losers. What a joke you all are.'

'Shut up, Mike,' snapped Kitty. 'There's only one joke here and it's you . . . why don't you leave Jimmy alone? He's done nothing to you.'

'Ooooh!' mocked Mike, with a high-pitched voice. 'Look at the little girl sticking up for the four-eyed loser. How are the lungs today, Jimmy Wheezer? Breathing okay?'

Jimmy felt his temper rising as he picked up his glasses and checked that they weren't broken again. They weren't, but as usual, a lens had popped out. He quickly slotted it back in place.

'He's not a loser!' shouted Kitty. 'And he's a way better rugby player than you'll ever be!"

Mike found this hilarious. 'Him?!' he cried, incredulous, and pointed at Jimmy, his finger jabbing the air just inches from Jimmy's nose. 'Are you serious? In what world could this four-eyed matchstick with lungs like an old granny be better than me?'

'This one,' said Jimmy coldly, and pushed Mike's finger away.

Mike snorted and leant in close to Jimmy, his breath sour and little flecks of spit spattering Jimmy's face as he talked. 'You think that just because Peter Clement has chosen you as his little puppy, you're going to become a decent rugby player. Well there's nothing on a rugby field that you could beat me at. Nothing.'

Jimmy held his ground, desperately trying to keep hold of his temper, remembering his mother's words *'no matter how much people goad you, Jimmy, never give them the satisfaction of seeing you react'*. He said nothing. He ignored the hot breath and spittle, but he took Mike's words and he buried them deep inside. He would use them again. And again. And again. One day he was going to shove them right down Mike's throat.

He was about to say something about Peter Clement never giving Mike the time of day, when someone spoke. It was Manu.

'Place kicking,' he said simply.

'What?' replied Mike, turning away from Jimmy and glaring at Manu. 'You're a bigger fool than he is. Have you forgotten who the place kicker for this school has been for the past two years? Me. And I never miss.'

'I don't care, he's still better than you,' said Manu nonchalantly, which seemed to increase Mike's rage. 'He'll beat you anytime, anyplace, anywhere. Just say when.'

'Oh, I love this!' barked Mike, looking over to his gang, who smirked back at their leader. 'A challenge that I can't lose.' He looked back at Manu. 'Tonight, six o'clock at The Rec.' Then, turning to Jimmy, he added, 'And don't be late like the last time you were supposed to meet someone there.' He burst out laughing and walked away. As he did, Mr Kane came around the corner and glanced suspiciously over at the tightly gathered group.

Jimmy said nothing as he watched Green and his gang saunter away. He waited until Mr Kane was out of earshot then he turned to Manu.

'Place kicking? Why on earth did you say place kicking?'

'Because you've been getting lessons, that's why,' said Manu laughing, 'it'll be a piece of cake!'

'Excellent. But I haven't been getting place kicking lessons, I've been getting lessons on kicking out of hand – spiral kicks. They've not spoken about place kicks at all.'

There was a long, awkward pause.

'Oh,' said Manu, the smile dropping from his face like a stone off a cliff. 'I didn't know that. Sorry, Jimmy boy.'

Everyone went quiet. Even Kitty, the most positive member of the group, said nothing.

After a quiet moment of thought, Jimmy spoke.

'Oh well, it's done now. Six o'clock it is. What's the worst that can happen?'

Nobody answered.

# WORDS OF WISDOM

Jimmy was sitting in front of his mum's iPad, searching YouTube for videos of the great rugby union place kickers, looking for tips that might help him in his contest with Mike. There was plenty of footage on there of all the greats: Neil Jenkins and Leigh Halfpenny of Wales, Michael Lynagh of Australia, Grant Fox and Dan Carter of New Zealand and Jonny Wilkinson and Owen Farrell of England. But he was frustrated. All the footage seemed to show close-ups of their faces, or was shot from a camera too far away to see exactly how these great kickers were preparing for their kicks. Also, they all did something completely different, especially Jonny Wilkinson. Jimmy paused and replayed one of his kicks several times, it looked as if he was doing a combination of sitting down and praying. He wouldn't be able to copy that in his contest with Mike, he was bound to be mocked if he did. Especially if he then missed.

Jimmy spent a good twenty minutes watching the films before he heard the call for tea from his mum. He was a little confused by all the different styles, but the one thing he noticed was that they all took their time. None of them rushed. That was interesting.

After the usual interview over tea by his mother – 'How was your day? What did you do? Did you behave yourself? Have you got any homework?' – Jimmy finished his food, had a large glass of water, picked up his boots and walked to the door.

'Down to The Rec again, love?' asked his mother. 'You'll be playing for the Wolves in no time! I was telling your dad how proud I am of all the hard work you're putting in. He's proud too. It'll all pay off for you when you need it most.'

*Tonight would be good,* thought Jimmy to himself, but just said, 'Thanks, Mum, see you later.'

As he walked out of the house, he turned towards The Rec. He thought he'd get there early and do some practising before everyone else turned up. He stopped. He felt nervous . . . he *never* felt nervous. Then he heard a familiar voice and turned around. It was his grandparents, walking slowly up the road, shopping bags in hands. He gave them a wave.

'Hello, Jimmy, love,' said his grandmother, Betty, with a smile. 'You off to play rugby again?'

Jimmy gave a half-hearted nod and an unconvincing smile.

'You all right, Jim?' asked Will, struck by the look on his grandson's face.

'What's the matter?' asked Betty, handing her shopping to Will and coming over to see him. 'You look like you've got the world on your shoulders. What's up, love?'

Jimmy thought of the previous few weeks – kicking the ball that hit Mr Kane, Mike stealing his inhaler, the detention, Mr

Kane ignoring him every day apart from when he was giving him a row and now today's confrontation with Mike. The kindness and concern in his grandmother's voice really got to him. He could feel tears welling, but he refused to cry, so did everything he could to stop them coming. But he could hide nothing from them.

'Come here, tell us all about it,' said Will softly and guided Jimmy towards their front door.

When they were inside and seated around the kitchen table, Jimmy told them.

Everything.

His grandparents sat there and didn't say a word, apart from the odd, loud angry 'tut' from his grandmother, until he was finished. Jimmy spoke for about five minutes, going into great detail about everything, talking non-stop. When he was done, his grandfather spoke for the first time.

'Okay. There are two basic issues here, this boy Green and your teacher.'

Jimmy nodded.

'I can help you with one, but you'll have to deal with other.'

Jimmy looked at his grandfather and waited for his explanation.

'As tough as it is, you're going to have to deal with Green yourself. It won't be easy, and it may not end overnight, but you are going to have to step up to him and take on the challenge. So, later, go down to The Rec and do your best. Whether you beat him or not doesn't matter, just do your best and win his respect.'

Jimmy felt crestfallen. He understood what his grandfather was getting at, but deep down he'd wanted more practical help.

'Do you really think that will work, Gramp?' he asked. 'I mean, I was just wondering if perhaps you came down with me and said something to him . . .'

Will looked at Jimmy, his heart aching over the obvious fear and confusion his beloved grandson was experiencing.

He reached out his hand and touched Jimmy's shoulder.

'You're going to have to trust me on this one, son. I might make things worse for you if I wade in and get involved. I know that Green family and they're not nice. If I inflame the situation, it could end up ten times worse for you.'

Jimmy nodded again, silently.

'The best thing is to avoid face-to-face conflict with him and try and win his respect in other ways . . . like using your rugby skills. It really will be the best way, son. Believe me.'

As disappointed as he felt at that moment, Jimmy understood what his grandfather was saying and knew that he was right.

'But, whatever you do – and your mother was right about this – don't get involved in retaliation and a confrontation. The bigger man is the one that can walk away with dignity. I know that's hard to understand right now, but you will as you get older.'

Betty agreed. 'Your grandfather's right, Jimmy. Turn the other cheek and walk away. Getting involved in silly confrontations will only make things worse. It's always the one who retaliates that gets into the biggest trouble. Always.'

'Okay,' said Jimmy. 'I'll try.'

'Now, as for young Mark Kane,' said his grandfather, bristling a little as he said the name. 'I'll deal with that. I know all about *him*.'

'What, you know him, Gramp?' asked Jimmy with surprise.

'Well, it's a long story, son, to be honest. But I'm pretty sure I know a reason why Kane has taken a dislike to you.'

'It's because I hit him with the ball – I embarrassed him.'

'Yes, that's certainly part of it. But there's something else. Do you know why his rugby career ended?'

'Kitty told me something about him getting an arm injury – I've seen the scar he has, it's horrible!'

'Exactly right. He broke it so badly that the surgeons could never strengthen it enough for it to be safe for him to play again.'

Jimmy nodded but he was still confused. 'What's any of that got to do with me? I didn't hit him on the arm.'

'Well, when the contract he had with one of his pro clubs ended he came back to live here for a while – this was before the injury. He asked the Wolves if he could train with them until the end of the season while his agent tried to land him a new contract somewhere. There was talk that he was going to play in France.'

'France?' exclaimed Jimmy. 'Was he that good then?'

'Let's put it this way,' replied Will, 'he was *effective*. He had about as much skill as this table, but they love a big, tough forward in France – and that's exactly what Mark Kane was. Anyway, he got quite fit with all the training and the Wolves had some injuries toward the end of their season, so he was asked to play in the last couple of games. The first of those games was home and I was there to watch it. Kane really shone that day, his extra power and . . . well . . . just nastiness really, had a big effect on the game.

'It was about ten minutes into the second half. The other team's hooker made a break from the edge of a ruck and headed to the wing. Kane has been hanging out wide in case the Wolves turned over the ball and just lined up the hooker as he came toward him. Then, instead of tackling him low, he just smashed into the hooker, really high and with a vicious swinging arm. It was an incredible collision – but, unfortunately for Kane, the hooker ducked his head at the last moment and Kane's forearm smashed into it.'

'Is that when he broke it?' asked Jimmy.

'Well, yes and no,' replied Will. 'The physio ran straight on and started examining his arm. He wasn't certain, but said it might be broken. Kane decided to play up to the crowd with his "Mr Tough Guy" act and started to argue with the physio, shouting loudly that he didn't want to come off, that he was fine. He kept saying to the physio, "Do you know it's broken a hundred per cent? I'm only going off if it is, otherwise I'm staying on!"

'The physio couldn't prove it was broken, so he didn't answer and just tried to lead Kane off so he could assess it further. Kane was furious and stopped dead in his tracks. "Unless you tell me it's broken, I'm staying on," he shouted. "You're useless!"

'The physio couldn't believe what he was hearing, so just looked at Kane with real anger in his eyes, picked up his medical bag and said, "Stay on then," and walked off.

'I think Kane was shocked, because I'm certain he really wanted to come off, but wanted the physio to make the decision for him – he didn't want to appear weak in front the crowd. But now he had no option but to stay on.'

'But surely, if the physio wasn't certain it was broken, it couldn't have been that bad. How could that injury end his career?' asked Jimmy.

'Because of what happened next. The game restarted and about a minute later, another forward charged at Kane and his shoulder caught Kane right on the spot of his injured arm – and the bone shattered. It was awful to see and to hear. He was treated on the pitch, then rushed to hospital. I think someone said he had about five operations, with various plates and screws put in over the following months – but it was never strong enough to play again. And that's one of the reasons why I think Kane has got it in for you.'

'Me? Why *me*? What's any of that got to do with *me?*' asked Jimmy in disbelief.

'Well, because Kane always told anyone who cared to listen that it was all the physio's fault. He blamed him for not telling him it was broken in the first place.'

'But the physio couldn't have known it was broken, surely?'

'Of course he couldn't,' replied Will, 'but Kane always blamed him. Still does, probably.'

Suddenly the truth hit Jimmy like a falling sandbag. 'The physio . . . it was Dad, wasn't it?'

Will nodded grimly. 'None of it was his fault, but Kane wanted someone to blame. And that someone was your dad. And now . . . well, I'm afraid Mark Kane has decided to shift some of that blame onto you, too.'

Jimmy sat in silence, trying to process this new information. It was all so unfair – how could he be to blame for Kane's ruined rugby career if his dad hadn't even been at fault in the first place? It was ridiculous! He flushed with anger at the injustice of it all.

'When have you got school rugby training next?'

'Thursday after school,' replied Jimmy.

'At The Rec?'

'Yes.'

'Good. I'll come and take a look, but, if you see me, ignore me, pretend you don't know me. Okay?'

'Why, grandpa?' asked Jimmy, now both extremely interested and a little worried about what Will had in mind.

'Don't worry about that. I have a little plan.'

Still, Jimmy didn't want to drop it. He was too intrigued. 'Even a hint?'

Will stopped and looked at his grandson.

'What do you know about loyalty, son?'

'Well, I . . . um . . . suppose . . . um . . . well, it's like having good friends and always being kind to them. I think,' said Jimmy, struggling to put words to the thoughts he had in his mind.

'Yes, that's certainly where it starts. But true loyalty can extend way beyond just friends. Let me explain.'

Will shuffled slightly on his chair to make himself comfortable, then began.

'Okay. You know I've often told you stories of my time in the armed forces?'

Jimmy nodded and smiled.

Will nodded, but his face, for once, remained serious.

'Now listen,' he said gravely. 'All the stories I've ever told you have been the fun ones, designed to make you have a laugh at what I got up to back then. But it's about time I told you some of the real stuff.'

Over the next fifteen minutes, Will gave his attentive grandson a mini master class in what it meant to serve in the armed forces. He explained the importance of loyalty to family, friends and people in need. Then he spoke about bravery and what that really means. He explained the different types of bravery the forces gave him by instilling a confidence in him about how he could handle any situation thrown at him. He explained this was achieved by total commitment and discipline – commitment to his training and a single-minded discipline to listen to instructions and carry out the lessons learned in his training. He also spoke at length about the importance of respect, good morals and decent manners and the dangers of being arrogant, rude and spiteful. In those few minutes, Jimmy began to understand more about his grandfather than he ever had before.

When Will had finished speaking, he picked up his tin mug, now filled with tea that would have been lukewarm at best and took a glug. His face was a mixture of seriousness, contentment and almost relief. Jimmy didn't take his eyes off him.

'I'm sorry if I went on a little bit,' said Will. 'It's just that sometimes I get a bit frustrated with young people like Mark Kane being poor role models to younger folk like you. I feel that people like him are helping let standards slip.'

He paused for a moment as if trying to find the right words.

'I'm not saying that every soldier I knew was a good bloke, because they weren't. But the bulk of us tried to be good soldiers and good people. I just wanted you to know everything that underpinned that, and that's what I'm going to try to bring to the attention of Mr Kane – to make him realise he has to change. I hope you understand where I'm coming from with this?'

'Yes, I do, Gramp. I do.'

'That's good,' said Will, smiling. 'Now, go down to The Rec and show that Green boy how good you are. Don't get sucked in to all the nonsense he'll give you, just focus on the rugby. Win his respect. It will change for you. I promise.'

'Okay, thanks, Gramp, I will.'

'And don't worry about your Mr Kane. You can leave him to me.

Just don't mention anything to him about your dad and his injury, the less said about that the better. Don't even tell your friends.'

'Okay,' nodded Jimmy.

Before he left, Jimmy stopped at the door and looked back. Despite understanding everything his grandfather had just told him about loyalty, bravery, respect, discipline and manners, he still didn't understand one thing. As much as Jimmy loved and respected his grandfather, he was in his sixties. Mr Kane was about half his age. He was also extremely fit, very strong and almost twice as big as his grandfather. Jimmy felt a little foolish, but he asked the question that was troubling him.

'I know what you said about bullies and how they are usually cowards, Gramp, but Mr Kane is huge and was apparently really nasty when he was a rugby player. So, when you go and speak to him, won't you be a bit . . . um . . . scared?'

Will smiled. 'Fear is all relative, son. In my time in the service, I was shot at, I was nearly captured by a group of enemy soldiers and I also had several hand-to-hand battles, out on the front lines. I was lucky that, thanks to my training, I got through all that without a scratch. One thing that happens as a result of those experiences is that you lose fear. I don't mean in a reckless way, I just mean that day-to-day problems and confrontations don't mean anything to me, especially when I remember the intensity and danger of some of those moments. I don't care how big or how nasty your Mr Kane is, he is way down the line in things that frighten your old Gramp. In fact, he's way behind spiders on that list. So don't worry about me.' And he gave his grandson a wink.

# THE KICKING COMPETITION

JIMMY LEFT his grandparents' house and headed over to The Rec. There waiting for him was Kitty.

'Hiya,' she said with a smile, 'fancy a warm up?'

'Yeah, why not?' he replied, grinning, and chipped her the ball.

Kitty caught it, turned and drilled a long spiral down the line, towards halfway.

'Not bad, Padawan, not bad . . .' he murmured and shot her a sideways glance.

'Thanks, Obi-Wan,' she said. 'Cool of you to pretend to be an old man while saying I'm a kick-ass young Jedi. You're probably about as fast as old Obi-Wan, too.'

Jimmy laughed and chased Kitty for the ball. No contest, she beat him by a yard.

As Kitty and Jimmy were passing the ball back and forth as quickly as they were trading insults, Matt and Manu turned up and joined them.

'Did you bring it?' Jimmy asked Manu.

'Yeah, of course, here it is,' replied Manu, bringing out a bright red kicking tee from his backpack. 'It's my brother's though, and he'll kill me if something happens to it.'

'I'll be careful,' said Jimmy, examining it in his hands with wonder. He'd never seen a kicking tee before, least of all used one. He placed it on the ground and tried to put his ball on it. It fell straight off.

'Look at the matchstick, he doesn't even know how to use a tee,' came Mike Green's crowing call. 'Did you remember to put your glasses on, Matchstick? Have a puff on that poxy inhaler of yours?'

Jimmy looked round to see Mike swaggering through the gates to The Rec with his small entourage in tow. *Just keep it together, Jimmy boy,* he told himself. *Remember what Gramp said.* He took a deep breath. It was going to be difficult.

'So, you ready to be humiliated then?' asked Mike as he reached them.

'Let's just get started, shall we?' said Jimmy through gritted teeth.

'Oh, it'll be my pleasure,' said Mike with a sneer. 'Come on, let's get this over with. We've got much better things to do than mess around with you idiots down here.' Behind him, Mike's friends all guffawed.

Jimmy, Kitty, Matt and Manu followed Mike and his cronies to the twenty-two-metre line at the far end of The Rec. When they got there, Mike laid out the rules.

'Right. It's best of three kicks. All on the twenty-two. One from the middle, one from the fifteen-metre line over to the right, then the last from five metres further to the right. If it's still equal after three kicks – which it won't be,' he added with a smirk, 'it'll be sudden death. Do you understand, or is that all a bit too complex for you?'

'I understand,' replied Jimmy coldly. 'Let's start. Who goes first?'

'I do, Matchstick. I'm the school kicking champion, not you.'

Jimmy ignored the stupid boast, picked up his kicking tee and moved to one side to join his friends. He looked at their faces for some moral support. They all looked worried sick. Apart from Manu. He looked as if he actually was *going* to be sick.

Green called to one of his gang, who ran over quickly and produced a green kicking tee and a brand new white and blue Gilbert match ball from his backpack. It looked magnificent.

Mike looked across to Jimmy, standing with his battered ball under his arm, so scuffed that the maker's mark was now illegible and shook his head. 'Typical. Look at the state of that ball you're using . . . just like you: hopeless!'

Once again, Jimmy ignored the insult.

Manu didn't.

'Look Mike, stop with all the sledging and just get on with it will you. None of us particularly want to be here with you either, so let's just get this done and keep your mouth shut.'

Green looked at Manu, but said nothing. Despite everything he did to hide it, Mike was a bit nervous around Manu. He'd played lots of rugby with the centre and knew how tough he was. He'd also seen Manu's older brothers, who were *huge*. If Manu grew up to be anything like their size – heck, even *half* their size – Mike needed to keep on his right side. Mike pretended he hadn't heard, but he stopped crowing and began to set up his first kick.

He walked forwards and placed his tee on the ground. He knelt down behind it, and placed the ball on top, lining it up with the middle of the posts ahead of him. The ball was angled upwards towards the posts like a torpedo. The bottom of the ball, raised off the ground by the tee, would be the bit that Mike would strike.

He stood up straight, positioned his right foot behind the ball, with his left one to the side. He dropped his arms to his hips and looked up at the posts. Then he marched back five deliberate paces, stopped, and moved two paces to the left. He glanced down at the ball, then up at the posts, then back down at the ball. He took one deep breath, then moved – quite elegantly – up to the ball and struck it perfectly, with a high follow-through. The ball sailed into the sky and straight towards the middle of the posts. It was a beauty.

1–0 to Green.

'Your turn, Matchstick,' said Mike as he picked up his tee.

Jimmy knelt down and basically repeated what Mike had done. He wasn't sure if he was doing it correctly as he'd never kicked a ball off a tee before, and he was having difficulty making sure that it even stayed upright.

'You really don't have a clue what you're doing, do you?' said Mike.

Jimmy ignored him.

When Jimmy was happy that the ball was balanced correctly, he stood up.

He remembered something he'd seen England's Owen Farrell doing on the YouTube film where he looked at the ball side on, then seemed to follow an imaginary path of the ball to the posts. He decided to do that.

He didn't know how many steps to take back, so he just did what felt comfortable, before deciding on three. When he stopped, he remembered to take his time. *Don't rush, don't rush,* he said to himself silently. Then he looked down to the ball and did the Owen Farrell thing again. He had no idea if it would work, but hoped it looked good.

He breathed in, then breathed out. Fortunately, he'd taken some puffs from his inhaler at his grandparents', so his chest felt fine. He relaxed his shoulders.

With one final look down at the ball, Jimmy moved forward and struck it with all his strength. The ball flew off the tee, but he had slipped slightly when he planted his left foot, which meant the kick wasn't going straight like Green's, instead it was heading slightly left.

Matt, Manu and Kitty all held their breath and watched silently as the ball flew towards the rusty and twisted old posts. They needn't have worried. Despite it heading left, Jimmy had struck it well enough for it to sneak in, just inside the left post, with a little room to spare.

'Lucky,' snarled Green as he took his tee and walked to the fifteen-metre line to his right.

One of his gang retrieved his ball and watched as Green followed the same routine as his first kick. He had the same result. The ball flew through the uprights perfectly. 2–1 to Green. Jimmy hated to admit it, but he was impressed. Mike could kick.

Matt tossed Jimmy his scruffy old ball. 'You can do it, bro,' he said.

And Jimmy did, slotting the ball through the posts, even though he hadn't connected with it perfectly.

2–2.

Before Jimmy could collect his thoughts, Mike had already set up his ball on the widest spot that they would kick from, out on the five-metre line. With the extra angle, it seemed a very long way, but it didn't seem to worry Mike.

He repeated his routine perfectly and drilled the ball high between the slightly uneven posts. He'd done it again. 3–2 to him and the pressure was back on Jimmy. If Jimmy missed, it was all over, Mike would've beaten him. Everyone was silent.

Strangely, Jimmy didn't feel any sense of pressure. He was concentrating completely on his task, he didn't hear any of the insults that Mike and his gang were starting to send his way, shattering the temporary silence.

He was in the zone.

Because of the extra distance, Jimmy took an extra stride back and the wider angle meant that he felt he needed to take a step to the left. He paused and breathed out. He felt completely relaxed. It was the best Jimmy had felt for any of the kicks. He did his 'Farrell', then stepped forward. He hit the ball absolutely perfectly, it sailed higher than any of Green's kicks and arrowed towards the posts. It was a magnificent kick.

Mike's face sank when he saw how brilliantly Jimmy had struck the ball.

However, high behind both groups of children, something happened that none of them saw. The flag on the top of the Wolves' grandstand, which had been hanging limp, suddenly sprang into life. A huge gust of wind caught the flag and would do only one thing . . . catch Jimmy's ball too.

As they watched, there seemed no way that Jimmy's kick could miss. But halfway to the posts, the freak gust of wind caught it, just enough to alter its path – just as it had done that day in the playground. And just like that fateful day, instead of the ball sailing through the narrow gap between the posts as it had been on target to do, it began to move to the left.

Manu held his breath. As did Kitty. As did Matt. Jimmy didn't. He knew. It was all over.

Jimmy's friends watched in horror as his kick, the best of the three he'd taken by far, smashed into the left-hand post on the full and flew back out onto the pitch. Jimmy had missed. Green had won 3–2. And he went bananas.

He screamed, he jumped, he shouted, he danced. He completely lost it. He ran around Jimmy with his thumb and forefinger across his forehead, shouting. 'Loser, loser, loooooooser!'

Jimmy just stood there, hands on hips, in disbelief. He was beyond gutted.

Suddenly, there was a flash. Jimmy looked up, and Jonathan, one of Mike's goons, had his phone out in front of him and had taken a picture. 'This loser is going to go viral later . . . you're going to be the Instafool on Instagram!' he cackled.

Jimmy knew what embarrassment that would bring but right now he couldn't care less. He sat down and stared at the grass. He'd never known disappointment like it.

# THE RACE

Jimmy was so gutted, he couldn't bring himself to say anything. He still couldn't believe he'd hit the post – he'd struck the ball so well. He just stayed there, staring at the grassy surface of The Rec, replaying the kick over and over in his mind. Cruelly, the spiteful mocking continued.

'Who-hoo! I knew it. You're rubbish! Leave the rugby to the big boys, Matchstick, you massive loser!' The mocking showed no sign of stopping. And there was nothing Jimmy could say. He'd lost the challenge, fair and square. It didn't matter that he'd never used a tee before. It didn't matter that Green was a superb kicker who had been doing it for the school team for two years. It didn't matter that it was just a freak gust of wind that had pushed his kick onto the post. All that mattered was that he'd lost. There was no getting away from it. And it was that fact that hurt Jimmy far more than the ridiculous comments Green continued to make.

Jimmy looked across at his loyal friends. He felt he'd let them all down.

Manu looked like he was ill, clearly distraught that it had been his daft suggestion that had put Jimmy in this position.

Matt looked across silently at both Jimmy and Manu. He had no words. He just walked across to stand beside Jimmy as Green continued with his mocking, and placed his hand on his shoulder.

'Haha, you're all nothing but a joke!' shouted Mike, getting hyper now. 'Give it up, the lot of you. None of you are good enough to play in our team, especially that loser,' he pointed at Jimmy. 'Just go back to Year 5 where you belong and take up knitting or something . . .' Then looking at Kitty, he said, 'You might as well set up a girls' team, that's all this lot are good for!'

Kitty had been boiling inside, only just keeping her temper under control. But this was one step too far. She exploded with rage.

'You're the joke!' she shouted. 'You're a horrible person and awful sportsman, and even worse than that, you just can't accept that girls can be equal to you!'

'What?' said Green, tilting his head as if he was suddenly studying a baffling puzzle. 'But you aren't equal to me! There is *nothing* you can beat me at.'

'Have a race then,' muttered Jimmy almost inaudibly. It was the first time he'd spoken since taking his last kick.

Mike's smile faltered for a moment.

'Yeah!' added Matt quickly, his eyes suddenly bright. 'Have a race with her. You're the big man who can win anything.'

Mike's whole expression was changing now. He'd never raced Kitty before, but he'd seen plenty who had – and now he was feeling worried. He should have shut up when Jimmy had missed his kick . . .

'Nah, I'm not racing a girl,' he said dismissively. 'That's just ridiculous, it would be a non-contest. Anyway, I came here to kick not run.'

'You just said there's nothing I can beat you at,' said Kitty. 'Changed your mind have you?'

'Go on, Greeno,' shouted one of his friends. 'She's just a stupid girl!'

Mike glared at the boy and hissed, 'Shut up!' If looks could kill, his friend would have exploded on the spot.

'Yeah,' cooed Kitty, examining her nails, 'I'm just a stupid girl. You could probably beat me running backwards. But why don't we try the usual way?'

Mike felt his stomach sinking. There was no way he could pull out now, he would lose too much face. Imagine if his dad or his brothers heard about it . . . But, even though he was just about the quickest in the rugby team – as a full back he had to be – he knew that Kitty was rapid.

'Right,' said Manu, taking the initiative. 'From this twenty-two to the other one.' He pointing down the pitch. 'That'll be about sixty metres . . . give or take.'

'I'm sure that'll be no bother for you, Greeno,' said Kitty in that same soft coo, and she moved to the line.

'I'll go down to the other line to see who wins,' said Matt.

'Go with him,' shouted Mike angrily to one of his gang. 'I don't trust him,' he said, pointing at Matt.

Matt just laughed. 'Pathetic,' he said loudly.

Normally, Mike Green wouldn't have allowed any of these losers to get away with speaking to him like that, but the word felt like a hammer blow to his chest. He swallowed and moved reluctantly to the start line.

Matt and Manu jogged down to the other twenty-two, followed by a few of Mike's lapdogs.

'The race will start when I drop my arm,' shouted Matt. Kitty nodded in response, Mike said nothing.

Jimmy sidled up to Kitty.

'This is silly, you don't have to do this,' he whispered to her. He didn't want her to suffer the same mocking he had taken from Mike if things didn't go well.

Kitty gave him a steely look that Jimmy had never seen from her before. 'Oh, I do,' she replied firmly, before looking away and down towards the finish line.

Jimmy nodded and gave her a light punch of encouragement on the arm before jogging down the field to join the others.

At the finishing line, Matt raised his arm.

'You know that you can't beat me,' Mike hissed desperately at Kitty.

Kitty's eyes didn't move. 'You know that I will,' she said, quietly.

Mike's face went pale. He looked up the field at Matt and set himself for the start.

Matt's arm dropped – and that's when Kitty made a mistake. As she watched for Matt's hand to come down, she waited for it to fall all the way down to his side before she moved. Mike didn't – he went as soon as Matt began to move. He had gained a metre before Kitty had even realised.

Mike ran faster than he had ever done in his life. He focused on the finishing line and on just getting his legs moving and pumping as fast as he could. He wasn't running out of determination or desire, he was running out of something that made a person run much faster. He was running out of fear.

Kitty cursed herself for giving him the edge at the start, but she put it out of her mind quickly and focused on her running. She was a beautiful, effortless runner. Mike was powerful but Kitty was a natural. Quite tall for a girl in Year 5, she managed to combine a long stride with incredibly fast leg speed which meant that she just ate up the ground.

But Kitty knew she had a lot to do after her silly mistake at the start. By the time they reached the halfway line, Green was still ahead and running well. By the time they passed the ten-metre line, Kitty was alongside and cruising. By the time they reached the twenty-two-metre finish line, her natural speed and ability had taken her ahead of Green and, just to be sure, she dipped at the line. She had seen athletes do that on TV and thought it looked cool, so she tried it. It didn't look cool. It looked awesome.

Predictably, Mike tried to claim it was a draw.

'Dead heat! Dead heat!' he shouted loudly. 'She didn't win, it was a draw, a draw!'

He desperately thought that if he shouted the lie loud and often enough, he would make it become the truth. But he had no chance – Manu had seen to that.

He walked straight across to Jonathan, the member of Mike's gang who had earlier taken the picture of Jimmy in despair and said he would send the picture of the 'loser' viral. Jonathan was shouting loudly alongside Mike, backing up his leader's claims that it had been a draw.

'She didn't beat him, a draw, it was a draw!' heckled Jonathan. He was dancing on the spot as if he was some sort of street gangster rapper. He even had his baseball cap on back to front. He looked ridiculous.

'Erm, no, it wasn't actually,' said Manu calmly.

'What do you know, fool?' replied Jonathan. 'If Greeno says it was a draw, it was a draw.'

'Yeah, I thought you might say that. Which is why I filmed it,' said Manu, holding up his phone.

'What?' shrieked Mike in horror.

'Yeah, I filmed the finish because I knew you lot would try something, and it shows clearly that Kitty beat you. She didn't even need to do the dip. Which looked particularly professional, Kitty, if I may say.'

Kitty laughed and gave a theatrical bow. 'Ah thank you, kind sir,' she said.

Mike and his mates went silent. Manu turned back to Jonathan.

'So if I were you, I'd delete that picture you took of Jimmy. Because if you don't, this film will be going viral too. I imagine it would be quite popular in school, bad Mikey Green being beaten in a race by a girl. Probably a bit more interesting than Jimmy's kick hitting the post.'

Mike turned to Jonathan instantly. 'Delete it. Delete it NOW!'

'All right, all right,' said Jonathan, fumbling to put his passcode in, before tapping furiously on the face of the phone. 'There done. It's gone.'

'And from the "recently deleted" bin.'

'Agh, all right.' There was a pause. 'There, done. See?'

Mike swung to Manu, 'And now you delete that film too.'

'Oh, I don't think so, Michael. I'll just keep it in case Jonny-boy there somehow finds a way to bring that pic of Jimmy back to life.'

Mike was about to say something, but for once, realised it was pointless. He turned to his gang and said quickly, 'Come on, let's go.'

And with that, they were gone. Maybe not forever, but at least for tonight.

Matt, Manu and Jimmy turned to Kitty.

'That was absolutely brilliant, Kit,' said Matt. 'I didn't think you'd catch him after that start.'

'Had to give him a little head start, didn't I,' laughed Kitty. 'Wouldn't have been fair to completely demolish him.'

Jimmy turned to Manu, with a smile as wide as the pitch on The Rec. 'Nice one Manu, what a brilliant idea to have recorded it on your phone!'

'I know, I know,' laughed Manu, 'I'm a genius, what can I say? But it could have been even better.'

'How do you mean?' asked Kitty

'Well, it might have helped if I'd actually pressed record.'

There were several seconds of stunned silence before the four friends fell into hysterical laughter that echoed around The Rec.

# GIRL POWER

On their way home from The Rec, Kitty and Jimmy couldn't stop laughing. Even though Jimmy was still down about not beating Mike in their kicking competition, the way that Kitty had beaten him in the race that followed had really lifted his spirits. It was all he talked about as he walked Kitty home.

Kitty and Jimmy had lived on the same street for as long as both could remember. They started nursery school on the same day, and then also went into the same Reception class together when they first went to Central Primary. Their friendship was as strong as anybody's in the school.

'You should have seen his face when you dipped over the line, Kitty, it was an absolute beauty,' said Jimmy.

'I wish I had,' she replied with a laugh, 'but I thought I'd messed it up with that start. I'm never going to let that happen again.'

'Yeah, I'm not gonna lie, I was a bit worried then, but you smoked him in the end!'

'Yeah, I did, didn't I? I smoked him!' said Kitty in the worst American accent Jimmy had ever heard, which reduced them both to fits of laughter again.

Across the road a door opened. It was Jimmy's mother coming out of his grandparents' house.

'What are you two laughing at?' she asked.

'Oh, nothing, Mum, it's just that Kitty's never going to be an actress, that's all.'

'Well that's just as well,' said Kitty primly, 'because I only want to be a rugby player anyway!' And with that, Kitty snatched the ball from Jimmy's arms and sprinted off down the street as if she was making a break for the All Blacks.

'Do you two want some supper before Kitty goes home?' asked Catherine.

'Oh, yes please, Mum, salad cream on toast for me!'

'Oh, Jimmy, what am I going to do with you? That's disgusting! All right, go and tell Kitty, and I'll just pop into her mum's to let them know.'

Ten minutes later, all three were sat around the kitchen table eating some supper. Jimmy was expertly squeezing the salad cream from the tube across all areas of his two pieces of toast, so not a millimetre of the golden bread could be seen.

Kitty stopped mid-chew to stare at him. 'How on earth can you eat that? It looks like cat sick.'

'Oi, it's delicious!' he cried in protest.

'He's done it since he was a little boy,' sighed Catherine. 'I'm just hoping he grows out of it soon.'

'Never!' exclaimed Jimmy, before taking a huge bite which saw salad cream oozing from either side of his mouth, before dropping right down the front of his blue t-shirt.

'Jimmy!' cried his mother. 'You little pig!'

'Yeah, man, that's rank,' added Kitty with a shake of her head, but all three of them collapsed into a fit of giggles.

As they wiped the last of the crumbs from their plates, Catherine turned to Kitty. 'So how's the rugby going, Kit? I hope these boys are looking after you.'

'Yeah, it's going really well, thanks, Mrs J. I'm really enjoying it. It's great fun and it's fantastic being part of a team. I just wish Jimmy was picked to play more often.'

'Oh, I will be soon, don't you worry about that,' came Jimmy's laid-back reply as he sat back in his chair and rubbed his full stomach.

'Tell me,' said Catherine, leaning forward to address Kitty directly. 'Why rugby? When I was in school, it was just rounders and netball. Rugby was considered too rough for us girls. We didn't even have a football team then.'

'You know,' said Kitty, wiping her hands on a napkin. 'My dad was once asked that by another parent who didn't understand why a girl would want to play rugby for a boys' team, and he said to the man – "Why *not* rugby?" – and that's how I feel about it, really. I've always played rugby on The Rec with Jimmy and the others, so it made no difference when we became old enough to try out for the school team.'

'Yes, but in a real game, you could get hurt, Kitty. Some of those boys are big. I do worry about you, love.'

Even though Kitty knew that Jimmy's mum was being caring, she was a little bit annoyed at what she was saying. But she didn't want to be rude to her.

'Well, my dad told me a long time ago to pick a sport you love and also pick a sport you're good at. That way, you'll make friends for life and will always have a good, strong level of fitness. I like football, too, but my favourite has always been rugby, so I just went for it. When my dad first realised that's what I wanted to do, he began to teach me about tackling and how to do it safely, so before I even started playing properly, he would make me practise tackling in the garden with one of his big punch bags. And then we'd spend hours watching *Massive Rugby Hits* on YouTube together, so that I could see for myself the best ways to tackle.'

'Ah, I watch that one too!' exclaimed Jimmy. 'It's awesome! Have you seen the one where Semi Radradra absolutely smashes Liam Williams when Fiji played Wales in the 2019 World Cup?'

'Yeah, it's brutal!' laughed Kitty. 'It was like a car crash!'

Catherine stared at them both, dumbfounded.

'Seriously, Mum,' said Jimmy, 'don't worry about Kitty, she's the best tackler of all of us, her dad has seen to that!'

'But what do the other girls think of you playing rugby with the boys, Kit? Surely some of them might think it's odd?'

Kitty thought for a moment. 'Well, there was one girl, Jessica Ryan, who said a couple of unkind things once, but I think she was just jealous that she wasn't very good at sport. All the other girls in school don't say anything, really. They just see it as normal. Lots of them come and watch the games, too, don't they, Jim?'

'Yeah, all the time. They're our "Barmy Army".'

Kitty laughed.

'Well, as long as you're happy, my love, that's fine, you go for it, girl!' said Catherine. 'But, I must admit, I think I'd be sticking to rounders. But who am I trying to kid, I was rubbish at that when I was in school!'

'What a surprise!' laughed Jimmy.

'Enough of your cheek, you,' said Catherine, 'or I'll set Kitty the monster tackler on you!'

'No thanks,' said Jimmy with his hands held up in mock surrender. 'I'd rather take my chances with Semi Radradra!'

# HANGING ON IN THERE

THE NEXT few days were a welcome change for Jimmy. Probably worried at the thought of Manu sharing the video of his sprinting defeat, Mike had kept out of Jimmy's way, leaving him and his friends alone. Whilst they were all relieved to be out of Mike's firing line for a while, they felt sorry for the other children in Year 5 who were now the target of his needling and abuse. 'He can't be allowed to carry on behaving like that to everyone,' Jimmy said to Matt one lunchtime. 'We're going to have to do something. It's just not right.'

Matt looked at Jimmy. Not only was Jimmy Matt's best friend, he had enormous respect for him too. But he also knew that tangling with Mike Green would only lead to more trouble.

'I know you're right, but you know what's going to happen if you mess with him, don't you?' asked Matt. Then, without waiting for Jimmy to reply, he continued. 'Green will just involve Mr Kane and you'll end up with more detentions, or even get suspended. And it would be the end of any chance you have to play rugby here.'

Jimmy was silent, thinking about what his friend had said. Matt was probably right. Even though Mr Kane had left Jimmy alone since the morning after the kicking competition with Mike – word had managed to spread through school about that and the race, even without the aid of the photo or the video – Mr Kane was still a long way from being friendly to Jimmy. In the week or so that had followed that evening, Jimmy had been just about the only person in his class that Mr Kane had not directly spoken to. At some point, every pupil had been asked to read out loud or answer a maths question or explain something in history or take part in a class experiment. But not Jimmy. It was like he didn't exist in Mr Kane's eyes.

If Jimmy did decide to step in and try and deal with Mike's bullying, Mr Kane, who absolutely loved Mike, would never believe Jimmy. He would always take Mike's side.

'Yeah, all right,' said Jimmy at last. 'It's probably best if we wait a while before dealing with Mike. But something needs to be done. You saw how quiet he went when Manu said that he had the video of him? Maybe that's what we need to do – find a way to embarrass him in front of everyone, and show him up as the coward he is?'

'How're you going to do that then?' asked Matt.

'Not sure yet. But there's nothing so public as a rugby match. Maybe we can do something then?'

But before he could think any more about it, around the corner of the teaching block and out onto the schoolyard came Mr Kane. As usual, he looked grumpy.

'Right, you lot, listen closely.' He glowered down at the group of children in front of him. 'This Thursday we've got the semi-final of the Cluster Cup against Western Primary. We will win and we will go and play in the final. You will not let me down. So, to make this happen, tomorrow after school, there's a last practice with the squad who will be taking part. It starts at 4.00 at The Rec. Don't be late.'

He turned and began to walk away. As he did, Kitty spoke.

'Sir? Does that include me?'

Mr Kane stopped, turned and looked at Kitty. He sighed before replying. He had begun to dislike Kitty as much as Jimmy, but knew that he dare not show that too publicly.

'Well, according to our head teacher, we're living in a world where girls can play in a man's game. So, to keep everyone satisfied, yes, you're in the squad.' The vein in his temple was throbbing.

Kitty flushed. Tokenism. That's all this was. She deserved to be in the team.

Again, Kane turned to walk away. This time it was Matt who spoke. 'Sir, the practice tomorrow. Does it include Jimmy too?'

Kane stopped in his tracks. He turned around slowly and, for the first time in an age, looked directly at Jimmy. There was a long pause before he spoke, as if he was searching for the right words to make his point as crystal clear as he could. 'George Stapleton was a very good fly-half,' he growled. 'He followed instructions, he listened to me and did what I said. He didn't kick when I told him not to. He didn't run and sidestep, because I told him to take contact, and he always gave the simple pass because I explained why that was important.' Kane's eyes were fixed on Jimmy's and didn't move. Then he glanced across to Matt. 'But your friend doesn't believe in any of those things, does he? Oh no, he thinks he knows it all and can do what he wants. A showboater. Well, not on my team.'

He kept looking at Matt, having seemingly dismissed Jimmy as an irrelevance.

'But to answer your question, it does include him – but only because Stapleton leaving the school has left me without anyone else to be a back-up fly-half. The key words there being "back-up".'

He threw out a thick, crooked finger at Jimmy, but still didn't look at him. 'So, count yourself lucky, boy. You're in the squad, but only because I have no other option.'

And with that, Kane turned and was off, walking towards Mike and his cronies on the other side of the yard.

Manu eventually broke the silence.

'Well that worked out well, Jim. But there is one way that you'll definitely get a game.'

'What's that?' asked Kitty and Matt together.

'Just ask George Stapleton's father to get Ollie Snell's dad a job in Swindon too!'

They all looked at Jimmy, who after a second, burst out laughing. They all joined in.

'Good idea, Manu,' said Jimmy. 'In fact, I might try and see if he can get a few more of the dads jobs there, too . . . I might end up as skipper in a fortnight!'

As the laughing friends made their way back to class, Jimmy reflected on something his grandfather had told him ages ago. *Humour is the key, Jimmy. If you can find it, in even the darkest of times, you won't be down for long. That's what we all did in the forces. Find the humour, son.*

Jimmy smiled as he thought of his grandfather. Mr Kane might be trying to keep him down, but he wouldn't manage it for long.

# THE NIGHTMARE CONTINUES

Jimmy took two huge puffs on his inhaler and put it back in his bag. He took off his glasses and went to place them inside too. His finger snagged on the rough edge of a piece of tape that was holding the left arm of his glasses in place. He'd broken them again that lunchtime, predictably, playing rugby in the yard. Miss Ayres had fixed them for him in class. Smoothing the tape down flat, Jimmy placed them next to his inhaler, then he reached for his gum shield and took it over to the tap to rinse, before shaking off the drips and tucking it into his sock. It was the last training session for the squad who would take part in the semi-final, and Jimmy was determined to enjoy it.

He jogged out of the changing room, along the concrete floor before making it outside. He loved the clacking sound his steel studs made on the hard surface before stepping off it onto the soft turf of the Rec. He loved rugby so much. He loved the anticipation of it, he loved the preparation for it and he loved the moment just before it started. He knew he was good at it – knew he was born to play it. He was just a little sad that, at the moment, he wasn't being given much opportunity to show that to anyone.

Or so he thought.

The whistle blew loudly.

'Right, get in here, you lot.' Mr Kane didn't look happy.

Jimmy joined everyone in the circle around the towering teacher. He was standing with Matt to his left, Mike Green to his right. Mike gave Jimmy a sharp dig with his elbow, trying to gain a reaction. Jimmy ignored it.

Mr Kane spoke.

'Right. We're going to do some training drills – just some running and passing to get you warmed up – so I want forwards over there in one group, and backs over here in another group. Unfortunately, I've just received news that Ollie Snell has had to go to the dentist. He won't be here tonight.' Then after a long pause, he added, 'Jimmy, as you're now the only one we've got, you're fly-half tonight.'

Jimmy couldn't believe it. He'd thought he was just going to be stood on the sidelines watching everything, but now he was actually going to be taking part. He was delighted. He also made a decision. He was going to do everything that Kane told him. Even if he disagreed with it. He was going to follow orders. This might be his only chance to make the team and that meant more to him than anything. If he had to do it Kane's way, so be it.

'Right then,' shouted Mr Kane as he tossed a ball, first to Tom Edmonds, his pack leader and then another to Mike, his full back and captain. 'I want you in lines, running from one side of the pitch to the other, gentle jogging and passing along the line and back. Off you go!' and with a shrill blow of his whistle, the players all rushed to the touchline to begin their drill.

Jimmy's group all followed Mike until they were lined up along the touchline, inside the twenty-two. 'Jimmy, next to me,' barked Mike, as everybody else lined up inside and to the left of Mike and Jimmy. Jimmy didn't understand why Mike was so insistent on having him next to him for a warm-up exercise, but he went along with it. Jimmy wasn't going to argue with anyone tonight, whatever happened.

Mike held the ball as he looked along the line to his left, with all the backs in the squad spread out along the length of the touchline, all the way over to Kitty who was at the far end. 'Ready?' he shouted and everyone signalled to show that they'd heard. Mike twirled the ball in his hand, started moving forward and shouted, 'Let's go then!' and with that, he fired a fast, hard, low spin pass straight at Jimmy's knees.

Jimmy had sensed that Mike was going to do something spiteful and sneaky, but even with that in his mind and his excellent reflexes, he was powerless to do anything with Mike's pass. He managed to get a thumb on it, but that only knocked the ball onto his knee before knocking it to the ground.

There was a loud whistle. Mr Kane had seen it. 'That was awful, Joseph!' shouted Kane. 'Any more mistakes like that and it'll be press-ups for you.' Jimmy thought of protesting, but remembered his promise to himself that he wouldn't say anything – and anyway, he knew it would be pointless.

Instead, Jimmy bent down, grabbed the ball and handed it to Matt. They swapped places in the line. Mike wouldn't be doing that to him again.

'Ready?' Jimmy asked Mike.

'Almost,' came the petulant reply and Mike shuffled down the line to stand on the other side of Jimmy. *Oh well,* thought Jimmy, *at least if I'm passing the ball to him, he can't deliver any more rubbish passes to me.*

Jimmy started to jog forward and as he collected the ball from Matt, delivered a perfect pass to Mike, just out in front of him, in the exact place for Mike to jog forwards and catch it without breaking his stride. It was the ideal rugby pass. Inexplicably, Mike slowed down at the moment that Jimmy passed, and shouted theatrically at the top of his voice, 'For Pete's sake!' as he let the pass sail ahead of him, making a desperate, lunging grasp to make it look as if Jimmy had thrown the pass too far forward.

There was another loud whistle. Thanks to Mike's screaming, Mr Kane had seen it again. 'That was rubbish!' he shouted at Jimmy again. 'I told you that your next mistake would cost you press-ups. Accuracy is required in passing, boy, so to make you understand that, ten press ups! Now!'

Jimmy sighed, but apart from that, he showed no obvious reaction to what was happening. He dropped to the floor and did his press-ups. Green was clearly trying to make Jimmy look bad in Mr Kane's eyes, but he vowed to himself that he wouldn't let Green win.

Mike collected the ball and moved to start the drill again with a pass to Jimmy. Matt could see what was happening, and suspected the same thing as Jimmy, so as Mike glanced over to see if Kane was watching, Matt rushed over and snatched the ball from him.

'Get over there, in line,' Matt hissed to Mike. 'Manu, here!' Manu jogged over and placed himself between Jimmy and Mike.

'Let's go!' shouted Matt, and moved forward, before making a perfect pass to Jimmy who caught it. Jimmy in turn made a perfect pass to Manu, who threw a very fast spin pass to Mike. The ball hit him right in the chest and bounced onto the floor in front of him.

'Sir! Knock on!' shouted Matt to Mr Kane.

'I didn't see it,' replied Kane, 'play on, play on!'

Matt went to answer Mr Kane back for his obvious favouritism, but Jimmy grabbed his arm. 'Leave it, Matt, don't you get involved too. It's fine, don't worry.'

Mike swept up the ball, jogged back in line and made a pass inside to Harrison, another Year 6 boy who was the other centre. He caught it, and passed the ball to Keegan, one of the wings. At last there was a string of passes being made, and now that Mike was no longer next to Jimmy, the group of backs made a full run across the field with no more dropped passes. They managed to complete another three runs, without incident, until Mr Kane ended the warm-up with his whistle.

'Right, come in,' he shouted, as he moved to the centre of the pitch. 'Time for contact.' He smiled and rubbed his hands together.

'In groups of five, I want one of you to take the ball into contact. I want the tackler to take you to the floor, then the ball-carrier to recycle the ball backwards. I then want two of you to run in and stand over the ball-carrier to form a ruck and the final one of you to pick up the ball and run around one of the sides. Then stop, and repeat again with all of you swapping roles. Understand?'

Everyone nodded.

'Okay,' said Mr Kane, 'first group, Mike, you're the ball-carrier, Manu and Harrison to follow up, Matt to collect the ball.' Then, with a sly smile, 'Joseph, you're the tackler.'

Jimmy nodded and jogged to his mark.

Kane blew the whistle and Mike ran straight at Jimmy. Jimmy made the tackle perfectly and, as instructed, brought Mike down to the floor to allow him to recycle the ball uncontested, so the drill could continue.

The whistle blew. 'That's playing the ball off your feet, Joseph – penalty! Don't you know the rules, boy? You need more discipline. Ten more press-ups. Now.'

Jimmy couldn't believe it, he'd done nothing wrong. His tackle had been perfect. He'd released Mike as soon as he hit the floor and he'd made no attempt to play the ball. He couldn't have executed the drill better. As he got down to do his press-ups, he glanced up at Mr Kane, who had a sick grin on his face. Jimmy almost erupted with fury. It was clear that Mr Kane was just picking on Jimmy for the sake of it, and his stupid grin – which all but confirmed it – nearly sent Jimmy over the edge . . . but he managed to hold on to his temper. Just.

Over in the corner of the field, unseen by many, somebody was watching. He was an older man, in his sixties, and he had the collar of his coat pulled up to keep out the stiff breeze. On his head was a cap, pulled down low so that the front of his face was obscured. It was Will, Jimmy's grandfather. He too was having trouble keeping hold of his temper.

# LEAVE THE BOY ALONE

THE TRAINING session went from bad to worse for Jimmy. If it wasn't Mike in his ear all the time, trying to put him off, it was Mr Kane coming down on him and telling him off for mistakes and errors that just never happened. The only good thing was that Mr Kane had stopped giving Jimmy press-ups to do – he must have got bored with it.

It was plain to see that Mr Kane had decided to make an example of Jimmy. And Will could hardly stand it. Finally, just before the end of the session, he couldn't take it anymore.

All the training drills had been done, all the tackles had been practised and all the set pieces had been finished. Apart from one. The line out.

Mr Kane set the line out and instructed Callum Robertson, the hooker, to throw it to the second row, Andrew Beasley, in the middle. His instruction was to catch the ball, then feed it instantly to Matt at scrum-half. Matt's instruction was to pass the ball as quickly as possible to Jimmy. Jimmy was given no instruction. Instead, Mr Kane turned to two of the reserve forwards, who he had told to stand on the opposition side of the line out at the back. Their job was to charge at the fly-half, Jimmy, as quickly as possible, to tackle him and prevent him passing. It was a simple drill.

All was set up, and on Mr Kane's whistle, Callum threw the ball into the line out. Unopposed, the giant lock, Beasley, soared above everyone to catch the ball. As he came back down to earth, he instantly popped the ball to Matt at scrum-half. By now, both the forwards were off and running at Jimmy. Then came the problem. Matt slightly fumbled the ball before he sent his pass out to Jimmy. That split-second fumble meant that the forwards were almost on Jimmy before he even had the ball. In the instant that the ball touched his hands, however, Jimmy had known what he was going to do. He didn't really catch the ball, instead he almost instantly dropped it down onto his right boot, and with the most gentle of touches, kicked the ball around the first of the onrushing forwards, who looked startled at having been deceived in such a way. Jimmy was off and around him as quick as a flash, and before the second forward could realise what had happened, Jimmy had scooped the ball up from the turf, and in the same movement sidestepped past him. There was just one more problem for Jimmy. In the couple of seconds that the move had taken him, one of the opposing centres had seen what Jimmy was doing and had come across to cover the second forward. Jimmy had seen the centre coming, and as the centre dived to tackle him, Jimmy stopped on the spot, moved his body to the right to let the desperate tackler dive through the air, grasping at nothing. Then, realising he now had space,

Jimmy steadied himself, and dropped the most perfect of goals from about twenty metres out. The ball flew high and handsome right through the middle of the rusty old uprights. It was an astonishing piece of rugby.

Hardly anyone on the pitch had said a word, as they watched the ball sailing between the dead centre of the posts.

Andrew Beasley was the first to do it. When the ball landed in the long grass behind the posts, he began clapping. He was joined almost at once by the rest of the forwards in the line out, and soon the rest of the players joined in. One of the forwards got up off the floor and walked up to Jimmy, 'Well done, mate,' he said, patting Jimmy on the shoulder, 'that was brilliant, fair dos.' Even Mike, of all people, was impressed. His instinct was to join in the clapping – he knew what he'd seen had been exceptional, and despite all his failings, Mike loved rugby. But Mike knew he had a reputation to keep, so he ignored his instinct and said and did nothing.

And then came the whistle. It was Mr Kane.

'Knock, on. I'd be giving a knock on if this was a game.' Looking at Jimmy, he said, 'You were not in control of that ball, and you dropped it forward. And what did I tell you? My instruction was for you to take the tackle.'

Jimmy had had enough. 'No, it wasn't. You never gave me an instruction. All you said was for Matt to pass to me and for the lads to take me down. You never said a word about what I should do – so I did what I would have done in a game, and made a break.'

'And that's why you'll never start a game for me!' roared Mr Kane. 'Your failure to do anything other than what you want to do. So get yourself off this field and get changed, I will not take answering-back from any players – especially *you.* Training's over!'

And with that, Mr Kane blew his whistle again and pointed to the changing rooms.

All the players, apart from Mike looked confused. Andrew Beasley looked at the centre, Harrison, and said, 'I don't understand . . . What Jimmy did then was brilliant, it was like watching Beauden Barrett!'

Another person would have agreed with Andrew if he'd heard him. Jimmy's grandfather.

As all the children walked off, Mr Kane walked towards the touchline on the far side of the pitch to fetch some bibs and cones that he'd left there. By the time he got there, Will was standing in front of him. Mr Kane didn't notice him at first, until Will reached out and gently grabbed the teacher by the left bicep with his right hand and began to firmly apply pressure. That got Mr Kane's attention.

'Can I help you?' asked Mr Kane, trying to wrestle his arm free from the surprisingly powerful grip. Will held Mr Kane's gaze for several long seconds before letting go.

'Yes, you can actually,' replied Will, coldly. 'I knew your father.'

'Oh, yeah?' said Mr Kane dismissively. 'Lots of people did.' Then he broke into a crooked grin. 'Hard bloke, my old man.'

'That's one way of describing him,' replied Will. 'We had another way . . . a bully.'

Will didn't take his eyes off Mr Kane as he delivered the insult. He wanted to look deep inside him to read his response.

Mr Kane was a little startled. He hadn't expected an insult. He was used to hearing all the old stories about his dad, always in the middle of confrontations and never backing down from anything.

'Hold on, what is this?' he spluttered. 'What did you just say about my old man?'

'I said he was a bully,' said Will calmly. 'And it seems to me that in your case, the apple hasn't fallen very far from the tree.' Again, he didn't take his eyes off the teacher.

'I beg your pardon?' said a startled Mr Kane, now standing up to his full six feet four inches and puffing out his chest. 'Who on earth are you anyway?'

'Don't worry about me,' said Will, 'this is about you. Why do you bully that little kid out there?'

'Which one? I don't bully anyone. What are you talking about?'

'I'm talking about the boy playing fly-half. I was walking past and saw the practice start so thought I'd have a quick look. I like my rugby. Then I saw what you did when Gary Green's boy messed up the lad's pass. Press-ups for that? What was that all about?' Before Kane could reply, Will pressed on, 'So I stayed and watched. Not the kids, mind, no, I stayed to watch you.'

'Oh, you did, did you?' said Mr Kane, his forehead scar beginning to wiggle. 'And what exactly did you see?'

'I'll tell you what I saw. I saw a grown man, a grown man of six feet four, decide to bully a ten-year-old kid. Is it because you're a failed rugby player? Well, I say rugby player, more a thug like your father, really – is that why you've decided to pick on the team's most talented player?'

'He's not talented, he's an arrogant show off!' spat Mr Kane. 'He needs to be put in his place.'

'No!' said Will, raising his voice for the first time. 'What I saw, was a ten-year-old kid with incredible ability who is just trying to do his best for his coach. Who is bullying him. It's you who needs putting in his place.'

'Look,' said Mr Kane, starting to go purple with anger. 'I don't know who you think you are, or what you think you saw, but I suggest that you walk away *now*, before you say something you regret. If anyone's going to put me in my place, it certainly won't be an old fossil like you.'

Will laughed. 'That's it, you threaten me instead. I've dealt with bullies all my life, far bigger and tougher than you.'

'I doubt it, old man,' replied Kane, with a chilling coldness. 'I doubt it.'

'Let me show you something,' said Will, still completely calm. He held out his right arm and pulled up the sleeve on his coat and jumper to expose a tattoo. It was about half the length of his forearm and depicted a dagger, with two poppies at the base of it. At the top, there was a scroll over the handle of the dagger that had two words: Royal Marines.

'Yes, I might appear an old man to you on the outside, but on the inside, I assure you I am not. If you want to take a chance at bullying anyone, have a go at me, but I warn you, this tattoo is my CV, and as a former Marine, I've never once backed out of a fight, nor lost one. And your father of all people knew that. On more than one occasion.' Will kept an icy gaze on Kane as he said every word.

Unnerved by the intensity of Will's speech, Kane took a step back. He was wary. Will had spotted a weakness when he first looked deep into Kane's eyes, it was there with all bullies. He rolled the sleeves back down.

'I've watched all the kids from this village over the years, and where I've been able to, I've helped many of them,' continued Will. 'I will not stand by and watch you come here and try and ruin one of them.'

Mr Kane ignored him. He just bent down and picked up the bibs and cones. He turned and walked away. After he'd got about ten yards ahead, he stopped and glanced over his shoulder.

'Why don't you just get lost you miserable old man.'

Will laughed. He couldn't believe that a grown man – and teacher at that – could behave so childishly – although he'd often noticed a childishness in bullies he'd encountered over the years, especially when they were confronted. 'You waited till you were all the way over there before you said anything? Pathetic.' He paused for a moment. 'I promise you this, I won't be getting lost – I'll be watching everything you do out here. Just remember that. Even if you can't see me . . . I'll be watching you. And don't make me have to come and confront you again. It won't end well for you, I can promise you that.'

Mr Kane scuttled off without saying another word, some beads of sweat breaking out onto his forehead, and he swore and cursed under his breath as he made his way back to the changing rooms.

Will didn't take his eyes off him. He done what he'd set out to achieve: place doubt in the bully's mind. He was also pleased that he hadn't had to bring up the issue about Kane's broken arm. He nearly had when he'd shown Kane the tattoo on his own arm, but thought it might actually make things worse for Jimmy. The confrontation might not alter things straight away, but he knew it was a start. He hoped that Kane would consider his future treatment of his beloved grandson. But whatever happened, Will would be watching and would step in again if needed. Then, this proud old man, feeling more alive than he had done in several years, pulled his collar back up and turned for home, happy that he'd been able to confront Kane, one to one, without anyone else witnessing their little chat.

But what Will hadn't realised was that someone else *had* been watching. Sitting unnoticed in his car at the top of The Rec, a man had watched with growing fury not only as he observed Will's confrontation with Kane, but also the whole sorry affair of Kane's treatment of Jimmy during the session.

'It's time I had a little chat with you, Mark Kane,' the man said to himself as he simultaneously watched Will walking away and Mr Kane ducking inside the changing rooms. Focussing back on the teacher he said. 'I will not tolerate bullying. Not at my school.'

It was Mr Davies, the headmaster.

# PICKING THE WRONG FIGHT

ON THE Monday of the following week, Manu was walking past Mr Davies' office. He could hear raised voices, so he stopped by the water cooler and pretended to fill his bottle. He couldn't make out exactly what was being said, but at various points he heard Mr Davies clearly say the words 'behaviour', 'bullying', 'fair play', 'tolerate' and one very clear phrase, because Mr Davies said it so loudly, 'they are primary school children, not professional rugby players!'

As he craned his neck to listen, the door to the office opened so quickly that Manu nearly dropped his bottle in surprise. He felt sure that Mr Kane would have a go at him but, surprisingly, he didn't even seem to notice that Manu was there as he strode angrily past him. Manu finally filled up his bottle, and was putting the lid on when he heard Mr Davies on the phone saying, 'Hello, can I speak to Mr Entwhistle, please?' *It must be serious*, thought Manu. Mr Entwhistle was the school's chair of governors and he usually only came into school when things went wrong. Just as Manu was thinking of pouring out his bottle so that he could continue listening, Mr Davies saw him and said, 'Can you close the door please, Manu, and get yourself back to class if you don't mind.'

'Yes sir,' said Manu instantly, closing the door and heading back to class. When he got there, Mr Kane was already sitting at the front, red-faced with anger.

'Where have you been, boy?' asked Mr Kane.

'To get some water, sir, Miss Ayres said it was okay.'

Mr Kane shot an angry glance towards Miss Ayres, who told him quickly that she had, in fact, given Manu permission.

As if ignoring his teaching assistant, he turned to the class and said, 'Nobody leaves this room without my permission. We are here to work not swan around the school getting drinks.'

Manu glanced across at Miss Ayres. It was her turn to have a face red with fury.

Later in the morning, Manu told Matt, Kitty and Jimmy what he'd heard. They were fascinated.

'Maybe it will all stop now, Jim,' said Kitty hopefully. 'Mr Davies can be really tough when he wants to be and it sounds like he has given Kane a right telling off.'

*Mmmm, maybe,* thought Jimmy. Perhaps things would change. After all, Mr Davies was in charge of everything at the school, so if he didn't like the way Kane was treating Jimmy, then he could put a stop to it. But from the little that Manu had heard, nobody could be sure that he had been talking about Jimmy at all. Maybe he was just telling Kane off for his attitude in general. Or maybe the way he handled rugby practice. Or maybe it was nothing at all, perhaps Manu had got it wrong.

Jimmy's mind was completely scrambled, he just didn't know what to think.

At lunch, Jimmy was placing his tray back on the trolley when he turned around and succeeded in knocking the tray out of the hand of the person behind him.

It was Mr Kane. It was also a total accident.

But not in Mr Kane's eyes.

'You, boy!' screamed Kane. 'Pick all that up! How dare you fool around and knock my tray out of my hand. Pick it up now, then get to my room. Detention for the rest of lunch and after school.'

Jimmy froze, hand over his mouth, not able to register what had just happened.

'Can't you hear me, boy? PICK. IT. UP!' bellowed Mr Kane. The way he emphasised each word with a pause frightened everyone in the hall. Except one.

'Mr Kane!' came a loud voice. 'Stop right there. I saw everything that just happened. It was a complete accident. That boy was simply turning away after placing his tray in the trolley. It was you who was not paying attention. I saw you looking down at your phone and you walked straight into him. How dare you speak to a child of this school like that and humiliate them, especially when it was all your own fault.'

It was all Mr Kane could do to contain his rage. He was so angry, he could hardly get his words out. He took a step towards the stranger, accidentally kicking his plate under a table as he did, before saying, 'Well what has it got to do with you anyway? You shouldn't even be in here.'

'Oh, I'm very much allowed to be in here Mr Kane. But perhaps, as we have not met, I should introduce myself.'

The man paused, as if for dramatic effect before he continued.

'My name is Entwhistle, Graham Entwhistle. I am the chair of governors for Central Primary.'

Tellingly, he didn't offer his hand to Mr Kane by way of a greeting. Instead, he just stared at him.

The realisation of the importance of this man hit Mark Kane like an Anthony Joshua punch.

'Ah. Oh, yes. Of course. Erm, I mean, yes, sir,' stuttered Mr Kane. 'Of course, erm, yes. I'm pleased to meet you.' Mr Kane's rage had left him completely. It was replaced by another strong emotion: panic. Blind panic. He continued, 'Yes, you're right, of course, I might have got that slightly wrong.'

Then, looking at Jimmy, Kane said, 'There we are, son, my fault, leave those plates. I'll pick them up now. You . . . erm . . . you just go out to play.' And with that he smiled at Jimmy.

*Smiled!*

Jimmy couldn't believe it, Mr Kane had barely looked at him in the weeks he had been teaching him, and here he was smiling at him – it was a bit like being smiled at by a great white shark, but it was a smile nevertheless. Jimmy realised there and then that what his grandfather had told him was one hundred per cent correct. Mr Kane was nothing but a coward – like most bullies. Maybe the tide was finally beginning to turn his way.

As he walked past Mr Entwhistle, the man looked at Jimmy and said, 'Are you all right, young man?'

Jimmy replied politely, 'Yes, sir. Thank you.'

Mr Entwhistle nodded, smiled and then looked back at Mr Kane, who was now on his hands and knees, trying to reach the plate he had kicked under the table. He walked up to Mr Kane and stopped. Mr Kane looked up at Mr Entwhistle, another grotesque smile appearing across his face. 'Can't quite reach the plate,' he said, a nervous bead of sweat dribbling down his cheek. 'It might be gone forever,' he said, trying to make a joke out of his predicament.

'Gone forever,' repeated Mr Entwhistle, 'how very prophetic, Mr Kane.'

With that, Mr Entwhistle walked off towards Mr Davies' office without saying another word.

Mr Kane reached the plate, dragged it from under the table and put it back on the tray, alongside the bowl and mug he'd already rescued. His panic had subsided and was now, again, being replaced by anger.

He walked over to the trolley and placed the tray on one of its shelves. As he walked away, he could only think of one thing. Jimmy Joseph. It was all his fault, *everything*. That damned Jimmy Joseph . . .

# A CHEAT'S CHARTER

THE FOLLOWING evening, it was the semi-final of the Cluster Cup. Central Primary were playing Western Primary, a school in the nearby village of Alderham.

Western Primary was a new-build, less than two years old. It had been built to accommodate two old, small primary schools that were less than a mile apart, but in neighbouring villages. The council had decided to merge the schools a few years before and, when they did, there had been protests from everyone in the area, saying it was unfair to close one and not the other. In the end, the council closed them both and built a new school. It had every bit of new equipment you could imagine a modern school might have – but the sports facilities stood out above everything else.

They had three sports pitches: one for rugby, one for football, and a 4G pitch. Each had a covered area for the coaches and subs, and the 4G pitch even had floodlights. But the best thing of all was the changing rooms. They were fantastic.

The battered old green minibus carrying the Central Primary players parked up next to two brand new gleaming white transit vans with 'Western Primary School – sponsored by Southville Garages' emblazoned along their sides. As Jimmy and his teammates trouped out, they couldn't help but feel a little embarrassed by their own mode of transport. Despite the dirt and the rust, the worst thing about the van was the lettering. There was a small sticker on each side of the van that said 'Central Primary', but it was still possible to make out the lettering from the previous owner underneath, which read 'Highview Rest Home – A place of Love'.

Some of the parents from Western could barely disguise their sniggers as they walked past the bus. Not that Jimmy could blame them. Everyone at Central thought the minibus was rubbish. *Oh well,* he thought to himself, *we're here to play rugby not take part in an episode of* Top Gear.

When the players from Central rounded the school and saw the playing fields, none of them could believe their eyes. Alongside the three pitches, and attached to the changing rooms they would be using, was a swimming pool. A real, brand new swimming pool. Every single one of them stopped to look through the huge glass windows. As they were tinted, they all put their bags on the floor, put their faces up to the glass, then cupped their hands around them to peer in. It was incredible. Twenty-five metres long, with eight lanes, steps into either end and with a diving board over in the corner.

'Look at this then,' exclaimed Manu to nobody in particular. 'It's like the blinkin' Olympics!'

Everybody laughed. But not for long.

'What're you all doing?' barked Mr Kane. 'Forget the sideshows, you need to focus on this game. Now pick your bags up and go and get changed . . . you've got a game to win for me.'

'*For me*?' thought Jimmy. Surely the game was for *them*.

After the players were changed and ready to go, Mr Kane told them all to sit down. 'Right then, all of you listen.' They did. Mr Kane wasn't the happiest at the best of times, but there was something extra unhappy about him this afternoon. He didn't mince his words.

'Central Primary and its approach to rugby isn't the school I thought it was going to be. When I went to it as a kid, it was a much better place to play rugby. No messing about, the strongest survived and if you weren't up to it, you were out. That's why we won the league and cup in one season – and I was captain. Nobody played for us if they weren't willing to try *everything* to win. We didn't care how we won, we just did whatever it took. Even if it was 3–0. We didn't care about attacking, pretty, fancy, silky rugby,' – he looked directly at Jimmy when he said this – 'we just cared about *winning* rugby.'

He paused for a moment, and scratched the scar that ran the length of his arm, as if Jimmy's face reminded him of when he got it. He continued, 'But now, all that's changed. Your head teacher tells me it's all about *inclusivity*, and *fairness* and *equality*. We even have *girls*.' He spat these words as if they tasted awful and couldn't bring himself to even look in Kitty's direction. Kitty couldn't bring herself to look at him either.

'But tonight, in this cup match, it's all about getting to the Final. AND YOU WILL DO IT!' he roared. 'Now, I know that some of you aren't good enough to make that happen, not all of you are as brave and strong as your captain.' Mike grinned smugly at the comment. 'But that's all right, because I'll be here to help you. I've agreed with the Western coach, that as he is playing at home, I will referee the game. So that means I will be right by your side, telling you all what to do.'

He paused again, making sure everyone knew and understood what he was about to say.

'And that means that you listen to everything I tell you. Right?'

There was no response.

'RIGHT?'

'Yes, sir!' they all shouted.

'Good. If I tell you to take the tackle, you take the tackle. There is no better way to get a penalty than in a tackle, the Western players will almost certainly infringe, so there will be plenty of penalties.'

He paused again, wiping away some spittle that had formed at the side of his mouth.

'When there's a scrum . . . and let me tell you, there will be plenty of scrums . . . make sure you engage before I say "set". I will not be penalising you for that today. I want you to really rough this lot up. Do you all understand?'

A slightly disbelieving murmur of, 'Yes, sir,' went around the dressing room. Nobody liked the sound of this. Jimmy glanced at Mike and was surprised to see that the smug grin had vanished to be replaced by a doubtful look on Mike's face.

'Good,' continued Mr Kane, ignoring the mood in the room. 'So, listen to me, do as I say, and you WILL win this game for me. I'll show that head teacher of yours what rugby is all about. It's all about winning and *crushing* the opposition.'

He turned to Mike.

'Right Mike, winning the toss for kick-off is vital. There's a strong wind out there at the moment but it's forecast to die down before the second half starts, so we need to take advantage of that. When I blow my whistle to call the two captains together for the coin toss to start the game, I'm going to pretend to have forgotten my coin. What I'll then do, is place my whistle in my hand, and put my hands behind my back. I'll then ask you to choose which hand – make sure you pick this one – my right,' and Mr Kane proceeded to show Mike exactly how he would put the whistle in his hand and place it behind his back. 'Remember, right hand, *right* hand. Okay?'

'Yes, sir, no problem. Right hand, right hand,' repeated Mike.

Jimmy was appalled. This was out-and-out cheating. The whole plan was. He knew that Mr Kane wasn't a very nice man, but even Jimmy couldn't believe he was willing to go to these lengths just to win a primary school game of rugby. It was terrible. Jimmy already knew that he wouldn't be starting the game, Ollie Snell had been picked, but part of him didn't even want to come on as replacement and be part of Mr Kane's cheating. But before Jimmy could consider the situation any further, Mr Kane spoke again.

'Let's get out there, then. And do what I say!' And with that, he strode out.

Matt turned to Jimmy and raised his eyebrows. 'Can you believe that? It's almost like he's going to cheat to get us to win the game.'

'He *is* going to cheat to win us the game,' replied Jimmy.

'Pathetic,' murmured Manu, leaning in towards them.

'I can't believe he would do this,' said Kitty, shaking her head. 'Cheating is the worst thing you can do in sport.'

Manu looked at them puzzled. 'That? No, I don't mean *that*. No, how pathetic are the changing rooms at The Rec compared to this? These are like Wembley! I can't wait for the end of the game, have you seen the shower room? It's like a palace in there! Better than the cold drips from the rusty old taps at The Rec!'

The other three just looked at each other. Then they laughed. Manu, as usual, was just on a completely different planet.

# FOUL PLAY

The whistle went to call the captains together for the start of the game. From the sidelines, Jimmy could see Mr Kane telling the two captains that he had forgotten the coin, before hiding the whistle behind his back.

But then, to everyone in Central Primary's surprise, Mike picked the wrong hand! What an idiot, thought Jimmy. Mr Kane turned his gargantuan face down to stare in disbelief at his captain before wordlessly holding out his empty hand. The Western captain clenched his fist in delight but before he could make his decision, Mr Kane stepped in and made it for him.

'Well done, boy,' he said gruffly, 'you get to kick off. Central will play this way.' He pointed downfield, the way the strong wind was blowing. He had done it so quickly and cleverly, nobody on the sidelines had noticed and the Western captain was too bemused to complain, but everyone in Central knew what was going on. Mr Kane's first piece of cheating was in play.

And it was about to get a whole lot worse.

What followed was the most terrible, most biased and most disgraceful refereeing display ever seen on a rugby pitch, anywhere. It was so bad, it nearly ended in a riot.

It started with the very first whistle. As Mr Kane blew it and the Western fly-half kicked the ball deep into the Central half, Mr Kane whistled again straight away.

'Offside!' he shouted. 'Chasing runners were in front of the ball, restart with a scrum to Central on halfway.'

Nobody could tell if Mr Kane was right or wrong. It wasn't the type of thing a referee would penalise players for in a primary school game. But the adults on the sidelines just shrugged their shoulders and carried on watching. All except one. Mr Davies, the Central headmaster, took out a small notebook and scribbled in it quickly.

At the game's first scrum, Mr Kane left nobody in any doubt about his intentions for the rest of the game. He called the two packs together, 'Crouch . . . bind . . .' and before he could say 'set', just as they had been told, the Central pack shoved into their opposition. 'Set!' said Mr Kane, but by then, Callum had already hooked the ball and it was in Matt's hands. It was blatant cheating but worse was to come.

Within the first ten minutes, Kane had ignored two obvious forward passes and a glaring knock on to give Central Primary three tries. Kitty, who was playing thanks to an injury to Keegan Miller, scored two of them, but was almost too embarrassed to touch down behind the posts for her second and the team's third. Her watching father shook his head in despair. What he was seeing went against everything he believed sport should be about.

Mr Kane's behaviour continued unabated. He gave seventeen penalties against Western Primary, without giving one against Central in the first half alone. This included ignoring a clothesline tackle by Manu that almost took his opposing centre's head off. In fairness to Manu, it was a complete accident, with him getting wrong-footed by his opponent's excellent sidestep, and instinctively throwing out his left arm in desperation, but slipping as he did. This resulted in him catching the player across the throat. Despite the howls from the parents of Western Primary, Kane threw his arms out in front of him, shouting, 'Play on, play on! The Western player ducked into the tackle, play on!'

The ball bounced from the stricken player's grasp and was swept up by Matt, but the penalty was so obvious – and the Western player in such clear distress as he hit the ground – that he instinctively kicked the ball into touch to stop the game. He, along with everyone else watching and playing, were then stunned when Mr Kane shouted, 'Brushed a Western sleeve, Line out to Central'.

Cries of protest thundered around the playing field, but Mr Kane appeared utterly oblivious to them all.

The second half was no better. After an amazing break from his own goal line, the Western winger, cleverly evading Kitty's diving tackle, tore up the line like a cheetah, before outsprinting Mike to dive and score in the corner. Thirty yards back, Mr Kane stood on the touchline, blowing his whistle which had initially been drowned out by the cheers of the Western parents. After blowing it several more times, he removed it from his mouth and shouted, 'Foot in touch, line out please. Central Primary ball.'

It was all too much for one of the Western Primary parents. Mrs Laura Edwards, mother of Western's tenacious hooker, Mike 'Spike' Edwards, walked towards Mr Kane. She was apoplectic with rage.

'Cheat! Cheat! You're nothing but a cheat!'

Mr Kane initially ignored the irate Mrs Edwards, but she wouldn't be stopped. 'You've ruined this game for these kids, it's not right, it's not right! You can't just cheat like this!'

Mark Kane turned around calmly to face his accuser, before nonchalantly saying, 'One more word from you madam, and I shall abandon this game and award it to Central Primary. We have played over three-quarters of the game, so I think you'll find that an abandonment will result in the match being defaulted and the game being awarded to Central Primary. Line out to Central, please!'

Mrs Edwards looked at her shattered son, considered her options and then delivered more than just one word to the referee. With that, Mr Kane blew his whistle, shouted out, 'Match abandoned due to crowd interference!' and marched off the pitch, telling all his players to go straight to the dressing room.

That turned out to be the wisest decision of Mr Kane's day because all hell broke loose on the touchline, with parents making all sorts of threats to the departing referee, but also to the parents of Central Primary, who they felt had been in support of Mr Kane's skulduggery and subterfuge. Naturally, being just as appalled as everyone else by his performance, the Central parents reacted badly to being called cheats and vigorously defended themselves. Soon, the mother of all arguments developed. It wasn't a pretty sight.

All the players from Western stood open-mouthed as the parents argued and shouted at one another, while the Central players did as they had been told and headed for the changing room. All except one.

Mike Green.

Surprisingly, Mike wasn't enjoying the chaos that had resulted from his favourite teacher's cheating. No, quite the opposite, in fact. For the first time in his life, Mike was considering his path in life. He had been more than happy to take advantage of Mr Kane's targeting of Jimmy Joseph, mainly because he knew it was what his father would have approved of, and even done himself in Mike's position. But now, seeing how victory in a game of rugby had been handed over to him, against a really good team who might easily have beaten Central with a fair referee, Mike felt no pleasure in the triumph and the idea of playing in front of the Wolves crowd in the final. In fact, he felt awful. He'd tried his hardest to give the Western side some advantage – picking the hand without the whistle before kick-off and then deliberately throwing some forward passes and dropping some balls – but it had been to no avail.

Something felt different inside him. It was like a light had been turned on in a dark room for the first time in years.

He decided that it was time he spoke to someone he hadn't seen in a long, long time.

# HARD TRUTHS

Unsurprisingly, it had been a very quiet trip home on the battered old minibus. Apart from telling everybody to fasten their seat belts and shouting at one of the parents as the bus left the parking space at Western Primary, Mr Kane didn't say a word. For the first time in his life, Jimmy was really glad he hadn't played a game of rugby. He, Matt, Kitty and Manu all sat in silence across the back row of seats, just trying to get their heads around things.

After about five minutes, Matt spoke. 'This isn't right,' he whispered, his eyes glancing up to make sure Mr Kane hadn't heard him.

But before any of the friends could reply, Mike, sitting alone in the seat in front, turned around and murmured, 'No, it isn't. It's not right at all.'

The four friends sat dumbstruck. Surely there was a sarcastic punchline to follow. But Mike just stared at them, stony faced, then turned back around and gazed out the window.

As soon as the bus pulled up at the school, Mike was the first one up and out of his seat. Jimmy didn't take his eyes off him as he watched Mike sling his bag over his shoulder and jog out of the school yard and turn right, down the road that led to The Rec.

*That's odd,* thought Jimmy as he watched his long-time nemesis pick up his jog into a run, *he lives in the other direction.*

Mike reached The Rec in record time. There were a few people playing down there, including Jimmy's brother, Jonny, who was playing touch rugby with some Year 8 boys from the Wolves' youth set up. But in truth, Mike hardly noticed them.

He slowed to a jog, then to a walk. He didn't want to be out of breath when he spoke. He knew it was going to be a tough enough phone call to make, and he didn't want to be huffing and puffing while doing it.

Mike made his way over to the far touchline of The Rec, where the fence was broken and an overgrown path led to a clearing that used to be a pound for horses some fifty years before. Amongst the moss-covered stones on the derelict walls of this long-abandoned farm compound was where Mike and his gang usually met up. For once, Mike felt uncomfortable in the surroundings.

He delved deep into his bag and rummaged for his phone. It was a new iPhone. His father had tossed it to him one night recently, saying, 'Don't say I don't give you anything, boy . . . and don't ask where it came from, either.'

Mike had learned long ago never to question his father about where things came from. Ever.

He held the phone up to his face. It quickly scanned his features and sprang to life. Mike tapped the green telephone icon, then tapped his list of contacts. He scrolled down to 'G' then found 'Mike Green – this phone'. He tapped the number it displayed, and the screen changed to show the call connecting. But the number wasn't for Mike's phone.

Within seconds, the call was answered by a worried voice. 'Mike . . . is that you? Are you okay?'

'Yeah, it's me, Martyn, and yeah, I'm fine. I just wanted to have a chat, that's all.'

Mike's eldest brother, Martyn, hadn't spoken to Mike, or any other member of the Green family, for over a year. Not since the showdown he'd had with their father. The next day, Martyn had met Mike after school and walked him to the edge of town. He had given Mike his new mobile number, told Mike to disguise it in his contacts and made him agree to ring him if ever he was in trouble at home. This was the first time Mike had used it.

Martyn sounded worried. 'Are you sure you're safe, Mike? What's the matter? Tell me.'

'It's nothing really, and I'm fine. It's just . . .' Mike's words stopped as he considered the enormity of what he was about to say. 'It's just I need to talk to you, Mart . . . I'm really not happy.' Mike stopped as he knew he was on the verge of tears.

'Oh, mate . . . Listen, where are you?'

'On the wall, by the pound. Behind The Rec.'

'Stay where you are. I'll be there in ten minutes.' The call disconnected.

Mike sat with the phone clutched in his hand, staring at his reflection in the dark depths of its blank screen. He wondered when he'd last properly looked at himself like this. And not just looked at his face, which was drawn and haunted-looking. At his whole self. His behaviours. His attitudes. Everything.

He looked up at the sound of crunching gravel and gave a half-hearted smile when he saw that it was Martyn. Without a word, Martyn strode through the long tufts of grass and across the boggy earth until he reached his brother – and he pulled him into a hug which felt like it lasted an age . . . and yet no time at all.

Finally pulling apart, Martyn cast an appraising eye over Mike, making sure he wasn't hurt or injured.

'What's going on, then, eh?' he said softly. 'Tell me all about it.'

It took a while for Mike to find the words and to then force them past the lump in his throat, but eventually he began to talk. He told Martyn about how their father had told him to form a gang among the largest and most intimidating boys in school. How he had become the toughest boy in that gang and how the rest of the school were afraid of him. He told him how lonely he felt, because none of those boys in the gang were really his friends. And what was the point of having a gang and people being afraid of you? It was all so empty and meaningless. And he'd done it all because their father . . . he hadn't been able to say more then, the words choking in his throat. But Martyn didn't need to hear more about that. When it came to their father, he knew it all.

Eventually, Mike wiped away the tears and began again. All he really wanted to do was play rugby. He wanted to be friends with his teammates, all of them, but especially the ones he respected the most – Jimmy, Matt, Manu and Kitty. But they all hated him. And he couldn't blame them. He hated himself as well. He explained about how he had taken advantage of Mr Kane's treatment of Jimmy to make his life a misery and sabotaging him at every chance he got. And finally, he told Martyn about the final straw – about how Mr Kane had cheated to win that day's match.

Once it was all over, the two brothers sat in silence. After a while, Martyn spoke.

'Why are you a bully, Mike?'

Mike was so surprised by the question that he took a moment to answer. 'What do you mean?'

Martyn calmly repeated the question.

'I'm not—'

'You are. Why?'

Mike's brow furrowed. Yeah he was tough . . . yeah, he liked to pick on people . . . but a bully? A *bully*?

Was he a bully?

Of course he was.

'Well . . .' he muttered at last. 'Because of Dad, I suppose. Because he is . . . I am. *All* of us are . . . except you.'

'Yeah, except me,' said Martyn. 'And why do you think that is, then?'

Mike took a moment to think again, before saying, 'Because you're like Mum, I suppose.'

'No, that's so wrong, Mike!' said Martyn raising his voice for the first time. 'Our dad's a bully. One of the worst. And Joe and Paul are, too. And that's what you've become as well. But you're not born a bully, Mike, and whatever you may think, you're not a bully because of Dad. You really need to understand that. Just because *he* is, it doesn't mean you have to be. Look at me, I'm not and I never have been. And you must know that's the reason why

I left. From as long ago as I remember, I refused to be a bully. And that has nothing to do with being like Mum. It's my own choice. I watched the way Dad goes about his life and I saw how wrong it was. His stealing, his bullying, his aggression, everything.'

Mike listened in silence.

'But I chose not to follow that path. Dad hated me for it, thought I was weak, but I knew it was right. A hundred per cent. Not following his path has been the best choice I've ever made in my life. And it can transform your life too, Mike. Nobody knows more than me how hard it is to stand up to a bully, especially when it's your own father, but honestly, Mike, I'll go back to my first question; do you know why you're a bully? Let me tell you. You're a bully because you've chosen to be one. It's been your choice, nobody else's. Yes, Dad has influenced you, of course he has, but it's *you* who's chosen to go along with it. It's a choice you have made, and – believe it or not – that's what's good.'

'*Good?* How can that be *good?*' asked Mike, astonished.

'It's good because the logic is quite simple: if a person chooses to be a bully, equally, they can choose not to be – at any point of their life, any day, any time. They can just stop. They are in control. We're all allowed to change our mind, Mike, about anything at all. And the good news is, it sounds to me like you are ready to change yours.'

Martyn paused for a second.

'So, I've got one last question for you. Are you ready to change? And tell me the truth now.'

Mike looked Martyn straight in the eye. Without hesitation he said, 'I am. I'm ready. I want to.'

The brothers spent the next half hour talking about how Mike could begin the change. Martyn told him that a bully can stop being a bully instantly, but needed to be aware that it can take a long time for other people, especially those he's bullied, to see and understand that. He also pointed out that even then, it can take a darn sight longer for people to forgive and forget. Mike understood. He really did.

Then they came up with a plan. It was a very simple one. The first thing was to change his behaviour, straight away. The second was to disband his gang and have nothing more to do with its members. This would be tougher, but it would break up easily enough without Mike as its ready leader. The third was to go and speak to Mr Davies, the headmaster, and tell him how Mr Kane had cheated in the match.

Mike dreaded the thought of it, but knew his brother was right. One thing that Martyn told Mike he didn't have to do, was tell his father anything. 'Just put up with him as best you can, but don't tell him anything. He'll only try to stop you.'

Mike couldn't hide his fear at this prospect.

'Look,' said Martyn, squeezing Mike's shoulder, 'if the worst comes to the worst, you can come and live with me. I've got a spare room and it's yours whenever you want it. For as long as you want it. Okay?'

Mike nodded and chewed on his lip, trying to stop himself from welling up again.

The final point of Martyn's plan was obviously going to be the toughest.

'Little brother, the last thing is the hard one. You're going to have to say sorry to a hell of a lot of people.'

Mike considered Martyn's words before whispering, 'I know, I know.'

'And sadly, some of them just won't want to know.'

'Yeah, I know that too,' said Mike solemnly.

# AN EARLY START

AT EIGHT o'clock the following morning, Mr Davies drove through the school gates and headed for his parking space. As he pulled through the yard he did a double-take – a boy was sitting outside the school reception.

Mr Davies collected his briefcase from the back seat and then headed across the yard, his brow furrowing when he recognised who it was.

'Good morning, Michael,' said Mr Davies. 'Is everything all right? What are you doing here so early?'

Mike stood up, straightening his jacket as he did so. He looked almost sick with nerves.

'I'd like to talk to you about yesterday's rugby match, please, sir,' he said in a barely audible whisper.

Mr Davies raised his eyebrows. How curious. He had already had a meeting with somebody about that match just half an hour earlier.

'Come on then,' said Mr Davies, his interest piqued, and he

beckoned Mike to follow him to his office.

Over the next ten minutes, Mike told Mr Davies pretty much everything he had told Martyn the night before. Mr Davies listened intently, nodding or murmuring in encouragement whenever Mike faltered slightly in his tale. When Mike finally finished, Mr Davies looked appraisingly at the young boy in front of him.

'Do you know, people often ask me what it's like being a teacher,' he mused. 'And I always tell them the same thing: no two days are the same and surprises lurk around every corner. And Mike, you have just proved that once again.'

Mike wasn't entirely sure where Mr Davies was going with this, but as Mr Davies wasn't shouting as he said it, he assumed it to be a good thing. So he risked half a smile.

'I admire your honesty and bravery completely, Mike,' continued Mr Davies. 'And let me assure you that everything you have told me here will remain completely confidential between us. But I want you to know how incredibly proud I am of you for coming to see me.'

Mike reddened and he realised it had been a long, long time since an adult had given him praise like this.

'You say you want to turn over a new leaf. I'm delighted to hear it. *Delighted*. Do you know something? It's easy to be an average person some of the time, but it's harder to be a good person all of the time. And it *will* be hard – but I guarantee you that you will have my help at every turn. You have made a very good start today, a very good start. Well done. You have, genuinely, made my day.'

And so that was it. One of the most significant encounters in

Mike Green's young life was over in just fifteen minutes.

As he left Mr Davies' office, Mike felt better than he had done in a long, long time.

# IT'S OVER

LATER THAT afternoon, the whole school was called into an assembly. They seldom had assembly on a Friday, it was usually only ever on a Monday or a Wednesday, and never in the afternoon, so this was a surprise. Another other odd thing was that there were no teachers present. The only staff there were the school's teaching assistants – apart from Miss Ayres. She wasn't there either.

After about thirty minutes of various songs, hymns and a chat by the Year 6 teaching assistant, Mrs Holledge, about what pupils could expect when they went up to the local comprehensive at the end of the term, the doors at the back of the hall opened, and in walked Mr Davies and the rest of the staff.

The headmaster walked straight onto the stage and began to address the assembled pupils.

'Good afternoon, children,' he said in a brisk, business-like tone. Could all classes up to Year 4 inclusive, please follow your teachers to your classrooms. Year 5 and Year 6, please stay where you are.'

As the other children began to file out of the hall, Jimmy realised that Mr Kane was nowhere to be seen. In fact, he hadn't been in school all day. Miss Ayres had explained this morning that he was on a course down at the County Hall, but Jimmy had expected him to be back by now.

Jimmy felt a sharp punch in his back, he swung round. It was Manu.

'He's gone, Jim. He's gone.'

Matt nodded in agreement. 'He must've, Jim, he must've.'

Sensing the rising tide of gossip, Mr Davies began to speak again. 'Thank you, Year 5 and Year 6, but let us sit in silence please while the other children leave the hall.'

After a few minutes of silence, where the bulk of Year 5 were just looking at each other with raised eyebrows and nods and winks, Mr Davies finally spoke.

'Thank you for your silence and your patience. I have an important announcement to make.' He paused for a moment, as if searching for the right words to say.

'As you are aware, halfway through this term, Mr Lloyd was sadly taken ill and was replaced by Mr Kane as a class teacher for Year 5. This was only ever intended to be a temporary appointment. Mr Kane was a former pupil at this school, and as he possessed a teaching qualification gained before he set out on his professional rugby career, his desire to return to teaching in the area that he grew up in fitted perfectly with the school's need to find a quick replacement for Mr Lloyd.'

Mr Davies paused again.

'However,' he continued, his voice suddenly more sombre. 'In recent weeks, it has become clear to me that Mr Kane's approach to teaching has not fallen in line with the approach that I, as head of Central Primary, demand from our staff. About ten days ago, I became aware of a role – in professional sport – that may have suited his skills and abilities better than the role of teaching in primary education. Fortunately for Mr Kane, he was offered the job on Monday this week.'

An 'Ooooh' rippled around the hall and Mr Davies waited for it to finish and for the silence to return.

'I had initially agreed with Mr Kane that he would wait until after half-term before leaving Central Primary and taking up his new role, but following events of last evening, it was agreed with all concerned, including the Board of Governors of the school, that Mr Kane be allowed to take up his new role with immediate effect.'

'He's gone, Jim, he's gone!' whispered Manu again, although it wasn't really a whisper this time and there was a cheer from nearly every pupil in Year 5.

'That's enough!' said Mr Davies firmly. 'Please refrain from shouting in assembly. Do you understand, Manu?'

'Yes, sir. Sorry, sir,' said Manu blushing.

'Good. And so, to finish. As from today, until half-term, I'm delighted to announce that Miss Ayres has agreed to step up to teach Year 5. Miss Ayres is a fully qualified teacher of great experience, but had taken a step back from teaching in recent years due to her family circumstances. However, she has kindly agreed to take over teaching duties until half term.'

This news was greeted by an outbreak of uncontrolled cheering from the Year 5 pupils. Miss Ayres beamed, unable to hide her delight.

'All right, thank you, thank you, that's enough now,' cried Mr Davies, holding his hands up to calm the pupils down and restore silence in the old hall. 'Now I know that this term has been quite disruptive for you – for some of you more than others,' – he glanced at Jimmy as he spoke – 'but I know that you will support Miss Ayres a hundred per cent as she brings much needed stability to your class. Will you all do that for me?'

'Yessssssssssss!' all the pupils of Year 5 shouted out.

As Mr Davies called for quiet again, one hand was left pointing high above everyone's heads, as they sat in their rows on the wooden floor. It was Jimmy.

'Yes, Jimmy, what is it?' asked Mr Davies.

'Sorry, sir, but I just wanted to ask about the rugby. What's going to happen with that? Are we still in the final after last night's game? A friend of my mother said that because the game was abandoned by Mr Kane, we've been thrown out of the competition.'

Every rugby-playing head in the assembly swung away from Jimmy and straight to Mr Davies.

'Well, your mother's friend is half right, Jimmy. Last night's match was completely unacceptable, and there is no way I would ever want a team from my school to benefit from anything that was deemed to be unfair. That simply is not a part of sport and never should be. So, I spoke to Mrs Payne, the headteacher of Western Primary, and offered her our place in the final, two weeks on Saturday, before the Wolves' match, at the Memorial Ground.'

A collective groan of disappointment spread around the hall. The only rugby players who remained silent were Jimmy and

Mike. Jimmy because he had already guessed this might have happened, Mike because he already knew the truth and had agreed with Mr Davies not to say a word.

Mr Davies coughed slightly before continuing. 'But Mrs Payne is an incredibly good, fair and understanding headteacher and, like me, she doesn't want her pupils to benefit from somebody else's misfortune when they are not directly to blame. So, in a wonderfully honourable gesture, Mrs Payne has agreed for the game to be replayed next Thursday afternoon, back at Western Primary.'

An audible buzz of excitement spread around the hall. Mr Davies held his hand up to bring the assembly back to silence.

'And will those of you lucky enough to take part in this rearranged game please inform your parents, guardians or carers that there will be a neutral referee in charge this time.'

Before the giggles reacting to this news spread to laughter, Mr Davies pressed on. 'As the school is now technically without a rugby coach, I will be taking the team myself, so I'll be looking forward to seeing those of you who would like to play in the game at The Rec after school on Monday. And I should stress,' Mr Davies added, emphasising this last, important point, 'that any of you, whatever age or size or gender you are, will be more than welcome to come along. I will ensure that we have a slightly different approach to rugby at this school from Monday onwards.'

# FUN, FUN, FUN

AFTER SCHOOL on the Monday, the rugby squad turned up to the first training session with Mr Davies. It was a dream.

First, Mr Davies got everyone together and gave them a quick pep talk. It was based around enjoying the game and trying to win the right way. He mentioned fair play a lot, but also stressed the importance of aiming to win.

'Winning isn't everything, because there are days when you will lose. But the whole point of sport is that it's based on competition, so we must all strive to win that competition, otherwise it's pointless taking part. However, if we do win, we will not brag or boast or crow about it, we will remember our opposition and how bad they must be feeling and treat them with respect. At all times. Similarly, if we lose, we will not moan or scream and shout, we will shake the hands of the opposition and congratulate them on a job well done. We can deal with our disappointment in private, afterwards.'

Jimmy loved this approach. It was exactly what he'd watched

on one of his grandfather's old Lions DVDs when the coach, Ian McGeechan, had explained what being a British & Irish Lion was all about. Jimmy felt the hairs on the back of his neck stand up when he watched that DVD and now he had the same sensation listening to his headmaster.

Mr Davies continued: 'I believe in sport, I believe in competition, I believe in winning, I believe in everyone trying to be the best they can be. But most of all I believe in enjoyment.'

Mr Davies scanned the face of every child who sat on that old Rec pitch in front of him. 'Enjoyment is the key to everything in sport. A happy player is an effective player, and an effective player can become a winning player. And in these last weeks, I've noticed that happiness in this squad has largely been absent.'

Almost every child nodded.

'So, starting tonight, rugby training is going to be fun and enjoyable. We will be trying to play fast, attractive and exciting running rugby and all our training will be based around that. On occasion, of course, we will need to take contact in the tackle and present the ball, but rugby is a much easier game if we avoid being tackled in the first place.'

This was all music to Jimmy's ears. He couldn't wait to get started.

'But one last thing before we begin,' said Mr Davies, with a serious tone to his voice. 'Every team needs a captain, and that captain has to be someone that the coach can trust to help deliver his methods and ideas out on the field. So I have chosen somebody I can trust to do just that.'

Almost every head turned to Jimmy. Jimmy blushed and looked down. Being named captain of the school team would be his greatest moment. He waited patiently for Mr Davies to confirm what everyone else suspected.

'So it gives me great pleasure to publicly name my captain, and I know you will all give him your complete support. Boys and girls, your captain . . . Mike Green.'

Jimmy's head snapped up at the same time that a collective groan came from everybody else. Nobody could believe it. Mike's reaction was awkward embarrassment and Jimmy looked at him closely as Mr Davies shook his hand. Normally, Mike would play to the crowd, especially to a reception like that, and Jimmy expected to see his angry, snarling face looking threateningly at anyone showing him disrespect, but this time he looked . . . different. There was a humbleness to his posture, an almost apologetic look in his eyes. He didn't say anything to anyone, just, 'I will do my very best, sir,' when Mr Davies said, 'Good luck, captain.'

With that, Mr Davies blew his whistle and asked everyone to stand.

'Okay, let's start with passing drills to warm up. Split up please, backs and forwards and then split into groups of five. Off you go!'

Manu, Matt and Kitty went straight over to Jimmy.

'Woah, what do you think of that?' breathed Matt.

'Old Mr D has lost his marbles!' hissed Manu.

'Mike captain again?' said Kitty, barely keeping her outrage under control. 'He shouldn't even still be *playing*, let alone *captain*. He took advantage of everything Mr Kane did to make your life a misery.'

'Come on you lot, get in a group,' chivvied Mr Davies. 'Let's get started and have some fun!'

Then, another voice.

'Get in this group, Jimmy, next to me. You guys, too.' It was Mike.

Jimmy stared at him.

'Listen,' said Mike, clearing his throat. His cheeks flushed as he tried to articulate the jumble of thoughts in his head. 'I've changed,' was all he eventually managed.

'What do you mean?' asked Jimmy, but Manu spoke over him.

'Whatever, Greeno. I dunno what you're trying to pull here, but you're not fooling us.'

They waited for the usual aggressive response, but none came.

'You'll see,' said Mike quietly and he bent down to pick up the ball. 'Ready?' he asked and indicated that they should form a line outside him.

'I . . . guess so . . .' said Jimmy slowly. He wasn't sure what Mike was playing at, but he wanted to get going so he joined Mike in the line, quickly followed by Matt, Manu and Kitty, and prepared himself for another sneaky tactic that would make him look a fool in front of Mr Davies.

'Let's go then,' said Mike Green jogging forward and then delivering the most perfect of passes to Jimmy – waist-height and just ahead of him to run on to.

And perfect summed up the way that Mike behaved for the rest of that session, and in all the practices leading up to the replay with Western Primary on the Thursday. Perfect.

## THE REPLAY

THE DAY of the match was disappointing for Jimmy. At lunchtime, Mr Davies came to find him in the yard and called him to his office. There he explained to Jimmy that whilst Mr Kane had treated him terribly, and that Jimmy was a truly excellent rugby player who would go on and play for Central Primary, and many other teams with great distinction, he had to be fair to the current fly-half, Ollie Snell.

'The only reason Ollie is starting the game ahead of you, Jimmy, is that he's in Year 6. The Cluster Cup is a Year 6 competition, and I really feel he deserves the opportunity to start the game. He's done nothing that merits being dropped from the team.'

Jimmy nodded. He understood, but he was massively disappointed. At the start of the week, most people had thought he would be made captain, and now here he was being told he wasn't even in the team.

'I hope you're not too disappointed,' said Mr Davies. 'I promise you'll get some game time. Then, if we are lucky enough to make the final, I'll consider both Ollie's and your performance when making that selection. But Ollie deserves this first chance. Do you understand?'

'Yes, sir,' said Jimmy. He understood what the head was telling him, even though, quietly, it was breaking his heart.

'Good boy. And, oh, can you do me a favour?'

'Yes, sir, of course.'

'Can you cut Mike Green a bit of slack? He's genuinely trying to turn his life around. He could do with some support from us all.'

This time, Jimmy's 'Yes, sir' was even less eager, but he had to admit to himself that he had noticed a change in Mike – although he still wasn't convinced it was permanent. Based on everything he knew about Mike, surely his new behaviour was some kind of trick.

'Good! Right, off you go . . . and remember, no kicking high bombs in the yard!'

Jimmy finally managed a smile as he remembered his disastrous introduction to Mr Kane, which was where all his troubles had begun. 'No, sir, never again!'

Following his disappointing meeting with the head, the afternoon still flew by and in next to no time Jimmy and the squad were pulling up at Western Primary in their scruffy minibus, and were walking to the wonderful changing facilities at the school. The players had been quite nervous arriving at Western, wondering what kind of reception they would receive – but they needn't have worried. They were warmly welcomed by everyone, the teachers, the parents – even the players. It was clear that Mrs Payne had spoken to all concerned and pinned the blame for everything that had occurred in the previous match, quite rightly, at the feet of Mr Kane. As a result, the game was replayed in a wonderful atmosphere – and what a game it was.

With all their superb sporting facilities, it was no surprise that – in a fairly refereed game – Western Primary were a high-quality team. Marshalled from fly-half by their excellent captain, Charlie Bateman, as good a player as Jimmy had ever seen, they attacked the game from the off.

Almost before any Central players had touched the ball, Bateman pounced on a loose kick from Ollie at the kick-off and, strangely, decided to run straight at Central's huge pack of forwards. Whether the boys weren't quite ready, or whether it was just a case of all of them assuming somebody else would make the tackle, young Bateman ran straight through the middle of them like a knife through butter, showing off some searing pace in the process.

Watching intently from the sidelines, Jimmy had only one word for it: 'Wow!'

After he'd flown through the pack, Bateman threw an outrageous sidestep which resulted in Kitty falling straight onto her backside, completely unable to make a tackle, and saw Bateman running straight for Mike at full back. Mike did everything correctly. He lined Bateman up, steadied himself and was set to deliver a thunderous tackle, designed to dislodge the ball from Bateman's grasp. However, at the very last second, Bateman decided to just dink the ball over Mike's head with the most delicate of kicks. This took Mike, and his thunder tackle, completely out of the game. Bateman sped past Mike, hacked the ball ahead with great control and swept it up before jogging under the posts for a try.

Surprisingly, even some of the Central team joined in the applause. Mr Davies loved that, and turned to his fellow headteacher, Mrs Payne. 'Isn't this just wonderful to see?' he beamed. 'A superb piece of rugby from your team and some excellent sportsmanship from mine. Just how it should be.'

'Well, it's certainly better than last time, Phil,' laughed Mrs Payne, vigorously joining the applause.

Matt caught the ball after the successful conversion, and decided that he had to do something quickly to get Central back into the game, otherwise there was a danger they'd be blown away within the first ten minutes. What he did was nothing short of brilliant.

From a knock on in the first play following Bateman's wonder try, Central were awarded the put-in at the resulting scrum. Matt picked up the ball from the back of the scrum and ran straight at Bateman. As he was tackled, Matt managed to free his arms, and as he and Bateman crashed to the ground, Matt was able to flip the ball around from behind Bateman's back into the hands of the onrushing Ollie Snell, who'd run outside Matt's break in support. Ollie collected the pass perfectly and, without breaking stride, ran at the first of the three players who were ahead of him to his right-hand side – a centre, the full back and the left wing. The others were on the opposite side of the scrum, having been taken by surprise by Matt's sharp break. Ollie powerfully brushed past the centre, and, deciding to take a leaf out of Mr Kane's book of rugby, smashed straight into the full back.

It wasn't a great attempt by the full back, and the weakness of his tackle easily allowed Ollie to keep his arms free with the ball to give him options to pass, just as Matt had done. The next thing he heard was Kitty calling on his right, and with the opposition wing not knowing whether to come in and try to stop Ollie passing or stay out and mark Kitty, he ended up in no man's land. Ollie delivered a simple pass to Kitty, leaving the opposition wing stranded, and Kitty sprinted the twenty metres, unopposed, to score under the gleaming white posts.

This time it was Mrs Payne's turn to congratulate Mr Davies, but the headteacher didn't hear his colleague as he just kept screaming, 'What a try, Kitty! What a try!'

From the sidelines, Jimmy noticed that the first person to rush to Kitty to offer his congratulations was Mike. Kitty's response was priceless: total surprise. It was the first time Mike had been nice to her in her life. Whether Mike saw it or not, he ignored Kitty's shock and ran next to Ollie Snell. 'Great work, Ollie, well done,' before running over to Matt, clasping him on the shoulders before shouting, 'What a break, Matt, what a break!'

Both Ollie and Matt didn't say a word. They just looked at each other with the same level of surprise on their faces that Kitty had shown. Again, Mike just jogged away to get the ball for the conversion. He quickly composed himself to pop the kick over for the two additional points. It was 7–7 after less than five minutes, leaving the crowd stunned. Jimmy was as stunned as anyone, but not at the rugby – at Mike's behaviour.

In a game of Under-11s rugby, the scoring team restarts the game by drop-kicking the ball back to the opposing team, unlike in senior rugby where the team that have conceded restarts the game. So Ollie took his place in the centre of the pitch for the restart. Now whether Ollie was getting carried away by his great start to the game, or whether it was a misjudgement, he knocked his drop-kick almost ten metres too far, and the ball flew directly into touch.

'Straight out!' called the referee. 'Scrum to Western back on halfway.'

Ollie's head dropped. He was a very talented player, but relied very much on his confidence being high in order for him to play well. This meant that when things went his way, he was as good as anyone around, but when he made mistakes, his game could quickly go to pieces. Jimmy noticed the change in his body language instantly.

From the resultant scrum, the Western scrum-half picked the ball up and passed quickly to Bateman who ran straight at Ollie. Ollie had been looking along the line, assuming Bateman was going to pass, so was caught slightly flat-footed. That was all Bateman needed. He spotted the lapse in Ollie's defence and left him stranded. Ollie was distraught. Luckily, Mike had spotted the danger and charged up from full back, making a tremendous tackle on Bateman, getting to his feet and winning the ball back for his team, before kicking the ball long, for a line out.

'Brilliant, Mike, brilliant! Well played!' shouted Mr Davies. Jimmy nodded in agreement. It had been an excellent piece of play.

From the resulting line out, big Andrew Beasley won the ball, towering over his opposite number, and tapped it down to Matt. With everyone expecting the scrum-half to pass out to Ollie, Matt did the complete opposite. Running straight at the gap in the line out created by Andrew Beasley as he accidentally brought down two of the Western forwards, Matt sprinted through the hole, and hared down the touchline. On his shoulder in support was Callum, the Central hooker, and as Matt was about to be shut down by the Western full back ten metres out from the try line, he popped the ball inside for his teammate to charge in under the posts.

After his now regular congratulations to all involved, Mike took the conversion and scored again. 14–7 to Central. And they weren't to lose the lead again. Incredibly, Central just blew Western away from that point on. Playing a brand of rugby that could only be described as one of sheer enjoyment, which clearly reflected Mr Davies' approach in his training sessions, Central scored another four excellent tries, all converted by Mike in an amazing display of kicking. At half-time, the score was 42–7.

Western Primary were shell shocked.

Mr Davies called everyone together, to hand out the oranges and give a team talk.

'Well done everyone. You've all played brilliantly, what a joy it's been to watch you.'

Everybody looked up at Mr Davies and smiled, for they all knew they'd done something special. All except Ollie Snell. He'd had no real involvement in the four tries, in fact, he'd nearly given a try away at the end of the half, when Bateman had only just missed intercepting his slow, looping pass, before knocking on. His confidence had gone completely.

If he noticed, Mr Davies didn't say anything, but Jimmy could see his friend was struggling. Despite this, Jimmy realised he would have to be patient and just wait for his chance. He felt sure it would come during the second-half.

'Right, everyone,' Mr Davies said, looking around at the squad, 'We've had a great first half, and whilst we will still have to play very well to stop Western getting back into the game, I think it's a good time to make some changes to give everyone a run-out today. I know nobody will let me down.'

Mr Davies looked at his replacements, all standing together at the side of the sweaty team who had started the first half. There were six of them. All dressed in their kit, and wearing yellow bibs. Alongside Jimmy were two forwards, two backs and Ryan Lewis. Ryan was a prop, and with no disrespect to him, Ryan wasn't an athlete of the highest standing. In addition, he wasn't very well. He had a stinking cold and had virtually not stopped sneezing since the previous Tuesday. But Ryan was one of the most committed pupils in Central Primary. He never missed school and he would certainly never miss a game of rugby.

Mr Davies looked at them all.

'Okay, the four of you next to Jimmy, you come on now,' he said, smiling at them all.

Then he turned to Ryan. 'How are you feeling, Ryan?'

Ryan's aggressive sneeze told Mr Davies all he needed to know. 'I don't think it's wise for you to play today, Ryan. You've shown your commitment by just being here when many might not have even made it to school. You just stay wrapped up warm, we'll only call you in an emergency!'

Ryan nodded in agreement, thrust his hands into his coat, and plucked out two mini pork pies from a four-pie pack. 'Starve a fever, feed a cold, sir,' he said, before stuffing a pie, whole, into his mouth. Mr Davies shook his head, just about managing not to burst out laughing in front of his pupils.

Jimmy glanced across at Mr Davies, and started to pull the bib over his head.

Mr Davies saw him, and walked quickly over.

'Can I have a quick word please, Jimmy?' Mr Davies put his arm around Jimmy's shoulder and, turning him away from the rest of the players, walked with him a few strides. Then he whispered in Jimmy's ear. 'Jimmy, I fully intended to bring you on with the others, but I'm going to delay it. It's because of poor Ollie. I'm scared of damaging his confidence if I take him off now. I want to give him ten minutes to try and do something positive, then I'll take him off. That sound okay to you?'

'Yes, sir. No problem at all,' said Jimmy and he meant it.

'Good lad, I knew you'd understand. And remember, you'll definitely be coming on, whatever happens.'

Jimmy nodded. He felt disappointed, but could see how down Ollie was. He really liked Ollie and realised it was a good thing to help. Jimmy actually remembered something his grandfather had said to him recently, when he took time to explain how his time in the Marines all worked out, 'You've often got to put the needs of others in front of your own. It's the only thing to do sometimes.'

Jimmy pulled his bib back down and took his place on the sidelines to watch the second half.

The referee blew for kick-off, and Bateman put a bit too much into his kick, and it went over the head of the forwards and bounced into touch.

They all jogged over to the line out, where the forwards lined up in their spaces. Mike ran up to Callum, the hooker, and whispered in his ear. Callum nodded. As Mike jogged back to his place, he ran in front of Ollie Snell and said quietly, 'He's throwing it long for you, Ollie. Catch it and make a break – you can do it.' Then he winked and ran off.

Ollie was as amazed as everyone else at this act of kindness, and was determined to banish his horror first half from everyone's memory.

As planned, from the hooker's throw, the ball flew straight over the tail of the line out, and into empty space. Most of the parents on the touchline saw a chance for Western to get the ball, but then, as if by magic, Ollie appeared as the ball bounced up off the turf and, running at top speed, he plucked the ball out of the air and ran straight at the Western back line. It was a brilliant piece of running, timed absolutely perfectly, and the way he just grasped the ball so cleanly in both hands, without missing a stride, drew a gasp from the crowd.

Ollie ran into the channel between Bateman at fly-half and his inside centre, and because the scrum-half was still out of position because of the line out, Ollie's plan was to sidestep inside Bateman and hit the gap left by the scrum-half.

But it all went wrong.

Just as Ollie began his sidestep, the studs under his right boot hit some soft turf and it gave way. Ollie staggered and slipped just as Bateman came in to tackle him and Ollie's right eye caught Bateman's knee.

You could hear the crack ring around the ground.

It was a complete accident, but the referee saw straight away that it was a bad one for both players, and blew up to stop the game.

Ollie was deemed to be the more serious of the two, so had treatment on the pitch from one of the fathers from Western, who was a doctor. For a few moments, everyone feared the worst, but fortunately, he had got away lightly. There were no broken bones, no cut, just a huge, golf-ball-sized swelling that formed instantly on the corner of his right eyebrow. Whilst he protested that he was alright to continue, the doctor was in no doubt about what to do.

'He'll have to come off. I'm sure he hasn't lost consciousness but we're not risking anything with a head injury.'

Mr Davies realised what this meant straight away. He looked across at Jimmy.

'You ready, Jimmy?'

Jimmy nodded and pulled his bib swiftly over his head.

'Come on, Ollie,' said Mr Davies kindly, helping the boy off and thanking the doctor on his way, before looking over to Jimmy and murmuring, 'Good luck!'

Jimmy jogged on, pulled his gumshield from his sock and did a few stretches. As he rebounded up from a particularly vigorous side bend, he felt a tap on his shoulder. It was Mike.

'Good luck, Jimmy. Play well.'

Jimmy stared at him for a moment and then jogged into position without saying anything in reply. He just couldn't believe that Mike wasn't up to something.

Mike returned to the backfield, clapping and shouting encouragingly at the rest of his team, remembering what his brother had said: *It's going to take some people a long time to come round.* He whispered some words of encouragement to himself as well.

The referee looked around, saw that Ollie was being treated off the pitch and that Jimmy had come on.

'Central were in possession of the ball at the point of stoppage, no infringement or advantage to either side, so scrum to restart, Central ball.'

Matt jogged across to Jimmy.

The scrum was to take place about twenty-five metres from the posts, and fifteen metres in-field.

'Drop-goal to get you into things, Jim?'

Jimmy nodded and shot Matt a grin. He knew that at this stage of the game it was a bit pointless to go for the drop-goal, such was the size of their lead, but Jimmy was frustrated. Frustrated that he'd had no involvement up to this point, so he wanted to show people what he could do. He viewed it as a shot-to-nothing.

The referee called the two packs together and set the scrum, and as soon as he'd shouted 'Set', Matt rolled the ball into the scrum, then nipped around the back of the scrum. As he arrived there, he glanced across to Jimmy, who was positioned at least five yards deeper than he would usually stand.

As soon as the ball appeared, Matt swept it up in one movement and rifled the most perfect spin pass to Jimmy. It went like a bullet.

To those who spoke about it later, they all agreed that it was as if Jimmy was in a trance. He didn't move a muscle when Matt delivered his pass, he just stood there, motionless. Then, just as the ball was reaching him from his left-hand side, Jimmy allowed the ball to drift across to the right side of his body, before catching then dropping it in one fluid movement. As the ball was about to hit the turf, Jimmy planted his left foot and swung his right foot through the ball, with the most amazing follow-through. The ball left his boot like a shell from a cannon and drew an 'Oooh!' from the assembled parents, as they all watched it fly higher and higher towards the posts.

It was a brilliant, brilliant drop-goal. And the brilliance didn't stop there.

The rest of the match was a masterclass. Jimmy showed everybody just how talented he was. He scored two tries and made three, one for Kitty with the most perfect kick ahead, that she beat the covering defence to, before scoring under the posts. It was an incredible performance. One person in particular was impressed, and if he hadn't been playing, he would have been taking notes: Charlie Bateman. He'd never seen or heard of Jimmy Joseph before this game, but he was blown away by his performance, as was the rest of his team.

The only other moment of note came right at the end of the game. There was only about a minute or two left, when Tom Edmonds, one of the Central props, bent his fingers back making a tackle and had to go off. As it was a scrum, Central needed a prop. Kitty's dad, who was watching, looked across and saw Ryan, eating his fifth Lockets menthol lozenge since half-time, and called across to him.

'Ryan,' he called, 'Ryan. You're on.'

Ryan looked up, reacted straight away and rushed to get ready.

Mr Davies saw what was happening, and stepped in. He called to the referee, Rob Whitehouse.

'He can't come on, Rob, the poor lad isn't well.'

'Well, without a prop, we can't restart, so I'm going to have to end the game now.'

'Oh no,' groaned Harrison, the inside centre. 'Can't we just get Ryan on to finish the game?' Harrison had already scored two tries, thanks to Jimmy, and fancied his first ever hat-trick.

'Well, it's up to you, Mr Davies,' said the referee, who was also keen to carry on.

'No, he's not well,' said Mr Davies, 'I can't let him on.'

With that, behind everyone on the touchline, there was a huge sneeze that made nearly everybody around jump out of their skins. When they looked over, they saw Ryan struggling – and failing – to get his coat over his head. 'What's 'appening then?' he shouted. 'Am I coming on or what? If I am, someone's gonna 'ave to 'elp me with this blinking coat, the zip has caught in my bib and I think it's got some of my skin!' And with that, struggling so much and not being able to see, he tripped over the little crate of water bottles and ended up in a heap on the floor.

The laughter was instantly drowned out by a long, loud blow on the whistle by the referee, who then joined in the laughter with everyone else.

Central had completed a crushing victory of 80 points to 7, and Jimmy's cameo had proved to be the starring role. He couldn't have been happier. But his thoughts were soon interrupted by the continued shouts from Ryan, rolling on the floor, calling out, 'Ow! My skin, my skin!' Then someone ran up to help him. It was Mike. Jimmy watched Mike help Ryan with care and good humour. And he couldn't help but whisper under his breath, 'Is this real, or not?'

He genuinely didn't know.

# THE BOMBSHELL

AT FIRST break the following morning, Mr Davies called a team meeting. He talked enthusiastically about the match and, in particular, Jimmy's incredible second-half performance. But then he delivered some news that stunned every single member of the team.

'Right boys and girls, I'm afraid I have to finish with some bad news. Unfortunately, with Mr Kane's sudden departure from the school, it has left me short of cover for the team. It has been a joy for me to work with you all and to enjoy such a brilliant team performance last evening, but I had made no plans for the final – that was all down to Mr Kane. Unfortunately, as he is no longer here, I do not have a teacher able to look after the team at the Memorial Ground next Saturday.'

There was a stunned silence.

Mr Davies continued, 'The problem this causes is that as the person legally responsible for the welfare of young people on an extracurricular school event, without the correct authorised supervision, I can't allow it to happen without a teacher. So, with

Mr Kane leaving, we have no other members of staff here who have attended the correct training courses in order to be allowed to supervise pupils in a competitive match. I'm qualified to do it, but next weekend I'm away attending a headteachers' conference in London that I'm unable to get out of.'

'So what does all this mean, sir?' asked Jimmy, a rising panic in his chest.

Again, Mr Davies paused. It wasn't going to be good news. 'I'm afraid it means that the game will probably have to be cancelled. I'm very, very sorry about that.'

Every player's head sunk with disappointment. As much as they all disliked Mr Kane and were glad that he'd left, the thought that they would now miss their chance to play on the Memorial Ground was heart-breaking.

'Right!' said Mr Davies, clapping his hands together, trying desperately to keep the children positive despite this blow. 'On your feet, please and off to class. Thank you all, and have a lovely day!'

The yard filled with noise and chatter as the children filed out and Jimmy was surprised to hear his name being bandied about. And not in a good way.

'It's Jimmy's fault – just because Mr Kane wouldn't pick him, he reported him.'

'I bet his grandfather had something to do with it, I heard he threatened Mr Kane.'

'I never liked Mr Kane, but if Jimmy had just played rugby like he was told, we'd still be going to the final.'

'I heard that Jimmy's brother told them in the senior school and they made Mr Davies sack him.'

The anger towards Jimmy got stronger as each story about him got taller.

But there was one person who had said nothing, but looked as angry as everyone else, and he wasn't going to keep quiet for long.

Mike Green.

He walked straight over to Jimmy and stopped right in front of him. Jimmy had seen him coming over from the moment they had come into the yard. He knew that Mike had loved Mr Kane and the true Mike was about to show his colours again – the loss of his chance to play the final added to the loss of his favourite teacher would just be too much for him. Jimmy braced himself for the onslaught.

'Lots of people are saying that this is all your fault, that it's all down to you,' said Mike. 'That because your grandfather had a go at Mr Kane and then told Mr Davies, that's why Mr Kane got sacked. They're all saying it's you.'

By now a decent crowd had gathered around them, watching with interest. Jimmy started to speak, to defend himself, but Mike stopped him with a dismissive swish of his arm, like he had done many times before. Then he turned to everyone watching.

'None of this is Jimmy's fault,' he said, fixing each of the watching crowd in the eye. 'What Mr Kane did to Jimmy was terrible, and I made the most of it. But if there's anyone to blame for Mr Kane leaving, it's me.'

A shocked 'Oooooh' rippled around the throng.

'I went to speak to Mr Davies and told him about Mr Kane's cheating. It had nothing to do with Jimmy. So if any of you want to have a go at anyone, have a go at me, not him.'

There was total silence. Nobody said a word. The bell went, signalling the end of break and the crowd began to dissipate.

Jimmy, however, didn't move. He looked at Mike in a curiously puzzled way. Mike turned and started when he saw the expression on Jimmy's face.

'I mean it,' said Mike, 'none of this is your fault.'

'You do mean it, don't you?' said Jimmy, as if he was beginning to work out a tricky maths problem.

'Yeah, I do . . . All of it.'

Jimmy looked at Mike for a long moment and then nodded. 'Thanks for sticking up for me.'

'No worries. It's the least I could do. And anyway, it's what you do when you're part of a team. I'm just sorry we're not getting a chance to show just how good a team we can all be. You know, make a statement.'

Jimmy's eyes widened at these words. *Make a statement.*

'You know what . . .' said Jimmy, his mind suddenly alight with possibility. 'There may still be a way for us to make this final happen . . .'

# A FINAL ROLL OF THE DICE

As soon as the bell went for the end of the day, Jimmy rushed out of school as quickly as his feet could carry him.

Normally, he'd wait for his friends and they'd walk home together, laughing and joking all the way. But today there was no time for that. Jimmy was on a mission.

He sprinted the whole way home, but instead of heading to his own house, he flew straight up the path and through the front door of his grandparents' house. He found Will and Betty sitting in the front room, sipping their tea and watching *Tipping Point* on the TV.

Usually, Jimmy would plonk himself down beside them on the settee and join them watching the show. But today he was distracted – so distracted he didn't react to the rugby question that host Ben Shephard then asked, 'Which country's rugby union team play their home matches at Murrayfield?'

'What's the matter, Jim?' asked his grandfather. 'I thought you'd have answered that straight away. Is everything okay?'

So Jimmy told them all about the cup final and the implications of Mr Kane's dismissal that nobody could have predicted. As he explained the news of the game being cancelled, his grandparents sat back in disappointment too. They had been so looking forward to it, especially with Kane now out of the way – and Will felt some guilt about his part in having Kane sacked. He knew it was the right course of action, but was so disappointed for his grandson that as a result of it, he would now miss out on his big day.

But then Jimmy told his grandparents about his idea.

'Gramp?' he said. 'How well do you know Peter Clement?'

'Quite well – I knew his father better. Why do you ask?'

'Well, from what Mr Davies said this morning, it seems that teachers need some sort of coaching qualification to be able to take a school team into a match against another team, and none of our teachers have one.'

'Yes, so you've just said. But in case you haven't noticed, Peter Clement isn't a teacher, he's a building society manager.'

'Yeah, I know,' replied Jimmy quickly, 'but he's a qualified coach, isn't he?'

Will paused for a moment in thought. 'So, you want me to ask Peter if he'll be willing to take your team to the final next week, maybe getting one of the teachers to come along to have overall responsibility for the pupils?'

'Yes, Gramp, exactly!' exclaimed Jimmy.

'Well, I suppose there's no harm in asking. Right, let's go over and speak to him together. We'll tell him everything and see if he can help.'

# THE MOST PRECIOUS PRIZE

Peter Clement answered the door. He was eating again.

'Hello, Will,' he said between mouthfuls. 'What can I do for you? Is it about this one playing for the Wolves first team . . . he's still a bit young!'

'Yes, that's a nice thought,' said Will, laughing. 'One day in the future, maybe. I was just wondering if we could have a quick word about something, but I can see this isn't a good time—'

'Nonsense, nonsense,' said Peter stepping back and waving them in. 'I've nearly finished, come in, come in. We'll have a cup of tea.'

He showed them through to the kitchen, finishing the last of his sandwich as he went, put the kettle on and made a big pint of squash for Jimmy before taking them through to his living room. Jimmy could barely believe that he was actually *inside* Peter Clement's house. There was rugby memorabilia everywhere. Team photos of the Wolves, the national team, the Warriors and Great Britain. Displayed on a side table was the cap Peter had been given when he first played for his country in rugby union and another for his first Test for Great Britain in rugby league. There were small shields and silver tankards, rugby balls scribbled with signatures and, in pride of place, a trophy cabinet. Jimmy could hardly take his eyes off it. Inside were jerseys, pennants, crystal glass and medals. Lots of medals. Some were gold and were lying in small leather boxes with the lid up, sitting on a piece of velvet. Some were small statuettes of rugby players, standing on top of a rugby ball. But one stood out above all others. It was enormous. It was silver and was the size of an actual rugby ball. It stood above a huge letter 'S' that represented 'Super League' and written around the black plinth that it stood on were the words 'Man of Steel'. It was magnificent. Jimmy couldn't take his eyes off it and his jaw dropped in wonder.

'Jimmy. Jimmy!'

It was his grandfather.

'Come on, Jimmy, you're supposed to be telling Peter about what Mr Davies said and what you want him to do, not gawping over there at the shiny stuff!'

Peter laughed. 'It's okay, people do tend to show a bit of interest in that stuff. It's all a long time ago now, though.' He sounded slightly embarrassed by the obvious success he had achieved in the game.

'Sorry,' said Jimmy, dragging his eyes from the cabinet. He began to explain everything that had happened since they'd last met, with Will interjecting every now and then with added bits of detail. Peter listened attentively, but when Will explained why they had come to see him – that they wanted him to help coach

Jimmy's team in the curtain-raiser before the Wolves match that Saturday – Peter looked grave.

'I'm not sure if I'm going to be able to help, I'm afraid,' he said, looking genuinely pained at having to let Jimmy down. 'The problem is the time. Your match kicks off before the Wolves game, and I won't have the time to take your match and prepare the Wolves too. I'm sorry, son, any other day and I would do it – but I've got so much to do on a match day, I really can't get involved.'

Jimmy felt like his stomach had turned to lead. Try as he might, he couldn't hide his disappointment. He had been so sure that he had come up with a solution. And now . . .

He waited a second or two before he spoke. He didn't want to make Peter feel bad, but more importantly, he didn't want to cry in front of his rugby hero either.

'It's okay,' he said quietly, and forced himself to smile. 'I understand—' He broke off, the lump in his throat about to crack his words.

'Are you all right, son?' asked Peter gently, placing a hand on Jimmy's shoulder.

Jimmy nodded and forced himself to speak normally. 'It's just that I feel sort of responsible for all of this,' he said, without looking up. 'I don't really know why Mr Kane didn't like me so much, but I think it's because of all of that, that he started to act really strange. Obviously, Mr Davies didn't like it either, so that's why he's gone. I just want to put things right—'

'Let me tell you a thing or two about Mark Kane,' interrupted Peter. 'I knew him when he was a youngster. He was a tidy rugby player, to be honest – very strong, very, very competitive.

But he was a bully. We all knew that . . . but sometimes, those traits – as unpleasant as they are – can be pretty handy for a rugby player. But Kane had another problem. He had terrible jealousy. And in particular, he was jealous of really skilful players. There was one at the club at the time, Kevin John. He reminded me of you a bit. Extraordinarily talented, fast, skilful and brave. Everyone was tipping him to play for the Wolves before he'd even turned seventeen. But Kane was jealous of him, so he made his life a misery. He was a year older than Kevin, and when you're a teenager, that year is a big difference. Kane did everything he could to upset Kevin, simply because Kevin could do things on a rugby pitch that Kane could never even dream of doing. All sorts of complaints were made to the club committee by Kevin's parents, but they never stood a chance. See, the chairman of the club was Reggie Kane . . . and have a guess whose father he was?'

Will tutted and shook his head as he remembered the story. 'Terrible man, terrible man,' he said.

'So what happened to Kevin?' asked Jimmy.

'He left. Joined the Blue and Blacks up the road, and eventually won his youth cap. But he got badly injured playing for the Reds – the regional team – and smashed his collarbone to bits. They had to put steel plates in and everything. He was never the same player again. Very sad. You know what, I always thought he was even better than me. Could have gone a long way, Kevin John. A tragedy, really.'

Jimmy's grandfather nodded in agreement. 'Last I heard, he'd gone to university to get his degree in sports science or something. Haven't heard anything more about him for years.'

This was turning into the most depressing conversation of Jimmy's life.

After a minute's silence, it was Jimmy who spoke next.

'Oh well, it can't be helped. Thanks for seeing us – it was nice to see all your trophies and stuff – all my friends at school will be well jealous. Hopefully I make the team next season and we get a chance to play in the Cluster Cup final again.' Jimmy and Will stood and made to head to the front door.

'Yes, thanks for seeing us, Peter—' began Will.

'What did you just say, son?' said Peter, looking up at Jimmy with surprise. His expression had changed completely.

'I said, I hope I can get in the team next year,' replied Jimmy.

'No, no. The cup, the cup! What cup did you say you were playing in?'

'Oh, it's called the Cluster Cup. It's between all the local primary schools that eventually combine in the senior school.'

'Oh, I know what the Cluster Cup is all about!' said Peter. 'I completely misunderstood – I thought the match was just a curtain raiser for the Wolves game – just like a friendly match or something.'

'It is a curtain raiser,' said Will, 'but it's not a friendly, it's a proper match, a cup final. 12.45 kick off, before your game at 2.30.'

Peter jumped up from his seat and, taking Jimmy by the arm, led him to the trophy cabinet. He stopped, looked around for a key, found it and opened it. Stepping away, he turned to Jimmy.

'Right, have a look at all of them, son, and point to my most precious one.'

Jimmy peered into the cabinet. There were dozens of items in there – medals, awards, certificates of all shapes and sizes. But there, in the middle, surrounded by all the others was Peter's most precious one. The biggest and most important one . . . The Man of Steel. Jimmy pointed at it.

'That one,' he said. 'It means you were the best rugby league player of the whole year. The Man of Steel.'

Peter coloured a little with pride, but he shook his head.

'No, it's not that one. Have a look behind it. That's my most precious one. Get it for me, will you?'

'Careful, Jimmy!' cried Will, spotting the potential disaster of dropped and smashed trophies going everywhere.

Jimmy didn't need to be told. He put his hand into the cabinet with the steadiness and accuracy of a brain surgeon. He moved the Man of Steel trophy slightly to the left, and saw a small plaque behind it.

It looked like one of those cheap, plastic awards you could buy in Poundland. He picked it up and brought it out of the cabinet.

'You mean this?' he asked doubtfully.

'Yes, that's the one. My most precious trophy.'

Peter took the small award and gazed at it proudly.

'This was the first thing I ever won. I was ten. It was the first final I ever played in, and was only the third rugby match of my life. I only got picked because our usual fly-half caught the measles a week before. I scored a try in the corner in the last minute and kicked the conversion to win the game 19–18.'

'Wow!' exclaimed Jimmy, 'You were the match-winner!'

'Yes, but that's not why it's special. It was a great team performance that won us that game – I was just lucky to finish things off. No, the reason why it's important to me and is my most precious trophy is that that day a man was watching who literally changed my life. He was coach of the Wolves at the time and he eventually picked me for the first team when I was sixteen and made me captain at eighteen. Those two decisions changed my life. He always said to me that if he hadn't seen me at that match, he would probably have never noticed me again as he didn't usually watch schoolboy rugby. From that day, he followed my career and eventually became my mentor, my coach. He taught me everything.' Peter's eyes glistened and he went silent for a moment. He handed the plaque back to Jimmy. 'Turn it over, read the back, it's a bit faded now.'

Jimmy flipped it over in his hand. The writing was small and barely legible. He slid his glasses up and, holding the plaque so close that it almost touched the tip of his nose, he began to read aloud. 'Nineteen . . . seventy . . . two . . . to . . . Nineteen . . . seventy . . . three . . . season. Erm . . . . The . . . Cluster . . . Cup.'

Jimmy's eyes rounded.

'It's the Cluster Cup, it says the Cluster Cup! You played in the Cluster Cup! Wow, that is so cool!'

'Yes, it is,' replied Peter with a laugh, 'very cool.' He paused for a moment and then said wistfully, 'Sometimes we can be guilty of forgetting what's really important in life.'

He looked down at Jimmy. 'Son, playing in the Cluster Cup final all those years ago changed my life forever. Let's see if it can't change yours. I'll get Liam to sort the warm-up for the Wolves. I'll do it – I'll look after your team at the final. You tell the head teacher I'll give him a ring tomorrow.'

Jimmy's scream of delight could be heard halfway to the Memorial Ground itself.

36

# GAME PREP

IT WAS the morning of the final. Jimmy had just experienced one of the best weeks of his life. Miss Ayres had been brilliant, giving really fun, interesting lessons . . . and had somehow even made the maths test entertaining.

But it had been the rugby that had been the most fantastic.

Peter Clement had done three after-school sessions on the Monday, Wednesday and Thursday. Every single one had been fast and fun and had involved everyone in the team. When Mr Kane put sessions on, they had usually involved getting the big boys like Andrew Beasley and his brother to just charge at the others, always focussing on 'contact, contact, contact'. Peter's sessions were completely different.

'Play rugby with your head up. The best rugby players play what they see in front of them. In other words, scan the field, look for space and then attack it – whether running into the space yourself, passing to someone in space or kicking into an area of the field that the defence have left unguarded.'

That was his primary lesson. Attack the space between the defenders. He also explained that it was all very well having plans for this and for that, but they were all pointless if the opposing team played in a different way than you expected. All week he had kept repeating to Jimmy, 'You have to be prepared to adapt to what you see in front of you. Keep your head up, play what you see . . . head up, play what you see.' Jimmy had loved every second of it.

He also loved that Peter was encouraging him to kick more, too.

'If we're under pressure, and you can get your kick away, use it!' he told him. 'You can kick it further than most in the Wolves team, so use it!'

On that first night, Peter gave Jimmy the news he had been dreaming of. Ollie Snell hadn't recovered from his injury, so had been ruled out of the final. Jimmy would start. Because of this news, and the quality of Peter's training sessions, Jimmy had spent a week in rugby heaven. A welcome bonus had been Mike's continuing change in behaviour. In every session he had been encouraging and helpful. And like Jimmy, he had completely bought into Peter's 'heads up rugby'. By the end of the week, Peter paid him the ultimate compliment of saying that Mike had been 'one of the best captains I've ever worked with'. Jimmy was strangely pleased for Mike – but he was still wary of him, too.

As usual before a match, Jimmy called in to see his grandparents. They had become his lucky charm. He had a lovely cup of tea with them and, as it was match day, his grandfather insisted that he have a Mars Bar – 'it will give you lots of energy' he told him. After his snack, Jimmy stood up and grabbed his stuff to leave.

'You know what, Jimmy,' said his grandfather, 'I don't think I've ever seen you looking so happy.'

Jimmy smiled and nodded in agreement.

'It reminds me of something I was told years ago, when I was in the Marines. "You've sometimes got to go through the bad times, to really appreciate the good ones". And that's what's happened to you. Me and your grandmother are so proud of the way you handled the whole Mr Kane thing, so now just go out there and enjoy the match. That's all you need to do.'

'Thanks,' said Jimmy and gave them both a hug as he left. He wanted to say more, but couldn't find the right words. But he gripped them tightly with each hug and hoped that that said enough.

'Oh, and Jimmy,' said his grandmother just before he left the house, 'you might be needing this.'

It was his asthma inhaler.

'Oops! Nice one, Grams,' said Jimmy, laughing.

He waved goodbye and made his way to The Rec, where Matt, Manu and Kitty were waiting for him.

'Jimmy boooooooooy,' shouted Manu when he saw him and Jimmy returned the call. He high-fived and fist-bumped them all and then they set off across The Rec for the Memorial Ground, Kitty chipping the ball to herself as they walked.

'Feeling nervous?' asked Matt to the group in general.

'Nah,' the others lied in reply.

'Yeah, me neither,' said Matt, gawping at the high stand as it rose up above them.

They followed the stand round to the entrance gates and trouped through them in silence, each of them taking a moment to enjoy their surroundings, barely able to believe that they were finally there as players, not just as spectators or ball boys or girls.

At last they reached the sign that read 'Players and Officials Only' and they all stopped for a moment to gaze at it.

'This is a big deal,' said Jimmy to break the silence.

Kitty ruffled his hair. 'Don't get nervous, fanboy. What did Peter say on Thursday? It's just another game.'

With that she headed down the tunnel, Manu behind her, followed by Matt.

'Just another game,' said Jimmy under his breath. He forced himself to relax and followed them in.

# THE TEAM TALK

AFTER GETTING changed into their kit and the usual high jinks involved in that, they were nearly ready. Apart from Ryan, the replacement prop. Now recovered from his Olympic sneezing fits of the week before, he'd somehow managed to put his boots on the wrong feet and was now struggling to get them off.

'It's not my fault, they're new! They never showed me in the shop. Go on, pull on them, Kit,' he said, sticking his left leg out for her to yank his boot off. They wouldn't budge.

'What have you done, Ryan, they're jammed on!' exclaimed Kitty, turning purple with the effort.

'Yeah, they're pretty tight. I think I might have left the paper inside them too.'

And with that, everyone burst out laughing. Ryan had certainly lightened the mood.

'That's what I like to see,' said Peter Clement, striding in, smiling. 'A happy dressing room is a winning dressing room.'

He called everyone together, and sat them down.

'First things first. Some great news. It's been agreed by both schools that as this is such a special occasion, we're going to use the whole pitch.'

Everyone cheered. It was all of their dreams to play on a full-sized pitch; it was much better than the half pitches they usually played on, which often didn't feel like a real game somehow.

'So, there'll be plenty of room out there to express yourselves and have fun today . . . make the most of it.' He nodded to Jimmy before continuing. 'Now, I'm not one for big speeches. Never have been. In fact, in my first match for Great Britain, all our coach said to us was, "Have a good game, lads. See you later . . . oh, and try and play well." And that's all I want to say to you all, really – try and play well.'

He waited a moment.

'But there's one other thing. For some of you, this will be the biggest rugby game you will ever play. For others, it will be the first of many big challenges you'll face. But here, today . . . well this is the most important game. Right here, right now. And you all owe it to yourselves to do one thing. Enjoy it.'

He paused again.

'Winning is great. We all want to win. But that's what the other coach next door will be saying – "Make sure you win". But he can't be sure of that, because he doesn't know what we are going to do. He doesn't know that we are really going to enjoy seeing Mike leading us out onto the pitch like the good captain I know he is. He doesn't know that we are going to really enjoy getting the ball out to Kitty, who is going to run like the wind. He doesn't know that we are really going to enjoy seeing Andrew leaping like a salmon at every line out before passing the ball to Matt. He doesn't know that we are really going to enjoy seeing Matt picking the ball up at the back of the scrum, before sending out one of his perfect spin passes to Jimmy. And he certainly doesn't know that we are really going to enjoy watching Jimmy do his thing. Because Jimmy does his thing better than any young fly-half I've ever seen.'

He scanned the room, looking every single player in the eye.

'So that's the key: enjoyment. Enjoy it, play to your best and the winning will take care of itself. What do you say?'

'Yes, sir!' they replied together.

'What do you say?' said Peter, louder and cupping his ear with his hand as if he couldn't hear.

'YES, SIR!' they screamed.

It was time.

# THE FINAL

THE PLAYERS all walked out together. Central Primary on the left, led by Mike; Rockwood Primary on the right, led by their captain, a big forward called Dale.

Leading everybody out were the referee and linesmen, all of whom were professional, full-time referees. The crowd that was arriving for the Wolves game that was to follow gave a huge cheer as the players emerged. The old grandstand was already half full.

'Jimmy, Jimmy!' a voice called out from the area by the dugout. Jimmy looked across. There, with a beaming grin, giving him a double thumbs up was Liam Wyatt. Beside him with his physio bag at his feet, was his dad. Jimmy had never seen him look so proud. A shiver ran down his back and the hairs on his neck stood on end. He felt ten feet tall. He was finally going to go out and play on the Memorial Ground where his grandfather and father had played before him. Where all the greats in the area had once played. *This is going to be a good day. No matter what happens, it's already perfect.*

As they walked onto the pitch Jimmy made sure to watch out for the step. Dale, however, was caught unawares, and he snagged his toe and staggered awkwardly as he tried to keep his balance. Jimmy grabbed him by the arm and just kept him from falling on his face.

'Oops, careful now,' said Jimmy, with a grin, which Dale returned with an awkward smile, his face flushing scarlet.

It was a near-perfect day for rugby. A cloudless, bluebell sky, just a whisper of wind blowing down from the mountains, the sun glinting on the last of the morning's dew clinging to the brilliant green grass. High above the posts at either end of the field, the metal wolves glared down, hackles raised, ready for the game to begin.

Rockwood won the toss and decided to play with the slight breeze at their backs, which meant Jimmy would kick off into it. He jogged over to Andrew Beasley, trying to avoid being noticed by the Rockwood players.

He whispered out of the side of his mouth to the giant second row, 'When the ref blows that whistle, just sprint like your life depends on it all the way to the ten-metre line. The ball will be there for you.' The giant, blond second row just nodded, and jogged off to the halfway line.

The referee called Jimmy over. 'Just wait for the whistle, okay, son?'

'Yes, sir, of course,' replied Jimmy politely.

He bounced the ball on its point a couple of times, then looked to his left where all the forwards were lined up. After looking down and bouncing the ball a couple more times, he glanced up and noticed that nearly all the Rockwood team had come across, and were looking at big Andrew Beasley. They had seen Jimmy's quick chat.

Peter's words flew into Jimmy's mind like a thunderbolt. *Play what's in front of you.*

'Have a good game, everyone, off we go,' shouted the ref, and blew his whistle.

Jimmy spun to his right, away from Andrew Beasley and the rest of the forwards, and drilled a long, raking kick over to the right wing. To Kitty. Jimmy had seen that the Rockwood winger had pushed a little too far up the field, so he aimed the kick into the space behind him.

Despite the wing having about a fifteen-metre head start on Kitty, the fact that he hadn't expected Jimmy to kick to his side meant that he had to turn to collect the ball – and this gave Kitty all the advantage she needed.

She began sprinting the moment the ball left Jimmy's boot. Passing her opposite number with ease, she reached the ball on its second bounce, grasped it tightly to her chest and ran for the posts.

The only player in her way was the Rockwood full back. He might as well have been invisible. Kitty surged past him with a bouncing sidestep and touched the ball down under the posts, unopposed. What a dramatic start!

Mike quickly added the conversion – although it wasn't his best of kicks. He seemed to be quite nervous standing over the ball and off balance when he struck it, and the ball barely made it over the crossbar. He ran back looking a little disappointed that he hadn't started the game very well.

Still, it was 7–0 to Central with less than a minute played. That wasn't bad.

'Good start, good start,' shouted Peter from the dugouts at the side of the pitch, clapping as he spoke, 'but back to your positions now, switch on, switch on.'

Jimmy ran back to his position in midfield, and looked all around him. Everyone looked focused and settled. All looked good.

As the Rockwood team lined up, an unfamiliar voice boomed out from the crowd. It was aggressive. It also sounded a bit drunk. It was Mike Green's dad. 'Come on, boy, time to do something. Show everyone how hard you are . . . Don't take no prisoners, boy, smash 'em!'

As awful as this sounded, for Gary Green, it was quite encouraging. But if his outburst was meant to inspire his son, it had the opposite effect. Nearly everyone on the team turned to look at Mike and they could see his head dropping. He suddenly felt like the whole world was on his shoulders. When he had got up that morning he had whispered a silent prayer for his dad not to come to the game. But sadly, those prayers hadn't been answered.

The referee's whistle went again, and following junior rugby rules, the scoring team had to kick possession back to their opponents. Jimmy restarted the game by sending his drop-kick straight into the arms of the Rockwood fly-half. It was a great opportunity for Rockwood to run the ball back at Central but, instead, the Rockwood fly-half decided to smash a huge kick back up the pitch, over everybody's heads and straight to Mike.

Mike shouted, 'Mine!' and got himself in the perfect position to catch the ball. But as the ball hung there in the sky, a voice called out from the crowd, 'Don't bloody drop the thing, boy!' It was his dad again.

It was unclear whether Mike took his eye off the ball or was distracted by his father's unhelpful comment, but whatever the reason, he totally messed it up, allowing the ball to clatter off his chest before he'd even got his arms together. The ball tumbled in front of him for a knock on.

Mike was mortified. The first thing he had had to do in the game was the conversion, which hadn't been great, then he'd messed up a simple catch. He screamed something inaudible at the top of his voice, before shaking his head and running back beneath the posts.

'Come on, boy, that was rubbish!' shouted his dad. 'Sort it out!'

Jimmy's grandfather was sitting two rows in front of Gary Green. He shook his head and tutted, before turning to Jimmy's mum, who was sitting next to him. 'Horrible man,' he muttered. 'Horrible. Why can't he just leave his son alone? Poor kid.' Catherine nodded sadly in agreement.

The referee called for the scrum and gave clear instructions to both packs. 'Listen to my words, boys. Crouch . . . bind . . . set!' Then, quick as a flash, the Rockwood scrum-half put the ball in the tunnel. It was hooked back instantly, and before anyone knew what was happening, the scrum-half passed the ball out to his fly-half. Jimmy and the rest of the Central defensive line tracked across field after the ball, but instead of keeping the ball going down the line of backs, the Rockwood fly-half passed back inside to his huge captain, Dale, who was coming out of the scrum. He burst into the space Jimmy had left between him and Matt. Manu had spotted the danger an instant before the rest of his backline and was haring back to tackle Dale – but in his eagerness to put in a heavy tackle, he mistimed it and failed to get a grip around Dale's legs. The Rockwood captain stepped out of the tackle and rampaged on, tucking the ball under his arm as he ran towards the last man in defence: Mike.

Dale, who was a very big lad for his age, had clearly taken a leaf out of the Mark Kane coaching manual and made no attempt to sidestep or avoid Mike – he just ran straight at him.

Mike, who had spent his entire school career threatening others and always trying to show off how tough he was, suddenly looked scared by what faced him. Instead of bracing himself for the tackle and wrapping his arms tightly around Dale's legs to bring him down, he half-heartedly threw himself towards the charging figure, as if hoping the impact of their collision would be enough to stop him. It wasn't. Mike was bumped off and sent spinning away.

As he rolled on the ground in obvious pain, Dale jogged on, over the line and touched down for a try.

Instantly, a voice boomed out from the stand. 'What the hell was that? Did you just chicken out of a tackle? Don't you dare embarrass me like that again, you should have smashed him!'

Gary's outburst was greeted by a chorus of boos and people calling for him to sit down and shut up. It appeared by his reaction that Gary wanted to argue with everyone. Will just tutted again and shook his head.

While the crowd were getting stirred up by Gary's antics, Peter ran on and checked that Mike was okay. He was, he had just been winded slightly.

Peter squeezed a wet sponge over his head. 'Come on, Mike, you're fine. You can come back from this. We've all missed tackles. You'll be fine.'

Mike got to his feet and tried to walk off his ignominy. He joined the rest of his teammates behind the posts and waited for the conversion. He didn't speak to, or look at, anyone.

The conversion was taken by the Rockwood full back, who looked even more nervous than Mike had been. So nervous, in fact, that he sliced his kick so wildly that the ball ended up nearer the corner flag than the posts. The conversion missed, Central held a slender 7–5 lead.

Game on.

The next ten minutes or so were largely uneventful. After all the action in the opening passages of play, both teams settled into the patterns of the game and basically tackled anything that moved. Despite playing on a bigger pitch than they usually did, both teams played as if they were on a much smaller area, continuing to bunch together. This made defending that much easier.

Despite this, Jimmy managed to make two beautiful breaks, gaining twenty or so metres each time – but on each occasion, when support arrived, Jimmy's pass was knocked on. Both were knocked on by Mike. He was having a nightmare of a game. Each of his mistakes was being booed loudly . . . by his own father.

Just before half-time, Mike spotted a chance to make amends. Big Dale tackled Jimmy and knocked the ball loose, but the tackle had been high. The referee had no option but to award a penalty to Central.

Mike ran up to take a quick tap to restart the game. He had seen a gap in the Rockwood defence, and thought that if he could take the tap quickly, he could launch a big pass out to Kitty to send her in for a try. But, in his haste, he got it all wrong, and only managed to spill the ball forward as he tried to collect it from his tap, handing possession straight back to Rockwood.

He was horrified. He couldn't believe what was happening to him. His confidence was shot to pieces. 'You're an embarrassment!' shouted his father. 'An embarrassment!'

Mike tried to ignored the taunts, but all he really wanted to do was run straight off the pitch and away from everyone. He had dreamed of this moment ever since he had started playing rugby – captaining a team on the Memorial Ground. How could it be going so horribly wrong? Was it some sort of cruel payback for all the times he'd been so horrible to others?

Fortunately for Mike and his team, Rockwood were unable to make anything from this surprise turnover, and the referee blew the whistle for half-time a few moments later. Everyone from the Central team jogged over to the side to see Peter in the dugout. He handed out drinks and slices of orange.

'There's no sugar on mine,' moaned Ryan. 'I can't eat oranges without sugar . . . too sour.'

Everyone laughed and rolled their eyes.

'Have a drink instead then,' said Peter.

'Don't like water. Have you got any Fanta? Low fat of course,' said the prop, rubbing his tummy.

This drew even more laughter, even from Peter, who just stood there shaking his head. Then, while the players took a drink and began to eat their slices of orange, he spoke.

'That was really good. We deserve to be in front, but we still have to carry on working hard if we want to keep it that way. They're a good side, excellent tacklers, but you have all tackled well, too. Well done.'

He took a sip of water himself, before turning to his two centres. 'Manu, Harrison, you've played some lovely stuff together, keep talking to each other, your communication has been excellent.' The boys punched each other on the arm in encouragement.

Then he turned to Kitty. 'You've been superb. Incredible actually.'

Kitty blushed, thrilled to bits.

'Everyone, we need to get the ball out wide to Kitty – nobody can catch her if she gets half a chance, especially with all this space. I think you all believe you're still playing on a mini pitch; let's use all the wonderful space that you've got,' he said, moving his arms to emphasise the size of the perfect, lush pitch. 'And above all else,' he continued, 'keep enjoying yourselves, it's been a joy to watch you all.'

As everyone finished off their oranges – apart from Ryan who was still searching for a can of Fanta – Peter looked for Mike. He saw him, sitting on his own, with his head in his hands.

'Come on, son, up you get,' he said kindly, crouching down beside Mike and resting his hand on his back. 'There's no point wallowing. That half is done. It's gone. There's nothing you can do about it now. But we've still got a game to win and we need you. You're a hell of a good player – all you need to do is go out there and show everyone.'

Mike hauled himself to his feet, wiping his eyes. He didn't say anything, but managed a nod and went to get himself a drink. Peter watched him trudge away and took a deep sigh. *Please let him show what he can do this half,* he thought.

In no time, the referee blew his whistle to clear the pitch and get ready for the restart.

Peter walked up to Jimmy and put his arm around his shoulder. He bent down and whispered in his ear. 'Mike's gone,' he said, tapping a finger to his forehead. 'He's shattered – but I can't take him off, it'll break him. You'll have to lead this team now.'

Jimmy nodded.

'You've been outstanding, son,' continued Peter. 'Keep it going. Take responsibility and don't be scared to make your own decisions, if it's right to run it, run it. If it's better to kick, then kick. Just play what's in front of you – from anywhere. These conditions are made for you.'

Jimmy nodded again.

'And remember,' said Peter, walking away, 'heads up rugby.'

For a final time, Jimmy nodded.

The referee restarted the game – and if Mike had thought that his nightmare might be over, he was sorely mistaken.

Sensing that the full back was the weak link in the excellent Central backline, the Rockwood fly-half drilled his restart straight at Mike. He knocked it on instantly. It was a carbon copy of the first half. Again, the shout came from the stand: 'Use your hands, boy! What the hell is wrong with you?'

As the referee set the scrum, Jimmy knew what was about to happen when Rockwood got the ball. They would repeat the move that brought them their first-half try. He looked at Mike. He seemed to be almost in a daze. Two months before, when Mike had been so horrible to Jimmy, he never thought he would feel sorry for him in a million years. But the change he had seen in him recently, the awful game he was having and the horrible abuse he was getting from his father, meant that Jimmy just didn't want to see him exposed again. He jogged over to Mike and said quickly, 'Mike, do me a big favour will you? I think I've just twisted my ankle a bit, can you go to fly-half for a minute and give me a quick rest back here?'

Mike looked up and saw big Dale getting ready to join the scrum. He knew what was likely to happen as well and didn't fancy having to face Dale on another rampage and risk further humiliation in front of his father.

'Okay,' he muttered, and moved up into the line.

'Crouch . . . bind . . . set!' cried the referee, and in the briefest of moments, the ball was into the scrum and heeled back by the Rockwood hooker again. The scrum-half spun the ball perfectly out to the fly-half again and, as Jimmy had predicted, in a perfect repeat of the move that had created their opening try, he passed it back inside to big Dale.

Manu got to him again but was almost as ineffective at bringing Dale down. Almost. This time, Manu managed to at least make Dale stumble and, as he did so, Jimmy rushed up and threw his shoulder into Dale's hips, wrapping his arms tightly around him at point of impact. It wasn't a textbook tackle but the impact was enough to topple Dale off balance. As he hit the ground, Dale heard the referee screaming, 'Release!', so let the ball go.

Quick as a flash, Jimmy bounced back to his feet and, very importantly staying onside, bent over Dale's body and plucked the ball up. As he did so, one of the Rockwood forwards flew at Jimmy – but Jimmy had seen him coming. Avoiding the flying player and standing up in one motion, Jimmy was off.

Because there was a scrum of forwards in front of him, all finding their feet again after Dale's break, Jimmy swerved to his left. As he did, he was greeted by the swinging arm of the Rockwood scrum-half, desperately trying to grasp part of Jimmy's jersey. Jimmy pirouetted and stepped outside it easily. A burst of speed took him to the left of the on-rushing fly-half and away from his desperate clutches. Next, stepping twice to his right to avoid another forward and one of the centres, Jimmy found himself in space.

In the split seconds that followed, he scanned the players in front of him and saw he was up against two props. He ran straight at them. Neither of the props could deal with his pace and before they could even move to close the gap between them, Jimmy was through.

Five metres became ten metres, ten metres became twenty and Jimmy was into the Rockwood half. There was only one player left to beat. The full back.

Jimmy looked at his options; the easier one was to keep running to his right – a more direct route to the line. However, the problem with that was that the full back could use the touchline as an extra defender and possibly tackle him out of play. Or he could try to step inside the defender – or chip him. *Play what's in front of you.*

Jimmy headed for the corner. Just as he feared, the full back tracked across and was just about to tackle him into touch. *Time for option two.* Jimmy threw all his weight onto his right foot, powered off it, and jagged like a lightning bolt to his left-hand side, leaving the full back for dead. It was so brilliantly done that even the Rockwood staff clapped as Jimmy touched the ball down under the posts, before jogging back to halfway and tossing the ball to Mike for the conversion.

High up in the stand, a man sitting alone and dressed in a black

Eagles jacket was impressed. He had a small notebook in front of him. He wrote down Jimmy's number – 10 – then followed it with, 'Superb vision, awareness and speed. Plays what's in front of him. Great hands. Needs to learn how to tackle.'

Then, in capital letters he wrote the word PROSPECT before circling it twice and underlining it.

Down on the pitch, Jimmy was receiving congratulations from his team.

'Thanks, cheers, ta,' he replied and then turned to watch the kick.

Mike set down his tee and placed the ball on it. He stepped back three paces. He looked down at the ball, then up at the posts. He was visibly shaking.

A shout rang out from the silent crowd. 'Don't you dare miss, boy.' Everyone knew who it was. Jimmy's grandfather gripped the edges of his seat in fury.

After the briefest of pauses, as if he just wanted to get it over with, Mike rushed forward to strike the ball. It was awful. He snatched at it and hooked it left, missing the target.

The groan was heard all around the Memorial Ground.

It was now 12–5 to Central.

'For God's sake, what are you doing, you're playing like an idiot!' Mike heard every word his father shouted and just wanted the torture to end.

The second half was played out almost exclusively like the first, apart from another error by Mike that allowed Rockwood in for another easy try under the posts. Fortunately, the Rockwood full back appeared as nervous as Mike. Perhaps it was because it was on a full-sized pitch, and the posts stretching metres above him, high into the sky, intimated him, but whatever it was, he hardly managed to get the ball off the ground. Conversion missed, Central kept a narrow lead, 12–10.

Following that try, the game became very tight again with both defences on top. Every time somebody made a break, there was either a great tackle, or somebody made a silly mistake and knocked it on. With just five minutes left, the score remained 12–10 to Central, but Rockwood were beginning to edge things and with momentum building in their attack they progressed deep into Central's half.

Following a scruffy line out and a hack ahead by one of the Rockwood props, the ball came to Mike just outside his twenty-two. Normally, he would have just run it back and taken the contact, as he was always told to do when Mr Kane was coaching him, but he was so short of confidence, he decided to collect the ball and kick it up field instead.

It was a shocker.

Despite having plenty of time, he sliced it hopelessly, and the ball went straight out into touch.

'Get him off! Put me out of my misery!' cried Gary Green. Again, boos rang out from people sitting nearby, but he didn't care. He'd never cared about anyone or anything. His son was an embarrassment. He deserved to be criticised.

Rockwood had an attacking line out, just a yard outside the Central twenty-two.

Dale called his forwards together. He had a plan.

Jimmy shouted to everyone to keep alert. 'Watch your man, and keep your width in defence. And get speed off the line!'

Then, just as the hooker was about to throw the ball in, Dale ran to the front of the line out to swap places with one of the props. Jimmy could see what was about to happen, but he was powerless to stop it.

The hooker threw the ball to the front of the line out, Dale caught it easily and threw it straight back to the hooker. The rest of the Central defence was wrong-footed by this, and were all moving in-field. Instead, the hooker sprinted straight down the line. At Kitty.

Jimmy shouted, 'Help Kitty!' at the top of his voice when he saw what was happening, but it was all too late. The hooker sprinted straight at her and despite the bravest of tackles that brought the hooker to his knees, his momentum took him over Kitty and he scored in the corner.

Nobody was more disappointed than Kitty, she thought she'd let everyone down, but Peter's voice put her straight on that, 'Brilliant effort, Kitty. Brilliant and very brave, that was unlucky!'

Jimmy jogged over to her. Before he could say anything, Kitty said, 'I should've stopped him, I should've . . .'

'Nah, don't worry about it,' he said. 'Just concentrate on the next job.' She nodded and walked towards the posts. Her jaw was set determinedly, but inside her heart was sinking, fearing that she might have just cost her team the cup – there was so little time left for them to get up the other end of the field to score.

As usual, the conversion was in front of the posts and easy. And for once, despite his earlier nerves, that's just how the Rockwood full back made it look – easy.

17–12 to Rockwood with less than three minutes remaining.

As Jimmy waited for the restart, he knew he had to do

something quickly to get the ball up the field. He guessed that the Rockwood fly-half would target Mike again, hoping for another knock on. If that happened it would be game over and the Cluster Cup would be on its way to Rockwood. Jimmy wasn't going to let that happen.

He ran over to his full back.

'You okay, Mike?'

Mike nodded, but said nothing.

'I think I'll just hang back here with you.'

There was no response. His awful game and the continued insults from his father had broken him.

The referee blew his whistle and, as Jimmy had predicted, the Rockwood fly-half struck the ball high towards them. Before Mike could even move, Jimmy was off.

'Mine!' he shouted loudly and sprinted towards the ball. He caught it effortlessly.

Then Jimmy took a gamble.

He knew that the Rockwood defence would expect him to run forward and try and break the line and probably not risk a pass and a knock on if he didn't have to. But Jimmy did the opposite.

Instead of sprinting forwards, he ran almost sideways, which completely bamboozled the Rockwood defence.

What confused the watching Peter Clement was that Jimmy was running towards Mike Green. Surely, he wasn't going to risk passing to him.

He was.

Jimmy ran straight towards a very surprised-looking Mike and just before he got to him, he shouted, 'Loop, Mike, loop!'

and passed the ball. Mike, for the first time in the match, caught it perfectly and drew a Rockwood tackler who was bearing down on them. Before the tackler could reach Mike, Jimmy had continued his run behind him and appeared on his left shoulder. Mike straightened his run, forcing the defender to commit to tackling him, but just before they collided, Mike slipped the ball outside to Jimmy and into space.

Jimmy was off like a bullet.

Only one player had seen what was happening, and that was the Rockwood left wing, who had begun moving across to the right of the field as soon as he saw Jimmy was going for the loop.

Jimmy was over the halfway line, going like a train. The field was opening up ahead of him – then he noticed the wing, coming from his right. He too was sprinting for his life.

Jimmy scanned the options ahead. If he changed direction and stepped to the right, it would give the wing more options to cover, as he would have a shorter distance to run. Jimmy had to go for the corner.

He was over the ten-metre line. The wing was gaining, his angle of run helping to close down the space between them.

A few strides more, and Jimmy was in the twenty-two. The wing was closing in fast.

Peter closed one of his eyes, he didn't think Jimmy could make it. The covering angle of the wing was perfect.

Jimmy kept going, straining every muscle and fibre in his body to get there.

Eight metres out, and it was clear that the wing was going to tackle Jimmy at the five-metre line and bundle him into touch. Jimmy knew it too. The wing had just been too fast.

Then Jimmy did an incredible thing.

Without breaking stride, Jimmy tucked the ball into his chest with both arms, and with all the power he had left in his aching legs, he threw himself forwards in a dive.

As Jimmy hit the ground, the turf was still damp enough for him to skid forward towards the try line. Just as he thought he was going to make it, the wing landed on Jimmy's back and legs following a dive of his own. But a combination of the speed of the wing and the fact that Jimmy was already on the ground, meant that he wasn't able to get a proper grip of Jimmy to push him into touch. Instead, he only succeeded in spinning Jimmy around slightly, before the wing sailed into touch himself. Jimmy came to a halt about a metre short of the line, but crucially, he was not in touch, or held by the wing.

Bouncing on the ground whilst cradling the ball had winded Jimmy slightly, but he had just enough energy to hop up and touch the ball down behind the line, before collapsing.

The crowd went wild.

Peter just turned to Liam and said, 'That boy is some player,' but his words were lost in the cacophony of applause from the crowd, the whoops of delight from Jimmy's family and the roar of his father as he raced around the dugout area punching the air in delight.

Up in the stands, the man in the black Eagles jacket opened his notebook again. Above the word PROSPECT he now wrote another one, EXCEPTIONAL. He circled that word twice too.

On the field, the Central players went crazy. They all swamped Jimmy with cheers of congratulations.

'Brilliant, Jimmy, brilliant!'

'What a try, incredible!'

'Fantastic run, Jimmy, absolutely fantastic . . . you've won us the cup!'

Jimmy swung round when he heard that one.

'No I haven't,' he wheezed, trying to get his breath back. 'It's 17-all. We need the conversation to win it.'

'That's okay,' shouted Manu, 'you won't miss from there. Easiest kick you'll ever take!'

Jimmy shook his head. 'Nah,' he said, 'I'm not taking it.'

39

# THE FINAL KICK

THE GROUND was hushed.

Jimmy's try had brought the game level at 17–17, and with only seconds left, the conversion would win the cup for Central, or see it shared between the two teams. There was never extra time in a Cluster Cup final.

Jimmy looked over to Mike, who quickly looked away and then turned his back as if doing so would somehow hide him.

'Hey, Mike, here you go,' said Jimmy, holding out the ball.

'I don't want it. You take it. I'll only miss.'

'Nah, you won't,' replied Jimmy lightly. 'Come on, go and win the match for us.'

'You only want me to take it so that I'll miss . . . to make you look good.'

'Hey,' said Jimmy sharply, which made Mike look at him for the first time. 'Don't be stupid. I don't want to share this cup, I want to win it. And the best chance we've got of winning it is with you. You've been brilliant these past few weeks, don't let him up there,' Jimmy pointed up to the grandstand to Mike's dad, 'get in there,' and he tapped Mike on the side of the head. 'You're much better than that . . . and him.'

Mike studied Jimmy's face and could tell he was being sincere.

'But what happens if I miss?'

'We'll never find that out,' replied Jimmy, 'because that's not going to happen.'

Mike paused for a moment.

'Why would you do this for me after I've been so horrible to you for so long?'

Jimmy thought of words that Will had once said to him. *You can be the most talented player in the world, but if you don't work with the team, if you don't support them and look after them, then they won't support and look after you. And without them, you'll achieve nothing.* 'Because everybody deserves a second chance,' he said, holding the ball out again. 'You're a much better player than you've shown everyone today – and a brilliant kicker. You deserve the chance to win it for us.'

Mike looked down at the ball and quietly said, 'Thanks.'

Mike took the tee from Ryan, who had brought it on while eating one of the Memorial Ground's legendary pasties, and then walked towards the posts to prepare for his kick. Jimmy called after him. 'Mike, you haven't been taking your correct run up today. Remember, five steps back, two to the left.'

Mike smiled as if a penny had dropped in his mind.

'And remember that deep breath too. Relax. I know you'll make this kick.'

With that, Jimmy turned around and jogged back to his teammates, ten metres away.

'Why have you let him take it, Jim?' spluttered Manu. 'He's been rubbish, he's going to miss.'

Mike heard every word. But ignored it.

Jimmy waved his hand to shush Manu. 'He needs to take it,' he whispered.

The referee walked up to Mike.

'Come on, son, you've taken enough time, get a move on.'

He looked down into the boy's eyes and saw nothing but fear. He felt sorry for him, so left him alone in his personal hell, to set the ball on the tee.

Mike looked down at the tee. He must have used it a hundred times, but as he placed it on the ground, it felt like a totally foreign object in his hand.

He placed the ball on it. It fell off. A slight 'Oooh' went up from the crowd.

Gary Green was about to shout out some more abuse, but then felt a tight grip on his wrist, followed by a voice, very firmly and very quietly saying, 'Do not say another word.' It was Mike's brother, Martyn.

Gary looked at his estranged son with unfettered hatred. His face coloured instantly, and he was about to speak, but Martyn cut him short.

'Look down there,' hissed Martyn, pointing at two policemen. 'Can you see one of them holding a letter?'

Gary could. He looked confused.

'That letter contains all the dates and times when you made me help you steal those Mercedes vans. It has all the details of who you sold them to and what you did with the money. I asked him to hold it for me for ten minutes. I told him that if I didn't come back, to open it.'

His father's jaw dropped open.

'If you say one more word to Mike out there, I'm walking out of this stadium, and out of your life forever. Until the trial of course, when I'll sing like a canary about what you get up to to earn your money. You'll be finished.' Martyn's eyes never left his father's.

Gary Green slumped back in his seat.

'Okay, okay,' he stammered. 'Go and get the letter, just go and get it, now.'

'After the kick.'

Gary nearly screamed, but it would have been to no avail – he was beaten.

Back on the pitch, Mike had finally managed to put the ball on the tee and stepped back. Three paces.

*Oh no,* thought Jimmy, *he's forgotten his routine again. Take five back, Mike, take five.* Jimmy was trying to send silent messages to Mike, hoping that, somehow, he'd hear.

Then, just as Mike was about to make his first movement forward, one of the famous sea breezes flew in from the coast, over the stand and down the length pitch. Because Mike hadn't placed the ball onto the tee properly, it toppled straight off. Mike looked in horror at the referee.

Not wishing to make the boy feel any worse, the referee looked at him and said softly, 'It's okay, lad, go and put it back on.'

Jimmy glanced up at the stand, expecting to hear some abuse from Mike's father. Nothing. There was complete silence.

Mike picked the ball up, and placed it back on the tee, this time remembering to line the ball up with the centre of the posts.

That seemed to jog his brain back into life, and he remembered that he usually stood up behind the ball at this point, and looked up at the posts. So that's exactly what he did. Then, somewhere deep in his memory, it was as if his brain automatically just took over. Almost without thinking, he took five large strides back. Stopped. Then took two to the left.

Jimmy smiled. *He's got it.*

Mike looked down at the ball, up to the posts, took a deep breath, then breathed out. Then, he took the five steps to the ball, planted his left foot to the side of it, and struck his right boot right through the back of the ball sending it skywards. As he did, another sea breeze hit the ground, but this one was kind. Instead of blowing Mike's ball off line, it simply lifted it high and handsome, right through the middle of the posts.

He had done it. The final whistle blew – Central had won 19–17, and the final had its most unlikely of heroes: Mike Green.

The main stand erupted into applause, not so much because Central had won, but more in relief that the young boy down on the pitch in front of them, who had just about played the worst match they had ever seen someone play, had conquered his demons and come out on top. That showed bravery. That showed character.

Before Mike had a chance to even see the ball land on the terracing behind the goal – so far had the wind blown it – he was jumped upon by his teammates. Ryan was the last to get there, pastie pastry all stuck to his bib, screaming, 'Pile on! Pile on!' And when he did pile on, he nearly killed poor Mike who was at the bottom.

As people rolled off, laughing, shouting and joking in total ecstasy, everyone was grabbing Mike and ruffling his hair or patting him on the back. He ignored everyone. He was looking for Jimmy. He couldn't see him at first, but then caught sight of him celebrating with Kitty, Matt and Manu, just behind where Ryan was organising another pile on.

Mike walked across and stretched out his hand.

'I'm really sorry I was so horrible to you for so long, I'm really, really sorry . . .' He was on the verge of tears.

The last thing Jimmy wanted was to make him break down and cry in front of everyone – what would be the point of that? A few weeks ago, he'd have loved to have seen it, but not now. Instead, Jimmy just took his hand and said, 'Forget about that, it's over now. You've changed and everybody knows it. Well done, mate.'

Mike was so relieved he felt completely lost for words. He smiled in grateful thanks.

Then hearing Ryan still shouting, 'Pile on! Pile on!' from the bottom of an increasingly big mountain of bodies, Jimmy looked at Mike and said, 'It would be rude not to . . .' Both roared with laughter and jumped on top of the pile.

Back up in the stand, Gary Green turned to his eldest son to order him again to get the letter from the policeman, but was horrified to see the seat was empty. During the excitement of the winning kick, his son had gone. Desperately, Gary looked down at the policeman. He was opening the letter. Before he had a chance to even break its seal, Gary was up out of his seat, barging past everyone before bolting for the exit. He was gone.

The policeman opened the letter, read its contents and showed his colleague, eyebrows raised.

It was a shopping list.

'Some people just love winding us up, don't they?' he said before crumpling the paper up and tossing it in the bin.

'He must have done it as a dare,' laughed his colleague.

The atmosphere in the ground was electric as everyone savoured what had been a truly fantastic game of school rugby. Most people who watched the game that day thought that the highlight was Jimmy's last-minute try. Not the players though. Their highlight was the enormous Fanta and pastie-filled burp that Ryan unleashed from the bottom of the pile that lasted a full eight seconds. Poor old Kitty copped the worst of it. 'Urgh, boys! You are so disgusting! I don't know why I bother hanging around with you sometimes!' she laughed as she clambered out of the pile.

Once order was restored, and Ryan was warned about his behaviour, it was time for the presentations.

Up first, to the committee box area behind the dug outs in the main stand, was Rockwood School. The Central team stood in front of the dug outs, clapping and cheering wildly for their much-respected opponents. As their captain, Dale, was presented with the runners-up shield, all the Central players shouted, 'Three cheers for Rockwood – hip-hip, hooray! Hip-hip, hooray! Hip-hip, hooray!'

Amid all the clapping and cheering given to the very deserving Rockwood team, Peter made his way over to Jimmy.

'I meant what I said earlier, son,' he said, laying a hand on his shoulder. 'For most of these kids today, on both sides, this will be the biggest game they will ever play in. It will be a memory for life for them playing on this pitch – the best rugby memory they'll ever have. But for you, Jimmy, it's just the start of a career full of memories. I saw things in you today that I hadn't seen before, or even thought possible, in one so young.'

Jimmy blushed and looked at the floor.

'It wasn't just in your play and your speed,' continued Peter. 'I expected that – no, it was in your decision-making and leadership. It was first class. When I saw you give the ball to Mike for that kick, I nearly ran on to stop you doing it – I certainly wouldn't have done it. But then I realised it was a hundred per cent the right thing to do. He *had* to take that kick, he would be finished otherwise. He might never have played again. That was an incredibly kind thing to do, and showed real maturity, son. Well done. Well done.'

As Jimmy smiled bashfully, he looked up and saw his mother, brother and sister alongside Jimmy's grandmother and grandfather cheering and waving. He also saw his dad, in his Wolves top in the dugout. He was beaming. Jimmy had never seen his family look so proud. He had never felt as happy. What a day, he thought.

'And now, your winners,' crackled the voice over the tannoy, 'let's hear it for Central Primary!'

A massive cheer went up and Mike turned to Jimmy to offer him the honour of leading them all up to collect the cup. He knew Jimmy was man of the match and deserved it more than anyone.

Jimmy shook his head. 'No skipper, thanks, but that's your job.'

Mike nodded and walked towards the committee box to get the cup. At the back of the line, Jimmy stood behind Matt, watching those in front get their medals. He glanced to his left and saw Peter walking off, back to the changing rooms.

'Peter,' shouted Jimmy, 'Peter, come up with us!'

'No,' replied Peter, 'this is your moment.' He shot Jimmy a broad grin and then added, 'And remember, son, this is the most important medal you'll ever win. The first one always is. Make sure it's the first of many.'

And with that, he was down the touchline, into the tunnel and gone.

Jimmy watched him disappear into the darkness, before saying under his breath, 'I'll make sure it will be. I'll make sure it will.'

# EPILOGUE

# THE LETTER

Dear Mrs Joseph,

I write on behalf on the Eagles Professional Rugby Club Limited, with regard to your son, Jimmy.

Following a match assessment I made in the recent Cluster Cup final at the Memorial Ground, I have decided that Jimmy has the required skills, abilities and attributes to become a potential Eagles player of the future.

Therefore, it's with great delight that I offer your son a place at the two-week summer residential training camp that will take place at the Eagles Training Academy. The course will run from Sunday 3rd August to Saturday 16th August. All board, lodging and pocket money will be provided. Transport there and back is also available and we will provide all kit, towels and toiletries. However, your son should bring his own gum shield and boots.

I hope this covers everything you require in terms of organisation for the training camp, however, should you require any further information, please do not hesitate to get in touch.

On a personal note, may I say how impressed I was with Jimmy's leadership qualities on the day of the final, the way he dealt with his horribly out-of-form captain was genuinely inspirational and should be commended. I would be grateful if you would pass on to Jimmy my thoughts regarding that matter.

Finally, I am delighted to announce that Eagles have secured the services of a former first-class rugby player of significant achievement and experience to lead Jimmy's age group in his camp. Please ensure that Jimmy makes himself known to the coach as soon as he arrives.

His name is Mark Kane.

With the kindest of regards,

*Stuart Withey*

Stuart Withey
Eagles Academy Director

# ACKNOWLEDGEMENTS

I had the idea for this book when I took my eldest son, Harrison, to a book fair and he couldn't find a rugby book for kids. That got me thinking – why don't I write one based on my own experiences? When I started considering my options for life after playing, I chatted to a family friend, the singer and broadcaster, Mal Pope, about my idea. He told me about a friend of his who was a sports writer and children's author and arranged for us to meet. From that very first day, David and I have been on the same page – excuse the pun! – and it has been a real pleasure working with him on the book. We decided that the best idea was to create a fictional school-aged version of 'me' and try to create a story that would appeal to rugby players everywhere who are starting out on their own rugby journeys.

The main idea was to share the overarching story of any life in rugby which will involve resilience, hard work, commitment, fair play, teamwork, sportsmanship and, above all, fun. David and I both hope that this book will not only inspire young readers, but will also entertain the adults in the family too – there is nothing better than grown-ups and children enjoying books together. We hope we've achieved that.

Books do not happen on their own, so David and I would both like to thank our wonderful agent who has also become a great friend – David Luxton. David, thanks for all the hard work you and all at David Luxton Associates have done, and continue to do, regarding this book. Also to Peter Burns and all at Polaris Publishing. Pete, thank you for your advice and friendship and for turning our dreams into reality. It's been a pleasure working with you on this and the upcoming books in the series. Thanks also to Helen Mockridge for all her marketing skills in promoting the book and getting it out there. Also grateful thanks to all my ex-teammates who willingly provided such kind and thoughtful reviews.

Finally, thanks to you, the reader, for choosing this book. David and I have been lucky enough to have careers based in sport, me playing and David writing. We have both been inspired throughout our lives by reading about sport. We sincerely hope that this book will inspire you to enjoy a life in sport, just like we have.

*James Hook, Swansea.*
*September 2020.*

# CHASING A RUGBY DREAM

## YOUTUBE SKILLS

Are you chasing a rugby dream like Jimmy and his friends? If you would like to learn new skills and take part in challenges to improve your game, check out my YouTube page: *Chasing a Rugby Dream with James Hook*

If you enjoy the videos, please like and share and leave any feedback or requests in the comments section.

And just remember Peter Clement's mantra: have fun!